D1494523

Ambition

Julie Burchill has written more than a dozen books,
with the TV adaptation of one of them, *Sugar Rush*,
winning an International Emmy. Her hobbies
include spite, luncheon, philanthropy and learning
Modern Hebrew. She is married and lives in
Brighton. She has been a journalist since the
age of 17 and is now 53 years old.

Julie Burchill
Ambition

CORVUS

First published in Great Britain in 1989 by The Bodley Head,
an imprint of Random House.

This edition published in paperback in Great Britain in 2013
by Corvus, an imprint of Atlantic Books Ltd.

10 9 8 7 6 5 4 3 2 1

A CIP catalogue record for this book is available from
the British Library.

Paperback ISBN: 978 1 78239 117 3
E-book ISBN: 978 1 78239 118 0
OME ISBN: 978 1 78239 154 8

Printed and bound by CPI Group (UK) Ltd, Croydon, CR0 4YY

Corvus
An imprint of Atlantic Books Ltd
Ormond House
26–27 Boswell Street
London
WC1N 3JZ

www.corvus-books.co.uk

AMBITION

ONE

There were two people in the Regency four-poster that swamped the suite overlooking the Brighton seafront but only one of them was breathing, deeply and evenly, as she sipped flat Bollinger Brut and decided what to do next.

Her name was Susan Street, and she was almost twenty-seven and almost beautiful with long dark hair, long pale legs and a short temper. Beside her lay a man who would never see fifty again and who now would never see sixty either. He had been, until half an hour ago, the editor of the *Sunday Best*, a tabloid with teeth whose circulation was three million and rising. Unfortunately he would never see · it reach four million, because his deputy editor Susan Street had just dispatched him to that big boardroom in the sky with a sexual performance of such singular virtuosity that his heart couldn't stand it.

His heart, like everything else about him, was weak, she thought as she kissed his still-warm lips.

She jumped from the bed in her Janet Reger teddy, looking like a call girl and thinking like a pimp. She saw herself in the mirror and reflected that the frail garment had to bear at least two-thirds of the responsibility for Charles Anstey's early death on its flimsy back. Men were so predictable, the helpful little sweeties: they all loved blowjobs, they all loved high heels and they all loved black Janet Reger teddies. If she ever made it up the Amazon and found a tribe totally untouched by both white man and *Playboy*, she just knew that once you got down to it they too would love blowjobs, high heels and Janet Reger teddies.

It was in the blood and under the skin of men. And who was she to withhold the addictive, destructive drug they craved so badly?

Who was she? She was Susan Street . . .

The smile slid from her face like the scribble from a child's Magic Slate, shaken suddenly. On her hands and knees she circled the deep pile of the red carpeted room, delicately picking up the small smashed phials which had contained the amyl nitrate. When she had covered the floor twice, she made a tiny glass mountain on a newspaper – yesterday's copy of the *Best* – pulled on her lethal red Blahnik heels and ground the glass into a fine powder. For one wild moment she thought of mixing it with talcum, taking it back to town and giving it to her best friend and worst enemy, Ingrid Irving. Ingrid was number three on a vastly more upmarket Sunday, a source of constant irritation and a complete and utter cokehead; her sinuses were so badly shot that she could snort straight Vim without missing a beat.

Then she looked at the man on the bed. She had done enough damage for one day.

Or nine lifetimes.

Grinding down the agent of Anstey's death on to the paper he had loved so much made her laugh hysterically. Who needs yesterday's paper, who needs yesterday's man? She sat down quickly on the bed as though she had received a fatal telegram, fighting her laughter. Tears came to her eyes.

It had been a sort of eternal triangle – not his wife, she wasn't important. But him, Susan and the *Best*. They had both loved it, both worked on it together for six years, both taken it so far and planned to take it further. To the top . . .

She jumped up and ran to the bathroom. Cry later. Tears on ice, shaken and stirred. She slid the glass into the bowl and flushed again and again until even the fussiest guest could have drunk their daiquiris from it. Then she walked into the bedroom, summoning back her hysteria. She brought her hands together to make a giant fist and smashed it into her stomach, hard, gasping with pain. Then she screamed, over and over, as (to be careful of her nails) she dialled 999 with the heavy black and gold Mont Blanc pen – Charles's first-ever present to her.

When the policeman answered, she gasped, 'Oh *please – quickly –* there's been a death, at the big hotel by the West Pier, the really big one . . . yes *that* one . . . Charles Anstey . . . no, I'm not, I'm an employee. My name is Susan Street. Thank you, yes, as soon as possible.'

She replaced the receiver carefully and smiled at her bright-eyed, wet-lipped reflection. She had never looked better. Wasn't this the way sappy male writers had their heroines looking after sex? No, sex had never done this for her; just blurred her mascara and kissed away her lipstick. Only power made a girl look this good . . .

'My name is Susan Street, and I am the youngest ever female newspaper editor in the world.'

The man on the bed jerked one more time, as if in agreement.

She rested her forehead against the window and watched the pretty Sussex countryside go by. All those people in all those houses . . . how many of them were teenage girls dreaming of escape? Thousands. And how many would make it? Not even a hundred.

She felt impossibly tired. Her ordeal, for the moment, was over. The police had seen the stained sheets and her long, long legs in their red shoes. They had listened silently to her tearful recitation of his medical history, including the

4

two small heart attacks before she met him. The younger constable – it was true about the police looking younger – had even gone pink around the edges.

She had mumbled something about his wife in Richmond and it all being horrid.

The older policeman said not to worry, miss, his lad would see to it personally, breaking the news to Madame Anstey. It was all she had been able to do to stop herself jumping up and offering to break the news to Madame Anstey herself: 'Oh, and by the way, Lorraine . . . his last words were "I'm coming, you bitch . . ." '

She leaned forward in her First Class train seat like a jockey in sight of the home stretch, urging the iron horse on. Hurry up, *please*. The country was for cows; the country was where you ran away from, or retired to, not where you *lived*, when you were young and almost beautiful. She loved the city, she needed the city, she *belonged* to the city . . .

And now the city belonged to her . . .

Once, all she had had of the city had been a map of the London Underground. In later years, when time had wrapped a tourniquet around the terrible anguish of her adolescence, she would always reply with a straight face, 'Harry Beck' when asked which artists she liked. Harry Beck was the man who had designed the map of the London Underground; the map under which she slept, wept and crossed the days off the calendars she kept beneath her winter clothes, as other adolescents kept dirty books. She knew that in the eyes of her friends and family, her maps and calendars would mark her out as being touched with something even worse than nymphomania.

Ambition.

But she slept beneath the map and she dreamed in tube stations: Angel, Marble Arch, White City. Once or twice a year she escaped alone and made the six hour round trip to her promised land where she would roam the streets wide-eyed, her tape recorder in her hand. At night she fell asleep to the sound of London, in dreams she saw it, and in the morning she wept to find herself beached in the backwater of the pretty West Country town she had been condemned to birth in.

But something rubbed off. By the age of fifteen she looked like a citizen of the Borough of Kensington and Chelsea, talked like a citizen of the Borough of Bow and thought like a citizen of the City. By now she knew that the country could never claim her and as if in retaliation the lost souls already sinking into its porous soil turned on the cocky cuckoo in the nest as they sank into the teenage quicksand of fiancé with room-temperature IQ, small screaming vampires in Viyella vests and le petit mortgage.

Right-wing ideas about the bond between people of a similar culture and pigmentation, and left-wing ideas about the bond between women left Susan Street early, flushed down the school toilets her former friends held her head down when they smelled a rat planning to leave the sinking ship of their youth. She was relieved of all illusions before she reached the age of consent, when she shed her tight and shrivelled adolescent skin

and emerged as a creature without conscience or scruples, with
an almost irritable desire to get on with it. When The Beat
ran the advert and she answered it on school notepaper (she
could have typed it, but let them drool over her immaculate
youth, old crumblies in their twenties who probably thought
that teenagers were mythical beast figments of their wildest,
wettest rock dreams), and they asked her to write something,
and she wrote it in her smudgiest, most schoolgirlish hand and
the editor, Sam Kelly, called the principal's office to summon
her from double Maths to offer her the job and she realized
she was going to work for the best and biggest music paper in
the world, she felt not elation but great relief and something
almost like . . . it was . . . disappointment.

It was all so predictable somehow, her irresistible rise. She
sat on the principal's window sill, biting her thumbnail and
looking out at the playground where her heart had been broken
and her fate had been sealed and she wished that somehow she
could have been given some choice in the matter of her ambition
and the success it would inevitably bring.

Six weeks later she was sitting in the lap, if not of luxury, then
of Gary Pride, sniffing amphetamine sulphate through a fifty-
pound note. In theory, she worked at The Beat during the day
and slept at the YWCA at night. In fact, she spent the day
slouching against the office partitions cleaning her nails with a
switchblade and sneering at her colleagues. In later years such
action would be known as a 'career move'.

At night she slept with Gary Pride in his coffin in Limehouse. Gary Pride was a rising young pop star of twenty-two who made awful records which contained the words 'Pride', 'Soul', 'Joy', 'Respect' and 'Dignity' repeated many times in various permutations. He said they were a homage to Motown. They sounded marginally less black than mid-period New Seekers. That didn't stop people buying them or Susan sleeping with him. Secretly, she held a deeply felt belief that he should be formally executed for crimes against the memory of black music.

Gary Pride had an ugly face and a beautiful smile which made you forget how basically worthless he was. At least, everyone but Susan. She thought he was a scumbag.

She slept with him because she had quickly learned that a teenage country girl with the legs of a dancer, the behind of a boy and the lips of a Port Said suck artist was a sitting Danish pastry for every disease-carrying flyboy in the shop window, not to mention the streets, offices and subways of the big city. Gary was her protection. By doing one unpleasant thing (Gary) she was made immune to the multitude of unpleasant things she might otherwise be cornered into doing. It was, if you wanted to be vulgar, immunization by injection. In later life she would calculate that at least eighty per cent of the girls she had known had tolerated their boyfriends for this same reason.

Of course, Gary Pride didn't know this. Like all shallow men he believed in True Love, taken frequently. He wrote songs for her – '(I Saw You) Dancing By Your Handbag' and 'Never Love A Soulboy'. She was so embarrassed she wanted to die, or preferably to kill him. Instead she accompanied him to the Top Of The Pops studio and to horrible places like Aylesbury where the band always tried out before London. She learned how to ignore the girls who hung around the stage door and spat at the band's girlfriends, even when it stuck to her face.

'You've got dignity, gel,' said Gary. (He liked that word.) 'You're just like the Queen Mum.'

He stayed faithful, by and large, to her because she was lividly young and pale, still uncalloused inside her Lewis Leathers second skin. Also because she worked on The Beat. ('Yeah, my girl's a writer,' she once heard him boasting to some fellow warbling cretin. 'Not some record company slag.')

Also because she had been a virgin.

His first!

He could laugh about it now, which he did loudly and lewdly and often, in front of his entourage, squeezing her thigh and referring smarmily to their first night of passion. It was like living in a Carry On film.

But at the time, he had almost killed her . . .

'You're a what?' Gary Pride jumped from the king-size coffin and stood in the middle of his Limehouse warehouse, naked except for a 666 tattoo on his shoulder.

'A virgin,' she whispered. Things had gone very quiet. Everyone was looking.

'Jesus, Susan!' He turned on the room, where his entourage lay sprawled on the flagstones watching The World At War

9

with the sound turned down and the 1910 Fruitgum Company on the Dansette, snorting, swigging, guzzling and groping yet another night away. 'Out, the lot of you liggers! OUT! Before I call the Bill!'

Shooting Susan poison looks, blaming her for displeasing their master and mealticket, the revellers staggered out into the cold night air. Gary Pride bolted the huge doors and stalked purposefully back to the coffin where Susan lay on her back with her eyes closed, trying to make herself look as much like the red silk lining as possible.

'Susan! God 'elp me, gel, if you don't open your eyes right now I'll close them for you permanent!'

She opened her grey eyes wide. The effect she was hoping for was that of those wretched Third World urchins with the big eyes and raggedy clothes in those awful Woolworth's prints her mother had such a liking for. She couldn't swear to it, but she thought they were called things like 'Chico'.

'Right. Now do you mean to tell me—' To her horror she noticed he was getting another erection. She hadn't seen anything so disgusting since her beloved grandmother had given up eating pigs' trotters on account of her dentures. Gary fastidiously threw a buffalo skin (Magnificent animal, innit, the buffalo? Sorter . . . majestic. Dignifield. I fink I'll write a song about a buffalo) on to her smooth white body. 'Do you mean to tell me you are an actual virgin?'

'Was.'

'Don't rub it in, gel!' He smote himself dramatically. 'WAS.'

'Yes.'

'Oh my God.' He sank on the stone floor theatrically, then jumped up as the chill flags touched his behind. 'People think I'm a wild sort of guy. I guess I am.' (He always assumed an American accent when talking about himself.) 'But I got my own code of honour. And do you know what the number one rule on my code of honour is?' He paused, one hand in the air, like Simon Rattle about to strut his stuff.

'No, Gary,' she whispered. She had always envisaged that getting shot of her virginity would be like having a tooth out: painful, boring, but basically banal and hopefully over quite quickly. She hadn't expected a cross between Twenty Questions and Armageddon.

'I don't sleep with virgins, that's what!' He glared vengefully.

'I'm sorry, Gary.' She thought he might strike her.

' 'Ow was you to know?' He looked at her with weary compassion. 'You ever read any books about knights?'

'Only Ivanhoe, at school.'

'That's bollocks. You wanna read the real stuff . . . the Crusaders, the Knights of Simon Templar . . . magic! Well, I see myself as a sort of urban parfait knight. You know what that is?'

'No, Gary.'

'They got a code, like all outlaws.' He thrust out his jaw, looking like something on loan from the Natural History Museum. 'AND VIRGINS IS RIGHT OUT!'

'I'm sorry, Gary.'

He shook his head with infinite wisdom. ' 'Ow was you to know? You're a good gel, Susan.' He lifted the buffalo skin and looked at her body, the gleam of infinite lechery dawning in his bloodshot eyes. Suddenly he vaulted back into the coffin, showing a remarkable agility. 'Might as well be hanged for a sheep as a lamb, I suppose!'

Before the night was over she was sitting on his face. Now she was sitting on his lap in his dressing room after a show at the Hammersmith Odeon, and he was shoving her towards an exotic-looking girl with a nose-ring. What a fucking parfait knight he was.

'I fancy a nice bit of dyke action,' he was whispering. Charming.

The crowd did a passable impersonation of après-ski Red Sea as Susan and the girl slid to the floor.

'What's your name?'

'Shira.'

'Mine's Susan.'

'Yes, I know. I see you around with the band.'

'Weren't you in Birmingham the other night?'

'Yes, right, when you . . .'

'Jesus H!' yelled Gary Pride. 'You want the room cleared so you can tell each other your life stories? Now eat it!'

The two girls slipped from their scuffed leather skins, under which they were naked. The silence dripped saliva. Shira had surprising emerald-green pubic hair and a tattoo just below her navel warning KEEP OFF THE GRASS. Susan got down to grazing, with a vengeance.

Gary Pride bought time.

He bought friends.

He bought a season ticket to Highbury, but he didn't dare go. (*More than my life's worth. I'd be ripped apart by the love of my people.*)

He bought books on the English Civil War, the code of the Samurai and the decline and fall of the Roman Empire, but he never read them. (*Life's too short, innit? Look, the snooker's on.*)

He bought suits of armour. Of course he never wore them. When they began to collect dust he had them packed in a crate and sent to his family in Kent. (*He claimed to be a Cockney; it was his whole raison d'être. His first album was called 'Cockney Pride'. There must have been a strong wind blowing south from the vicinity of Bow Bells the day Gary Pride was born, Susan secretly thought.*)

He bought lutes, mandolins and lyres and threw them down in fits of pique when they failed to respond in exactly the same way as a 1976 Fender bass.

But most of all, he bought drugs. And these he certainly knew what to do with. Hash, speed, cocaine, opium and LSD. It was the acid that broke the cretin's back. He woke up in the coffin one morning screaming about the Rotarians. And the Freemasons. And the Tongs. Through a lurching amphetamine fog hangover Susan saw him pull on his nearest clothing (a

Samurai ceremonial robe – was he going to get stopped at Customs!) and rifle through the bureau for his passport. She never heard from him again. A month or so later his record company told her he had gone to the volcanic island of Vanuatu to get his head together.

She was eighteen and sick to the back teeth of asking crooning morons too stoned to remember their own phone numbers what their views were on the situation in Rhodesia, which had become as essential to a Beat interview as a favourite colour was to the teenybopper magazines. If you failed to ask them to their stupid faces you had to call them at home and pop the question, and doing it in isolation made you feel even dumber. Then a posh cow called Rebecca called her at the office one day and asked if they could have a drink.

In a bar in Jermyn Street Rebecca sighed deeply into her Kir Royale and murmured something about New Blood. About the Street. About the Blank Generation. Susan watched, fascinated. Rebecca talked into her drink like a ventriloquist drinking a glass of water while screeching 'Gottle of geer!' and sounded like a Labour Party Manifesto. Then suddenly she rounded on Susan, looking her straight in the eye, and said in a completely different, mid-Atlantic voice, 'Well?'

'Sorry?'

'Fifteen thousand a year, pathetic really, no car, expenses, as much depilatory as you can use and endless free samples, well, of everything really.' Rebecca fished in her Fendi bag and threw a glossy magazine on to the bar. A girl in a tux pouted furiously at them. PARVENU. 'We'll call you associate ed, if you want. Doesn't mean anything. But everyone else is an editor, even the messenger, so you might as well be.' Her mission complete, Rebecca wilted elegantly again and began to murmur into her cocktail about Working Class Energy.

Susan knew of Parvenu. It was a magazine which proclaimed, subtitled on the cover of every issue, 'LIFE IS A PARTY'. It was frivolous, snobbish and shallow. But after The Beat, where thirty-year-old men looked for the meaning of life in plastic platters, it came as a breath of fresh carbon monoxide. So she murmured into her Black Russian about a Time For Everything and the New Selfishness. Displaying a healthy measure of it, Rebecca shot off five minutes later leaving Susan to pay for the drinks.

In her two years at Parvenu Susan learned how to call dinner lunch, how to call enemies 'Darling', how to dress, how to drink and how to tell the perfect lie. She also learned things about men that made Gary Pride look like a verger.

One afternoon after a fashion shoot she went to bed with three male models. In the morning one of them asked her if she had ever done it with an Afghan.

'Guerrilla?'

He ruffled her hair and laughed. 'Hound, silly.'

Then she interviewed a hot young actor at a hotel in Kensington. They stayed in his room for a week, ordering cocaine, champagne and caviar from the hotel's various pantries. On the day of his departure he was very quiet. He didn't look at her as he packed and she guessed that he was already psyching himself into his next role: that of loving, faithful boyfriend to the filthy rich Manhattan heiress he was engaged to.

'Aren't you going to give me anything to remember you by?' she finally asked flirtatiously and desperately from the bed.

He pulled on his cowboy boots, stood up and looked down at her. 'I have,' he said quietly. 'Herpes.' Then he was out of the door, carrying the one canvas tote bag that made up his luggage, a man-of-the-people affectation that had charmed her a week ago and now revolted her.

It took two weeks, a week's wages and a private clinic before she was sure he was just a sadist with a kooky sense of humour. Herpes was the new urban folk demon; people told jokes against it as if to inoculate themselves. What do the couple who have everything have embroidered on their towels? 'HIS' and 'HERPES'.

She shared a flat in SW10 with a cousin of Isabella's, the girl at the next desk in the Parvenu office. The girl called herself Trash. She was impossibly rich, had five A-levels and worked in an Arab clip joint in W1. Her family were related by marriage to a certain Family who shall be nameless and blameless. She wore her evening clothes only once: on coming home, around four in the morning, she dropped them into the matt black dustbin as other more frugal girls might drop them carelessly on to the floor after a hard day at the office. Occasionally, she burned that night's dress in the sink, scat singing arias from Madame Butterfly as she did so.

Trash had two hyphens, not one, in her surname. Susan once didn't see or hear her for six weeks. They never talked. Trash seemed to regard conversation as a breach of good manners. Once Susan, a little drunk and lonely, stopped her as they passed in the hallway and asked her why she needed a flatmate. Trash smiled like a game-show host.

'Because I can't stand a cold toilet seat.'

When she killed herself in the bath one Monday morning, Susan discovered that Trash had really been Georgia. 'But I always called her Trash!' she said to Isabella as they waited for the lift down one night. Somehow it seemed very important.

Isabella smiled absently. 'Oh, don't worry. Everyone called her Trash. Even her ma.'

'That's not the point.'

'Sorry?'

Who, what, why, where, when? This was supposed to be the mantra of journalism. It went through her head, more and more, like the slick black backbeat of a soul song. She couldn't answer any of them. She read cereal packets and racing results to find an answer. She spent a preternatural amount of time listening to the lyrics of popular songs. A song called 'Boogie Oogie Oogie' drove her to distraction for a few weeks; she bought the single and stayed at home in the evenings with the stylus on auto, listening to it fifty times in a row. She was convinced it was trying to tell her something.

She got drunk every night and every morning woke up with a headache where her memory had once been. The thought of suicide was always there, comforting, like old money to be fallen back on in desperate times. Sometimes only the thought of death made life bearable. A greyhound winner called Too Much Too Young made her laugh for half an hour. WHO, WHAT, WHY, WHERE, WHEN?

Then she met Matthew.

Matthew Stockbridge sat at his desk in the big South London hospital and looked across at the pretty, sick-looking girl who was trying to insert a cheese sandwich into her tape recorder.

'I'm ver' sorry,' she slurred. 'Some sort of malpractice.'

He laughed, a little shocked. 'No, Miss Street, you came here to ask me about malpractice suits. Didn't you?'

'Malpractice. No, malfunction.' She dropped the sandwich on to the desk and stared at it. 'Oh look,' she said brightly. 'I wondered where that got to.' She looked up at him, her pupils almost completely covering her grey irises.

'Miss Street, which drug are you on?'

She rifled through her bag and triumphantly shoved a twist of foil under his nose. 'Sulphate. Almost pure. Want some?'

'No thank you.'

Now she was gazing over his shoulder into the far corner of the room with something between amusement and terror.

'What's wrong?'

'There's a bird in that corner. It's the Roadrunner,' she said matter-of-factly.

'Really?'

'Oh yes. It's the Roadrunner and it's doing the Charleston.'

'Miss Street, I assure you it's not. It's amphetamine sulphate, which has gone to your liver and been transformed into mescalin due to extreme abuse and lack of food and sleep. Am I right?'

She smiled knowingly at him. Then she leaned across the desk and shot the best part of the litre bottle of Perrier water she had been drinking into his lap. Then she began to laugh, so hard that she fell off her chair. She lay on her back, retching up a vile yellow bile and laughing.

Matthew Stockbridge dodged around the desk and knelt beside her. She looked at him.

'Who, what, why, where, when?' she asked weakly.

'Whatever you want.' He laughed too. 'It's all right now, Susan.'

That had been seven years ago. Time, the great vandal, had had its bash at them, and love had gone about halfway through, but she still hadn't got around to moving out. When you were both busy moderns, there was very little time for elaborate things like leaving. You were always too busy buying things and signing things and throwing things, from dinner parties to dishes. There weren't enough hours in the day for you to move out. Even when everything else had gone.

***

She was twenty when she met Charles Anstey, a man with a mission to take the void out of tabloid, at London Fashion Week. He was with his tall, dark and ugly clothesaholic French wife Lorraine. Twenty years ago she must have seemed like good value to a provincial boy in the outer suburbs of his youth but now she had the bitter, disappointed face and grudgingly anorexic body of the fading fashion victim in danger of becoming a fashion fatality.

They sat on either side of Charles, Lorraine nagging for clothes, Susan hustling for a job, like cross caricatures of pre- and post-feminist woman.

'The young reader,' Susan elaborated enthusiastically, telling him things he knew already but doing it in such an excited way that he couldn't help but nod seriously, 'that's what you want – no one needs a dying readership. Get them young. And the women readers – don't marginalize them. Think about them on every page. Newspapers aren't just about news any more. You should be taking readers from the women's magazines – not just from each other.'

She never found out if Lorraine got what she wanted from Charles Anstey – but she did. A week later he called her at Parvenu and asked her if she would like a job as a feature writer on the new Sunday Best.

She was a good journalist, but not that good. She had once thrown a scare into a rentboy trying to sell the dirt on a Labour

MP just because she was young and idealistic and believed in the things he stood for. And because he was fun to lunch. She wouldn't do that now, she thought. And a really good tabloid reporter would never have done it. She had been pleased when promotion to features editor lifted her out of the scramble for stories. And then for almost two years she had been deputy editor and next in line to the editor's chair. Until now.

She was jolted in her seat and out of her dreams. The train had arrived.

And so had she.

TWO

The next day was a Tuesday, first day of the working week for the Sunday papers. She slept like a baby – one hour sleeping, one hour crying, and so on – rose early and dressed carefully.

Her best Azzedine Alaïa, plain and black and respectful. Ok, so it was tight as a tourniquet and had only a passing acquaintance with her thighs. But Charles had always been a leg man. Her earrings were small and jet, Cobra and Bellamy, and her shoes were simple and black, Kurt Geiger, with a very modest four-inch heel.

Talking of shoes, she expected it would be fairly easy to step into Charles's, and she didn't mean the ones still waiting patiently outside the Brighton bedroom fresh from their overnight cleaning. Poor Charles; he had died not with his boots on but his hard on.

The *Best*'s proprietor, Lord Tooth, was a sweetie, and a fairly senile one at that. Susan's protégée, Zero, called anyone over forty a Senile Citizen, and Lord Tooth qualified nicely. He was fond of Susan, thought her very young and daring, and always asked her if the Beatles had re-formed yet. She didn't have the heart to tell him that one of them was really dead and the other three were brain dead. It was a cinch.

It was nothing of the sort.

As she walked into the open-plan office, people sniggered in small groups. She thought she heard someone hum a few bars of the Dead March from *Saul*. Holding her head high she walked into her room and shut the door.

When Susan picked up one of the three telephones that squatted smugly on her desk, she was greeted by the noise she most dreaded hearing, that of five smacking wet kisses in a row. It was in this way that Ingrid Irving invariably greeted her. A few steps behind Susan but climbing fast, and well connected to a long line of dukes and judges in a way Susan could only dream of, Ingrid was a regular fixture on BBC panel games – telegenic and, if her grasp of gossip was anything to go by, telepathic. She was always described in print as 'vivacious', which meant that she giggled a lot and sucked up to anything in boxer shorts. She was the only person Susan knew who wore taffeta before noon. An old song of Frank Sinatra's that her mother had played to death came to Susan's mind, slightly subbed, at the thought of Ingrid. *Picture a tarantula in tulle . . . that's Ingrid with the grinning skull.*

Now the five kisses exploded wetly in her ear, making her wince. 'Darling, tell me *everything!* Did he die with his boots on? Or his trousers?'

'So far as I know, he died with his overcoat on. Hello, Ingrid.'

'Hello, darling.' There was a barrage of popping corks at the other end of the phone, much shrieking and a few bars of 'Tomorrow Belongs To Me'.

'Why are you at home, Ingrid?'

'Oh, I'm not, darling. Nose to the grindstone. Come on, you know what it's like . . . even the seccies stay drunk until Friday. Just having a few mates over – Jasper, *stop* it. Leave that poor little messenger *alone*.'

'Listen, Ingrid, I know even less about this terrible thing than you. I'm going to find Oliver and get the story. See you anon, OK?'

'See you for lunch, sweetie.'

Not if I see you first, *sweetie*.

She rose grimly to her feet and walked next door into Oliver Fane's office; number three on the paper and a prize snoot to boot. Like the rest of his colleagues he loathed her – for her age, her gender and a horde of less important reasons, such as believing that she was spectacularly untalented. 'A woman's place is on the woman's page,' said a memo on her desk soon after her promotion. She was sure it came from him.

He was lounging, with a smile on his face and his feet on the desk, but jumped up when he saw her.

'Susan, Susan!' He came round the desk and took her consolingly by the arm. 'Have a seat! Heard the news? No, of course not, you've been too . . . upset.'

'News?'

'We've been sold!'

'Sold?' She sat down quickly.

'Sold!' he said triumphantly, like a gleeful auctioneer unloading a naff antique. 'This very morning!'

'But . . .'

'To Tobias Pope!' He leered. 'Not very good news, is it? Especially considering what a . . . special relationship you had with old Tooth.' *That* put the tail-switching little counterjumper in her place. *He* had a 2:1 from Oxford *and* had trained at the *Times and* done the mandatory NUJ stint at the provincial hellhole. There was nothing he hated more than someone who hadn't paid their dues – unless it was someone who got paid more than him. Susan Street was both.

Susan Street was stunned. Tobias Pope was as different a prospect from old Lord Tooth as you could imagine. With a reputation somewhere between Rupert Murdoch, G. Gordon Liddy and the Marquis de Sade, he ruled his communications empire with fear and loathing – his employees feared him, and he loathed them. He had been heard to refer to the people in his pay and his pocket as 'my reps' – short not for representatives, but for reptiles. If Lord Tooth would have seen Silly Putty in her hands, Tobias Pope was going to be US Steel.

Oliver Fane was burbling on. 'Apparently it's been on the cards for months. Only that idiot Tooth didn't have the heart to tell Charles. He thought he'd be upset or something, because of their *special relationship* – I think that means he bonked Charles's mother on a house party thirty years ago. Anyway, he planned to tell him today, but as the fickle finger of fate would have it . . . Susan?'

There was a thump. Susan Street had fainted.

When she came to she was being slapped, much harder than was absolutely necessary. A suntanned man in his fifties, the lines on his face a conspiracy between climate and a cruel nature, was hitting her rhythmically around the face with a black-gloved hand. 'Ah, here it is!' he said, looking straight into her wide-open eyes and smiling. Taking a glass of water from Oliver Fane's secretary, he threw it straight at her chest.

She gasped in shock and horror. The skintight Alaïa seemed as though it might burst open like a peach hit by a hammer under the weight and wetness of her breasts. The assembled staff of the *Sunday Best* stood around and gaped. In their wildest, wettest dreams, the rude awakening of Susan Street had never been so beautifully, humiliatingly realized.

The man laughed. 'You seem refreshed, my dear.' He hauled her to her feet and shook her hand delicately. 'Allow me. My name is Tobias X. Pope and I am your new owner.' He turned on his heel, a flurry of flunkies swelling on all sides. 'Oh, and by the way – you're fired. Have a nice day!'

Matthew Stockbridge sat on the bed, clean-cut even at nine in the evening, wearing a blue Czech & Speake bathrobe, with a bottle of Badoit and a Virago paperback by his side. Handsome, sensitive, successful – and completely undesirable, she reflected sourly as she looked at his image in the five mirrors of her dressing table. Five Matthews! She couldn't find the correct use for *one* any more.

Matthew was fair in both temperament and colouring; a basic blond dreamboat to be eaten up with the eyes and toyed with by the other senses until it sank in with some surprise that he was intelligent and droll, with a smile around the eyes that rarely reached his mouth and therefore seemed all the more genuine. He was the English Popular Schoolboy grown up: with a broken voice and a brace of broken hearts behind him, he was still putting his best foot forward. He was the boy who *did* like games, but also liked Henry James; defender of the weak and seducer of the sleek. He had never given his mother a sleepless night or his girls edible underwear and sexually transmitted diseases. Some would have said he was the perfect New Man.

Susan's Zero, though, said the only New Man women had time for was *Paul*. For such lines was Zero paid 45K p.a. by Susan and referred to as 'The Executive Toy' by her

28

colleagues. She was also known as Caligula's Little Pony, because the boy emperor had been powerful, wilful and foolish enough to make his horse a senator.

Zero said that Matthew was a big *girl*, and when would men discover the obvious fact that strong women wanted strong men, or real girls, but certainly not some tepid hybrid of the two? Sometimes when Susan was drunk, she agreed. Occasionally, when she was seriously drunk, she said it to his face.

Tonight was not one of those nights: why waste time tweaking the monkey's testicles when the organ grinder's got his foot on your neck? As men went he looked decent if dull from where she was sitting. She had been brooding over the object of her hostility while making three-quarters of a bottle of Stolichnaya disappear since leaving the office in a state of shock this morning and now, when she jumped up and began to pace the room, cursing, Matthew was not the target, or even the target practice, of the poison arrows shot from the bow of her wounded pride.

'*Everyone* will be *talking* about me!' she said yet again, and was struck unpleasantly by how little removed this major fear of hers was from her mother's concern to keep the neighbours from talking. You've come a long way, baby, but you can't escape the long armlock of the neighbours, even if they do go under the name of your peer group in this tax bracket. '*Laughing* at me. *Me!* This is just what they've been praying for, those miserable bastards.'

'Come on, Sue,' Matthew said soothingly. 'That's called paranoia.'

'It's called an educated guess where I come from.' She flung herself down on the bed and stared at the ceiling. 'Why in hell did this have to happen *now*? Just when everything was going so wonderfully.'

'Susan,' he reprimanded her quietly. 'The sudden, painful and early death of a man who advanced your career beyond all others can hardly be described as wonderful.'

'You know what I mean. Objectively. Career-wise. Oh, don't go getting all Hippocratic on me, Matthew. And then there's the son – this is the *real* joke. The *Best* is going to be used as some sort of sacrificial lamb, some sort of fatted calf killed to tempt the prodigal son back into the fold – a toy, stuffed into the toe of some rich brat's Christmas stocking! A toy – *my* life, *my* paper!'

'Yours?' He smiled.

'You talk about "my hospital"! Anyway, it *would* have been mine – in every sense of the word. I'd be editor right now, if not for Pope. You know that!'

He looked at her and thought how true it was that some women were beautiful when they were angry. Drink and temper had flushed her face and swollen her lips, and her eyes flashed like neon. He leaned over and stroked her hair. 'Hey. Calm down. It's not the end of the world.'

'I can't calm down.'

'Maybe I can help you.'

He slid down the bed, peeled off her tights and parted her legs.

She sighed inwardly. Oh, no, on top of her other troubles, Matthew had chosen this moment to be Good In Bed. She had heard of a time before the Seventies when women were always complaining to each other about how Bad In Bed men were – and Bad In Bed, it always transpired, was polite English for a refusal to contemplate cunnilingus. Oh, ignorant bliss.

Then suddenly it was the Seventies and, ever since Susan Street could remember, men were launching themselves like ground-to-air missiles at your groin with their tongues hanging out the second after they'd first shaken hands with you. Some sort of mass, subliminal brainwashing seemed to have convinced them that a quick lick won them instant promotion to the Demon Lover league and elevated their victim to the realms of convulsive ecstasy.

How shocked they'd be if they knew how bored most girls were by it! And the ones who really liked it usually became lesbians – because when you got down to it, or went down to it, no one knew better than a girl what a girl liked.

Her mind wandered as he got stuck in. That was the one good thing about cunnilingus: like ironing, it freed your mind to dwell on higher things.

Just a small corner of her consciousness remained tethered to the bed, and there she felt just a faint irritation; the physical equivalent of hearing a fly buzzing to get out against a closed window on a hot summer's day when you were laid up in traction and couldn't move a muscle to free it. Neither heaven nor hell but one long, annoying limbo, that's what the act had become. She fought the temptation to swat at his eager little head, as if he was that poor pesky fly.

Cunnilingus is the waiting-room of sex, she decided, and felt a flash of nostalgia for those days she had never known, when men thought it was disgusting. Men who were Bad In Bed were no bother: two minutes' acting, five minutes' reassurance and you could go on to do something more fun. Men who were Good In Bed were another matter: five hours' acting, two hours' rave reviews and by then they were ready to go again. People made a fuss about Bruce Springsteen doing four hours on stage – big deal! The level of showmanship and stamina a modern girl needed nightly in the sack made him look like a two-minute wonder.

She wondered once more just why she kept Matthew on in there when he could be out sticking his tongue up some deserving and grateful girl. And she knew that it was because once you had a man these days, you hung on to him until something better came along. You didn't just throw the paddle out of the boat and leave yourself up the creek waiting for something else to float by. Because the chances were it wouldn't.

Susan knew that there wasn't officially a man shortage; she had run a survey in the paper only two weeks previously which told her that there was actually a glut of young men in the developed countries of the West, an extra one million in the USA alone. The trouble was that half of them were called Jasper – and the other half weren't good enough. There wasn't a *man* shortage, but there was a Superman shortage.

Ingrid Irving had a theory that there had been a war that no one had told them about, in which all the heterosexual men under forty, over six foot and earning more than fifty K a year had been wiped out. 'They used this weapon which was sort of a very sophisticated version of the neutron bomb,' explained Ingrid. 'You know – that left buildings standing but wiped out people. Well, *this* bomb – the Talent-Taker – wiped out all the hunks and left the jerks standing. The sort of men that used to be called 4F: fags, failures, fatsos and freaks.'

Women, unlike men, were raised on the pornography of perfection; first pop stars, then romantic fiction heroes. The higher they climbed, and the more they were told they could have it all, the less inclined to compromise they became; an inferior man would cast doubts on their hard-won status. Sexually speaking, successful women had become fussy eaters.

Men, on the other hand, learned early to make the best of things. They had a dream girl, but until that came along, their hormones urged them to look on the bright side. There were no female counterparts of such pragmatically obscene sayings as 'Who looks at the mantelpiece when you're poking the fire?' and 'All cats are grey in the dark'. Long before they graduated to the stapled *smorgasbord* of the centrefold, they learned to appreciate the cheap and cheerful girls of the downmarket end of so-called adult books (which might be more accurately described as magazines for masturbating juveniles). They learned sexual compromise: she's got cross eyes, but great legs! No teeth, but look at the tits on it!

They were lucky, Susan thought as she lay on the bed. Every time she considered leaving Matthew, she only had to look at him to realize what a bargain he was. He was handsome, successful, intelligent and solvent; she couldn't settle for anything less. She'd just have to wait until she could get something more.

The phone rang and automatically she reached across the bed to answer it.

'Ignore it,' begged Matthew, raising his head for a minute before carrying on where he'd left off.

She ignored him instead. 'Hello?'

'Susan?'

'Who is this?'

'This is Tobias Pope. I was wondering whether you would like your job back. Or even your dead boyfriend's job.'

A whimpering noise escaped her, which was more than Matthew's mouth had achieved in a quarter of an hour. What could she say? Yes sounded pathetic, no sounded suicidal. She was literally speechless.

'Hello? Are you there, Susan? Speak up, girl. Do you want the job or don't you?'

'Yes,' she said sulkily.

'Good. I've booked a table at Le Drive for ten; actually I've booked all the tables. Can you be there in time? If not, I'll ask someone else.'

'I can be there.'

'Good. I like black dresses. Make sure you wear one.'

She gaped into the vacant phone.

'Who was that?' asked Matthew softly. Oh, he'd stopped. She hadn't noticed.

'A friend.' She swung her legs gracefully over his head, got up and walked over to her wardrobe, throwing open the door and gazing at her row of clothes without seeing anything. 'A friend and benefactor.' She grabbed at a black Rifat Ozbek and pulled it over her head. Snatching up her Mason-Pearson hairbrush and her Etienne Augier briefcase, she ran down the stairs.

At the front door it occurred to her that she hadn't said goodbye to Matthew. She yelled it up the stairs. But it was a big house, and she couldn't be sure he'd heard her. And she didn't have any time to waste.

'Punctuality! One of the great virtues!' Tobias Pope smiled at her across the table as though she was the entrée and he planned to have her flambéed in brandy. 'And so much more important than all those milk-and-water so-called virtues like honesty, decency and loyalty. On the contrary, I call those vices: soul-sapping things only to be indulged in by those who've cancelled their subscription to the human race. Don't you agree, Susan?'

'Absolutely.' She looked at his face with interest; it was an unmistakably American face of the type that can be traced from Mount Rushmore to American soap opera patriarchs. It was stubborn, obsessively individualistic and it led with its jaw; his hair was a shade best described as Pentagon Pewter, and his eyes were bright blue, too blue, bright and beautiful in his weather-beaten and wolverine face. They looked unreal, transplants stolen from a screen idol, and they made her uncomfortable. She pretended an interest in the decor of Le Dive, done out in the matt black and lacquered red of a designer opium den; those colors which the rag hags predicted would be replaced by pastels every year, and which never were.

It really was empty, for the first time in the three years since it had opened. He really had booked all the tables; it must have cost him thousands of pounds sterling. Just a tip in the ocean, she guessed.

'Really, Mr Pope, a Big Mac would have done nicely.'

'A cheap date, too!' He laughed. 'Oh, that's a good one. I like that. I like *you*, Susan. I like you so much I'll level with you.'

He leaned across the table, close. She could smell his aftershave, something very old and expensive that made her think of the time when New York phone numbers had been preceded by codes like 'Rhinelander' and 'Plaza'. She couldn't place it, and not being able to place a man's aftershave for once – and thus not being able to write him off with one pertinent put-down – made her feel oddly disorientated and powerless.

'I can get a lot of women,' he said. 'Too many, in fact. There is such a thing, believe me. In some countries, though I shan't say which, I can literally get any woman I want, from the strutting little generalissimo's wife down to the last sad *muchacha* in shanty town. Here in your fine country, where the women are fair, the policemen are wonderful and the guys like nothing more than to dress up in frocks and play football, I can get up to – let's see, arriviste minor royalty. Easily.

'But they're just blue-blooded bimbos, basically, and once you've had them they're as much fun as some dumb wetback wench who can't speak a word of American. They're worse, because you can't pretend you don't speak their language. And I'm so sick of bimbo talk, and bimbos. Do you know why, Susan?'

'Because you want an old-fashioned girl?' She gulped at her vodka martini.

He laughed again. 'Well caught. But no. It's because I'm bored with breaking bimbos. It's no fun, no challenge, no sport – it's like putting Sugar Ray in the ring with a crippled midget. No. Strong, hard career girls – they're the new *filet mignon* of females. They're the new frontier for a man. Girls like you. Oh, I'd have fun breaking you, Susan.' He frowned at her plate. 'Eat your dinner, you're too thin.' His tone was grotesquely paternal.

She poked at her sautéed chicken in bourbon. Her throat was so tight she couldn't have swallowed a peanut. She wondered if it would be bad form to ask for her next martini intravenously.

He was mad. He wanted to hurt her.

She wanted to hear more. She must be mad, too.

She looked at him. 'I don't think I understand you.'

'Oh, I think you do.' He took a pecan from her plate. 'I'll tell you how I see the schedule. You've read about the twelve labours of Hercules, I suppose?' He laughed. 'I take it you can read?'

'Oh yes. Especially between the lines.'

'Good girl.' Bourbon from the pilfered pecan ran down his chin. He looked even more like the king of the concrete jungle at feeding time. How do you like your blood sacrifice, sir? Rare, please. 'Well, let's think about this proposition in a classical vein. Let's call it the six labours of Susan. See how modest my demands are? And believe me, my imagination runs well into telephone numbers. International calls at that. But you have only six tasks to complete. Of course, there is no logical reason at all why I should give you your job back, let alone your victim's. Your conduct was disgraceful, unprofessional and indefensible.' He sighed 'Yet you have a dream and I have a whim.'

She laid down her knife and stared him straight in the eye. 'What is it?'

'You do what I want, and you get what you want.' He snapped a breadstick neatly in two. 'Or you break.'

He had his driver take her home. He didn't touch her. He didn't need to. He told her to report for work on time the next morning. And he told her to sleep on it.

She thought that it might be marginally less difficult sleeping on a bed of nails . . .

But things looked brighter the next day. At the editor's desk she found a stuttering, sarcastic Australian called Bryan O'Brien, a Pope Communications corporate man notorious as a first-rate caretaker editor but nothing more. He posed no threat and might even turn into an advantage; like most Australians he adored English girls and abhorred English men, especially educated ones. Which meant that Fane, for one, was back where he belonged – eating expense-account humble pie.

And she was still deputy. People were respectful, if not friendly, again – when had they ever been? The thought of how her dear colleagues would dance on her desk if a new editor was brought in over her head made her fists clench and the room swim. She felt she would do anything to save her face. Anything. Even sacrifice her soul.

'Kathy, when Blondell gets here send her straight in, would you?'

Now Charles was gone and before Bryan was won over, her protégée would be her only ally in the office. A tall, slender bottle-blonde from Tiger Bay, Zero Blondell had marched into Susan's office slightly more than a year ago and announced that she was Miss Street's temp. Barely looking at her, Susan had handed her a pile of routine letters to type. The girl had thanked her politely and returned three-quarters of an hour later to lay a pile of foolscap paper on her desk. The letters were there, beautifully typed. But beneath them, also immaculate, was a two-thousand-word rant, wanderfully written, on the sorry state of 1980s man. It was called 'WHERE'S THE BEEF?' and it was signed 'Zero Blondell'.

'That's my new name. That's who I want to be,' the girl said simply when Susan called her in to explain herself. 'I don't think I look like a Pratt, do you?' Zero had been Myfanwy Pratt then. 'No, don't answer that. But as you can see, I type beautifully and I give great shorthand too. See, I was trained as a secretary and then one day I thought, "Why should I fritter my young life away copying down these decrepit old men's stupid thoughts all day when mine are so much better?" So I saved up and came here six months ago. I've been temping, and I've tried slipping my own stuff in at various magazines before. But no one takes you seriously if you bleach your hair and walk with wiggle. Until now.' She smiled seductively at Susan, showing a mouthful of pale primrose teeth, some cracked and chipped for good measure. They were incongruous behind the high gloss of her Schiaparelli hot pink pout. 'Would you like me to be your secretary, Miss Street? I'll sit on your lap. And take dic—'

'No thank you, Miss Pratt,' said Susan firmly. 'I think your talents might be somewhat wasted making tea.'

'Then can I be a writer?' Zero Blondell literally wrung her hands, like a Dickens orphan. 'Oh, *please* can I?'

'Let me think.' She thought, and decided in double-quick time that this strange young person could be just what the chief sales rep ordered to secure the elusive ABC1 young professional audience every paper craved. They enjoyed a bit of controversy served up over Sunday brunch, and all the *Best* could boast by way of provocation was a middle-aged *enfant terrible* whose vitriol had been watered down with gin over the years and who was usually too drunk to actually write the column. Instead assorted hacks rallied round with stray squibs about the royal family and popular entertainers and why their bad behaviour was emblematic of a moral decline – and their star took more than fifty thousand pounds a year just for use of an old photograph and a byline. Looking at Zero Blondell's hot copy and eager face, this didn't look much like a bargain any more. 'Let me talk to the editor. Take your piece away with you, and if you want to work in your lunch hour and cut it by six hundred words – well, I can't make any promises.'

'Oh, thank you, Miss Street! You angel! You saint!' The beautiful girl leaned across the desk and squeezed her tight, leaving a faint but unmistakable odour of halitosis. Well, no one was perfect.

It took all Susan's powers of persuasion and promises of the capture of the mythical young and female readerships to get her a licence for Zero from Charles. At first he had been appalled by Zero's spite and spleen. Within a month he had realized that, unlike ninety per cent of the people employed in newspapers, she really could write. This presented its own set of problems. Unlike the more mediocre hacks, she was fierce about the subediting of what she wrote; she once walked up to a dozing sub just back from the pub and a liquid lunch, slapped his face and hissed, 'I refuse to believe that you could derive full job satisfaction anywhere outside of an abattoir in the rush hour.' Tantrum followed tantrum until Susan stepped in and took the task upon herself. Since then Zero had been sweetness and light. She could afford to be. At twenty-three, she was earning more than any other writer in the office and only slightly less than the editors.

As if this wasn't enough to distinguish her, she was flamboyantly and violently lesbian.

'Why do you hate men so much?' Susan had asked her as they lounged over martinis at the Groucho.

'I was married to one.' Zero laughed.

'Fuck. Off. I make two-fifty a word, so that just cost you a fiver,' she spat at a middle-aged reporter who tried to

42

put his arm around her in a fit of drunken bonhomie one Christmas Eve. She was civil only to Charles, Susan – and the secretaries. She made them coffee and tried to look up their skirts when they went up stepladders in search of research material. 'Zero, back to your desk!' Susan would scold if she caught her at either. 'You are not being paid to make either tea or whoopee. You are being paid to write!' Zero would pout furiously, as she always did on being found out.

'When in doubt, pout,' she once told Susan was her philosophy of life.

For someone who didn't like men, Susan thought as she waited for the girl to arrive, Zero could do a pretty good imitation of the very worst sort. What a bastard she could be. Susan had seen literally groups of girls – three, four – sniffing and weeping in the street outside the *Best*'s main entrance while Zero sneaked in the back way in her veiled black pillbox and trenchcoat. She pretended to be appalled by the sensation she created, but when she wasn't working hard at it her genuine glee crept through. 'Look at them, Susie!' she would hiss, leaning out of Susan's window and squinting at her fan club below as they chainsmoked, compared case histories and complained shrilly to each other. 'Look at the brunette! She's Italian – what a beaut! I had her last week – no strings, no promises. Now she thinks we're engaged or something, she's threatening to get her brother on to me! Dig the redhead! What a dog, but what

43

a pair! Her father's in the FO – she wants to move in with me! Me, the milkman's daughter!'

'Zero, have you always had this effect on women?'

'Oh no, bach, only since I was seventeen. Right after I was married. It went awful from the start; I was a good chapel girl, knew nothing about the dirty deed. I couldn't ever fancy fucking the pig. I thought I was frigid, he told me enough times I was. He was a right slag, even after we were married. So, I was sitting in the doctor's waiting-room one night waiting for my monthly supply of instant thrombosis and I read in some magazine about how to improve your marriage. Well, mine could use the improving. And rule one was "Interest yourself in your husband's hobby". And I realized that Dai's hobbies were rugby and women. I'm not athletic, so women were all that was left. So I interested myself in them.' Zero sighed at the memory. 'All those coffee mornings and girls' nights out. There certainly wasn't any lack of opportunity. You'd be amazed how easy it was, Susan bach. Men are such bad fucks that a girl can get a girl as easy as *that*' – she snapped her fingers – 'when the lights are low and the Babycham is flowing. Well, within a year I was the Lothario of the valleys. You bet I had to leave town! So I came here, to sin city. I had my typing, didn't I, the working-class girl's weapon. And I made a point of temping for media women. So within weeks I learned about the Muffia, and I knew that was the world for me.' She pouted. 'But all those other media tarts just wanted my

44

body, not my copy. You're the first editor to love me for my mind, not my behind.'

Zero maintained the existence of something called the Muffia, a loose affiliation of media lesbians who spent their lives laying, lunching and launching each other up the ladder of success. Susan had never caught a whiff of it in all her ten years of journalism. But maybe she had been looking – or sniffing – in the wrong places.

'Zero, why are you so mean to those girls?' she had asked.

'Oh, I don't mean to be mean, bach. But girls are such pretty things, and there's so many of them in this city. It's a city full of pretty girls. You think you're having drinks with the cutest girl in the world, and then you look up into the waitress's eyes and you could drown in them. You can't help yourself leaving your card with the tip. I always write on mine, "Heaven is seven numbers away." '

Susan made a retching noise.

'No, it's an old lie about girls being nicer to girls than men. They're not, they're just more fun. Going with girls, no Pill or pregnancy or losing your figure – why, it's just like being a teenager all your life! You should try it, babes, you really should.'

'It sounds wonderful. There's just one snag.'

'What?'

'I don't fancy girls.'

Now the girl herself was walking through the door wearing one of her legion of black dresses, this one plain except for a striking tail proudly standing out behind. She carried the trade press, which she threw on to Susan's desk. 'Hi, babes. Seen these?'

'TOOTH OUT – POPE INFALLIBLE?' they screamed. Susan shook her head. 'God, the standard of journalism in this country.' They laughed.

'So what's happening to you? Being kicked upstairs?'

'Yes. Right into his bedroom.'

Zero made wide eyes. 'No!'

'Seriously. You wouldn't believe what he wants me to do.'

'I'd believe anything of men.'

'He wants me to do six tasks for him. Just do what he wants six times.'

'Isn't that just like a man?' Zero laughed. 'It's called being married. Only it doesn't end after six times.'

'Should I do it?'

'What do you get?'

'I think I get the editorship. Don't tell anyone.'

'Don't tell anyone, but I think you should do it.'

'Do you think I could?'

'I don't see why not.' Zero's face went very young and hard, as it never failed to do when talking about sex with men. Specifically, about Susan having sex with men. 'You don't love Matthew. Charles wasn't the most appetizing morsel of man-meat I've seen in my young life. In fact he was a real dog. But you did *that*.' She pouted accusingly. 'For *years*.'

46

'I *liked* Charles.'

'I fail to see exactly where or why your feelings have to be engaged. It's business, not pleasure.'

'YOU wouldn't do it.'

'Ah, but I'm not a career girl. I'm a congenital genius. If I *were* a career girl, and one of many after the same thing, I'd use anything I had to get it. I would work on a Protean basis – I would recreate myself constantly. I'd be a bitch in the boardroom and a slave in the sack. I'd be what I had to be until I could be what I want. We're lucky: we're women. We can recreate ourselves in a way men can't because artifice doesn't become second nature to them in childhood as it does to us.'

Susan looked at her suspiciously. 'Did you swallow a thesaurus?'

Zero giggled. 'No, I ate out a Kenyan girl, second-year PPE at Oxford. God, did we have some classy pillow talk.'

'So what you're saying, stop me if I'm wrong, is that I should behave like a whore?'

Zero shrugged elaborately. 'You become a whore the minute you sleep with a man. I'm just asking you to be a pro.'

'I think you're horrible.'

'Yeah, well, go and ask your girly boyfriend what you should do if you want the blushing broad angle.'

'But he's over *fifty*.'

'All the better for you. How much can it take to keep him happy?' Zero rifled through the 'Strictly Confidential' file. 'God, is that all Pascoe's getting? No wonder he gives me the fish eye. You know the new metropolitan measure of how well you're doing? You have to get your age in thousands. At *least*. Where's the wife?'

'In the Sunny von Bulow Clinic, I think. Upstate New York. Stop that, Zero. Rich alkie or something.'

'Where's the son?'

'America. Big daddy has yet to persuade him to check out his new toy printing set.'

'Didn't he used to hang around with Caroline Malaise? The old man, I mean?'

'God, yes. I'd forgotten. All those pictures of them in Dempster three years ago leaving Langan's.'

'Talk about Beauty and the Beast! Wasn't she some sort of vague royal? – the blue-blooded bimbo they used to call her. Now *there*'s a career that spontaneously combusted.'

'Didn't some French director say she was the new Catherine Deneuve?'

'Do me a favour. They didn't know what to do with the old one once she lost her milk teeth, But Caroline Malaise! Well – and now he wants you – little Susan Street from Nowhere-on-Sea!'

He wanted her, she thought. He did. But not half as much as she wanted power.

'Well' – Zero rose, straightening her tail fastidiously –

'It's all up to you, I suppose. You're the one who's got to do the dirty deed. Deeds. But I'll tell you one thing for nothing.' She paused with her hand on the handle. 'There are forty-four ugly, stupid men in this office, give or take a messenger boy or two. Not one of them isn't bitter and doesn't hate women and because of that not one of them hasn't crystallized his fear and loathing of modern women in you. And right now every one of them spends a good part of his waking hours wetting himself with glee because he's got a ringside seat for the downfall of Susan Street. If you fail, you're not just failing for yourself. You're in the inspiration game now, babes. I'd hate you to sleep with Pope, you know that. You must know I'm in love with you. But more than anything I'd hate to see you fail.' She closed the door quietly.

Susan sat at her desk staring into space for at least an hour, and by the time the phone rang and Kathy said it was Mr Pope from Munich, her mind was made up.

'I'll do it,' she said flatly. 'I'll do anything.'

THREE

As the car turned into the weeping neon wasteland of Saturday night King's Cross, Tobias Pope whooped with all the good-humoured excitement of a young American boy at a baseball game.

'Fast, Susan! Fast food and fast sex! I love it! These are our people, Susan – just the place for a fast mover like you to end up!'

Beside him in the back seat, Susan Street shivered inside her Nicole Farhi overcoat and clenched her fists. End up? What did *that* mean? The simmering fear that her first task might be to turn a trick came bubbling up inside her, making her heart pump hot blood into her cheeks.

'Ah, here we are. Come up and see my etchings, my dear.'

Up two flights of stairs, between a place which called itself Family Fun and was filled with middle-aged men staring hungrily at young boys feeding endless coins into shrill and fruitless fruit machines, and a fast-food restaurant called the Meat Machine (though this name would have done just as well for the alleged amusement arcade, she reflected sourly as she followed three steps behind the eager Pope looking for all the world like a sullen Muslim bride), Susan faced her first task.

The taskmaster turned out to be a large man wearing a rubber apron and scratching a greasy pigtail, looking suspiciously at Tobias Pope as the immaculate American pumped his hand enthusiastically.

'Let me shake the hand of artistry, my good man! And are your services available at this very moment?'

The man's expression changed to one Susan recognized as Let's-Skin-The-Tourist. 'Yep. Which one you want?' He gestured around the room.

On the walls, liberally interspersed with colour photographs of the Princess of Wales torn from tabloids, smiling down like a Madonna of the mezzobrows, were dozens of ornate, scrolled designs, of ships, wild beasts, hotrod cars.

'Not me, my good artisan. My daughter here. A more elegant and subtle motif, don't you think?'

Susan sat down quickly, conveniently in the subject's chair. She was in a tattoo parlour! Of course she'd read about them; she had even commissioned a feature on them when she worked at *Parvenu*. She and Isabella had screamed with laughter and pantomimed retching over the photographs taken to accompany the piece until the editor came out to investigate the racket. The sheer ugliness of the blank-eyed human flotsam who cared so little for themselves that they had reduced themselves to the level of walls to be mired in graffiti had appalled and repulsed her, despite her laughter. If anyone had told her she would one day be sitting in such a hellhole, not as an observer but an offering, she would have offered to call the men in white coats for them.

She got to her feet and, like the mythical drowning man, the faces of every man who had doubted her determination and ability to get to the top seemed to pass before her eyes, stopping at the assembled male mass of the *Sunday Best*. Dozens of ugly, resentful men, laughing, chattering, pointing as she cleared out her desk and walked through the newsroom and out the door for the last time. She could almost taste the salty tears of rage that coursed down her face.

No, no, no! Anything but that . . .

It might be a small design. In some hidden place. She knew that some bold girls about town had discreet lizards or birds on shoulders and ankles. She sat down.

Pope was conferring with the tattooist, smiling at her over the man's shoulder. She gestured to him frantically.

'Excuse me, my good man.' He crossed the room and looked down at her contemptuously. 'What's wrong with you? Not refusing at the first jump, are we? Like a common little carthorse.'

'Do you seriously intend for me to have one of these things?'

'Just a small one.'

'You mean a life-size representation of the HMS *Brazen*?'

'Just a small one.'

'How small?'

'Just a four-letter word. In letters no bigger than those of an upper-case typeface.'

Her mind raced, furtively thumbing and speed-reading the pages in her memory bank's dictionary of obscenity. 'Cunt?' she whispered finally.

Pope drew back and made a little moue of disgust. 'My dear Susan. You make your origins horribly obvious at times. No, *not* your job description; we both know that already.' He chuckled. 'A *clean* word. The cleanest word in the world, expressing all the beauty and symmetry of the free market.'

She shook her head blankly.

'You'll soon see, my dear.'

The tattooist cleared his throat in Technicolor.

'But lo, the muse is tugging at the sleeve of our primitive genius, bidding him hurry.' He patted her arm. 'I suggest we close our eyes.'

She closed her eyes. She felt a hand pin back her thick dark fringe. She heard the little cocktail tray of paints being wheeled up beside her. She heard the miniature dentist's drill being switched on. She heard the tattooist telling her to relax and starting a long rambling story about a Hell's Angel client who collapsed while having a Harley Davidson inscribed on his scrotum, which really helped her trepidation.

Then suddenly the pain started, filling her entire head with white sound. It was as though a laser beam of pain, no bigger than the point of a needle and as sharp, was moving across the centre of her forehead. She was just about to scream when it stopped. The room danced red and gold before her open eyes and she collapsed against Tobias Pope. The smell of his aftershave was grotesquely reassuring.

Money and a bandage changed hands, and then he carried her out to the car as though she was something infinitely precious to him, and laid her along the back seat.

'Drive,' he said.

'Where, sir?'

'Just drive.'

He slipped a silver flask between her lips and she gulped Hine brandy hungrily. He smoothed back her fringe and tugged gently at the bandage. She winced. He took a small flashlight from his pocket and examined his new *objet d'art*.

'Hmm, not bad. It's bleeding a little, and beginning to swell, but do you know what? I think it will look rather smart when it clears up.' He replaced the bandage.

'More brandy.'

'You've been very brave, Susan. That's enough, you don't want to go home drunk as a sailor on shore leave. *Very* brave. Some men would have collapsed. Proves what I say about women being the stronger sex. And getting stronger all the time: soon we men will just be used as house-boys, changing fuses and such. You've got much stronger stomachs already, I've always said so. Men couldn't work as prostitutes *en masse*, they'd be throwing up every time a new baggy body came through the door. They couldn't give birth, they'd die of fright. They can't take a tattoo without passing out. I admire the strength of you women, I really do.' He shone the flashlight in her face. 'Hmm, you don't look quite as green as you did a minute ago. Ready to go home?'

She nodded painfully.

'Good girl.' Leaning forward, he tapped on the glass. 'The first Saturday night of next month, Susan. Keep it free.'

He had picked her up just around the corner from the *Best* at nine, and he had her home before ten. She had told Matthew she was going to Tiger Bay with Zero for the weekend, so of course he was out drowning his sorrows – in alcohol-free lager, naturally. She fell into bed fully clothed, grateful for her thick dark fringe. But when she awoke, late on Saturday morning, Matthew was looking sternly down at her and her brow was bare. She grasped feebly at her missing fringe. Too late.

'Susan, you appear to have a tattoo on your face. Do you for a moment begin to comprehend what this can do to your blood? And the danger of infection from those wretched needles is beyond belief. In this day and age, and with your knowledge of the subject, I particularly thought you might . . .'

On he droned, about AIDS and Hep B and the whole yucky kit and caboodle. This was typical of the way their relationship had gone. Not WHY?, but a Government Health Warning. It wasn't much fun living with a pamphlet.

Finally, after touching briefly on the social stigma of tattoos in contemporary society, he asked her how it had happened.

'Zero and me had dinner at 192 and got so drunk on Velvet Hammers we missed the sleeper from Paddington. She dared me.'

He looked at her dubiously.

'I was drunk, Matt! You should see Zero! She's got a Sandinista on her thigh!'

'Left or right?'

'Left, of course.'

He sighed. 'You're impossible, Susan.' Rolling off the bed he pulled on his tracksuit. 'I'm going jogging. See you.'

She lay there miserably for a few minutes, then when she heard the door slam jumped out of bed and ran to the window. She touched her forehead gingerly; the bandage had fallen off and she could feel small brittle beads of dry blood. Slowly she pulled aside the curtain, picked up a hand mirror and stepped out on to the balcony.

The righteous light of the sun shone mercilessly into Susan Street's face, clearly picking out a word in small red capital letters on her forehead.

SOLD.

The beautiful black girl who had been born Sharon Sealey and was now Serena Soixante-Neuf laughed so loudly that the reporters peeking at her through the glass porthole in Susan's door recoiled with shock. Wrapped from head to toe in Donna Karan's soft red leather and sitting on Susan's desk, she recrossed her legs and lit a small cigar.

'Well, Sue?' she asked boldly, looking Susan straight in the eyes. They had met for the first time only half an hour earlier, but Serena was not one for gradually getting to know people. Instant intimacy was her business.

Susan clicked off the machine and pocketed the tape. 'Wonderful work. Thank you very much.'

Serena preened and smiled slyly. 'And you're offering . . . ?'

'That's not my job, I'm afraid. You'll have to talk to our money man.' She picked up a phone and punched an in-house number. 'Kathy, can you tell Max we're ready for him now? Thanks. Tell him Miss . . . Miss . . . Soixante-Neuf is here with the recording.'

Serena screamed with laughter once more. The only thing she liked more than the sound of her own voice was the sound of her own name on embarrassed lips.

Mr Maxwell Sadkin, family man and pillar of his Reform synagogue, took one look at Serena, blanched and offered up a prayer to his God for protection – though whether from Serena or his own affectionate nature he could not be sure. Susan left them alone to negotiate, Serena towering over the quaking money man. Holding the tape tight in her pocket, she knocked on Bryan O'Brien's door. 'Bryan? I've got the Lejeune tape. Got a minute?'

Of course he had; he knew a hot putative front page when he smelled one. And this one had it all: sex, financial scandal and the supernatural, the Holy Trinity of the tabloids – even those with pretensions to uptown.

Two years ago Constantine Lejeune had been an unknown Black Country clairvoyant who had turned up on the doorstep of a breakfast TV company claiming to know the whereabouts of a kidnapped knitwear heiress. On the air he went into a trance; on the air the police located the girl, broke down a door and arrested her kidnappers. Since then Lejeune had risen irresistibly to a position unparalleled by any other supernatural superstar.

He could stop clocks – once, spectacularly, Big Ben – bend cutlery – once, controversially, every fork on the yacht HMS *Britannia* – and find bodies. But he was not content to be an entertainer or even a detective.

He held meetings which one journalist had compared scathingly to Nuremberg rallies – but then British journalists had a bad habit of comparing any public meeting with a charismatic speaker and an audience which extended into double figures to a Nuremberg rally. But Lejeune did spout a strong populist line at his meetings: against immigration and international finance, he managed to implicate a Second Coming into race riots and hinted strongly at having the ear of God. A Yorkshireman of alleged Franco-Greek extraction whose blunt speech was peppered with Gallic exclamations, his greasy good looks and rabble-rousing rhetoric assured him a massive following amongst middle-aged women and overgrown boys. A book and several long-playing records of prophecy ('Prophet with a profit', Lejeune's detractors were fond of calling him) had sold millions.

Yes, if there were two things that Constantine Lejeune particularly hated they were miscegenation and high finance. And now here was a tape which not only had him engaged in sexual congress with a prostitute whose St Lucian accent was clearly in evidence, but also breaking off from his exertions to receive calls from his broker. Constantine Lejeune, hater of high finance and people's friend, was using his strange gift to make quite a killing on the stock market.

'I don't know quite how he could make such a stupid mistake,' Serena had said. 'I only know he's not the first famous bastard I've done business with. They all seem to think that if you're on the game you're automatically deaf, dumb and blind too. But this is the first one I've been really interested in nailing. Call it personal, because he's a racist jerk, or call it business because he's the biggest name I've had yet, and I know you'll pay through the nose for him. Anyway, you can take that to the bank.' With that she had tossed the tape on to Susan's desk. 'You know all that stuff he peddles about the Second Coming? I've got it all down here. And the third, and the fourth . . .'

Now that unmistakable Black Country-on-Seine voice groaned from O'Brien's tape machine . . .'*Sacré bleu* bah gum . . .' The Australian laughed and clicked it off.

'Good work, Sue. I think I can do you a front page for this little beaut. "As Told To" suit you?'

'Suits me fine.' Susan Street smiled.

FOUR

'If Bangkok is a bar girl and Paris is an expensive mistress, then Rio is an orgiast,' Tobias Pope proclaimed from his mobile Olympus as it moved through the clouds, as fluffy and yielding as a Fifties pin-up blonde, above the Atlantic Ocean.

By his side Susan Street slept, sulked and stared blankly at the pages of her Tama Janowitz novel. 'Really?' she said, in a voice which dripped boredom.

'But certainly. Brazil is sometimes called the Thailand of Lat Am, but personally I've always found Thai women essentially joyless and resentful types behind that grateful façade. If it wasn't for the hard cash, they wouldn't touch you with a six-foot dildo. The *carioca* girls, on the other hand . . . superb beasts. Glossy, healthy brutes. Pre-AIDS, that is. They're still as loose as ever, though. They'd do it for fun, if it came to that. Which, praise God and the dollar, it never will.'

Susan sighed and put her book away into her Etienne Augier briefcase. Every time she tried to read, Pope pinched an excruciatingly tiny and tender amount of flesh at the top of her inner thigh which her mini-skirted grey wool Alaïa suit left achingly vulnerable. Her Bruce Oldfield tights were already laddered due to numerous digital rebukes. In the interest of her wardrobe, it might be wise to converse with him.

'If Rio is an orgiast, and Paris is a mistress, then what's London?' she asked patiently.

He turned and laughed into her face. He'd been hoping for this one, she could tell. 'A whore. Down on its luck. Two-bit. A two-bit whore whose speciality is getting down on its knees and sucking the dick of any rich American who crosses its path. That's what your countrywomen are famous for, isn't it? What did they say about English girls during the war? One Yank—'

'—and they're off,' Susan finished wearily. It was a revelation hearing Tobias Pope's witticisms and wisdoms. Somehow she hadn't excepted the head of one the biggest communications empires in the world to have a marginally less sophisticated sense of humour than a stand-up comic in a North Country working-men's club.

He chuckled happily at his joke. 'Yes, yes. I've always thought it strange, you know, that only Italy should be shaped like a part of the human physiognomy. If there was any natural justice in the world, the British land mass would be a Y-shaped pair of open legs and the tip of the United States would be thrusting into it. It would be appropriate, wouldn't it? Economically, militarily and sexually.'

'Isn't it a coincidence,' Susan said sarcastically, 'that the women of countries suddenly become so wildly attracted to rich Americans when their countries are being screwed in every other way by the United States. This animal magnetism couldn't have anything to do with a certain little thing called financial necessity, could it?'

'As in your case, you mean?' Tobias Pope sipped his J&B thoughtfully. 'Yes, I do see your point. It must be torment trying to struggle by on fifty-five thousand pounds sterling per annum plus expenses. No wonder you're a whore.'

She thought about asking the stewardess for some earplugs on the pretence of trying to sleep.

'Yes, a remarkable country, Brazil. A country of paradoxes. The people are a unique racial inter-marriage of African, Indian and European, but the stratification of their society is still savage. Which is as it should be. Dark-skinned on the coastal north of Rio, light-skinned to the south.'

'South Africa-on-Sea,' she muttered.

'Speak up, young woman, don't mumble. Yes, in the seventy years up to 1950 Brazil took in four and a half million Europeans, and something like fifty thousand a year since then.' His upper lip winced in mild distaste.

'The Japs have moved in recently, unfortunately. There's a fair number of them in coffee. Some mornings in the business quarter you feel like an extra in *Bridge Over The River Kwai*.'

She had to smile. Just like Joe Blow in the street, Tobias Pope had a deep and violent dislike of the Japanese. She had asked him why at the airport that evening, as he stared with disapproval at the camera-clacking hordes of Japanese tourists taking a photographs of the planes, the people, even litter bins. 'Because the women are ugly and the men are clever. That's not how the yellow races should be. Or any race but the Americans, come to that.'

'Brazil, as I'm sure you know by now, thanks to the ecology gangsters who run our TV channels, has the largest virgin rain forest in the world which contains one third of the world's trees and covers an area larger than Europe. But in the last sixty years, praise God, a quarter has been destroyed and another four per cent goes every year. It's a terrible thing, conservation – it makes cowards out of the people. The rain forest is being pulled down with no thought for anything but a fast buck. Which is just as it should be. A brave and optimistic people. Riddled with AIDS, naturally. You can buy a woman for the price of a piña colada. It has been a biggest gap between rich and poor of any country in the world. That fact alone is proof the United States is not what is used to be. Yes, it's a wonderful country. Healthy.'

Susan took a deep breath. Here was where laying out the financial pages of the *Best* came in useful. 'So healthy that if it declared itself bankrupt, the world banking system would probably collapse? So healthy that it owes one hundred billion dollars and can't even pay back the interest?'

'You shouldn't believe everything you read in the papers, Susan.' He leaned back in his seat and closed his eyes. 'Especially if you read it in one of mine.'

From the window of her hotel suite on the Avenida Atlantica, she could see the pure white beaches of Rio, resembling a *smorgasbord* of spilled cocaine, and the banquet of tanned flesh barely tethered by the briefest of tangas that used it as a catwalk, hoping to exchange almost criminal beauty for legal tender. These girls were not professionals, though, just beautiful and poor in the wrong place and hoping for a man who was as kind as he was rich. The robust earthiness of their beauty robbed even this situation of its exploitative sordidness and, despite herself, she smiled as the soundtrack to a travel advert floated through her head – 'Brasil', 'Rio', 'The Girl From Ipanema'.

She turned her head idly to the right, and gasped.

Less than two hundred yards from her window, level with her eyes, was a man-made mountain of trash. On it, children, dogs and rats competed on equal terms for the pickings. Around its base stood flimsy wooden shacks and around these stood weary women looking helplessly and hopelessly at the children. Rag and bone, she thought dazedly, these people are made of rag and bone.

'The *favelas*,' said Tobias Pope behind her. 'No sanitation, power or water. They ring every big city here, living off the waste. A very *ecological* system. I think of the *favelas* as a frame; their repulsiveness makes the beauty of Rio proper even more of dazzling.'

'I don't think Rio's beautiful. All those skyscrapers and freeways and flyovers and armies of people scuttling along like survivalist ants. It's like a corrupt Legoland.' She gestured towards the *favelas*. 'And now this—'

'Put your sunglasses on,' said Pope impatiently 'It will help your vision and your conscience.'

'It's like heaven and hell in the same place. It's *horrible*.'

He laughed patiently. 'But Susan, you're describing your own country, or any rich Western country. America is one thing for me, but it certainly doubles as hell for the poor. The same with you and British. You just don't have to look it in the face, that's all. You sit in the West End drinking Piper and talking about socialism and you don't have to look at the East End or the North Country. At least they're honest here. Go down to Copacabana or Flamengo for a swim carrying a camera or wearing jewellery and you'll be lucky to come back with your bikini. The poor get a good shot at the rich here.'

'And vice versa.' She gestured at the girls on the beach.

They talked about Two Nations at home; they didn't know the half of it. Brazil was both Disneyland

and Dante's Inferno: the poor and the rich; the ugly and the beautiful; the sexual invitation of the beach girls and the huge billboards which purported to warn against AIDS but, due to the beauty of the models and the carefree smiles which could have been pushing stockings or lipstick, only served to act as further stimuli in this already over-heated city. The Brazilian people seemed a lot like the rain forests themselves: natural wonders mown down by what passed for civilization but were really the most base urges of the First World: the pursuit of sex and money. If Rio was the Bangkok of Latin America it was only that the recklessness of the desperate was always wilfully mistaken for sensuality by the people who sought to exploit it. To call the Brazilians hedonistic was like saying that American ghetto blacks were hedonistic because they took drugs, caught AIDS and otherwise destroyed themselves. Brazil was a ghetto and, like most ghettos, it doubled as a playground for the rich. Physically and fiscally, Brazil was being screwed.

'Charming animals, aren't they?' said Pope at her shoulder, tracing her gaze to the beach. They stood at the window in the Avenida Atlantica joined by a kind of understanding. They could both comprehend the massive unfairness of the fact that this beautiful and lively people were condemned to strutting their stuff for their supper in a city that was little more than a brothel. The only difference was that he approved of the arrangement and she didn't.

The only difference! How her priorities were changing already! She drew back and looked at him.

He recoiled and laughed almost tenderly at the expression on her face. 'Oh, Susan! You're *so* English! Look at your face! The Roman haughtiness of the nose, the Norman disdain of the eyes, the Teutonic disapproval of the mouth, the Viking iciness of the bearing – perfect English girl!' He sighed. 'You'll never understand how to go about having fun, you Euros, will you? You'll never understand that the only way not to feel the world's pain is to go at it like a pig at a trough. Otherwise you're lost. Look at that beautiful mess out there. Wallow in it. *Enjoy* the craziness of it. Or it will be your downfall. You won't sleep at night and you won't be happy. Believe me, I know what I'm talking about.'

'What do you know?' she said sulkily.

'I know, young lady, believe me.' He opened his mouth, then closed it, then blurted, 'I was a Communist at your age!'

Her head shot round.

He was relaxed again. He laughed. 'I'm not lying. Whatever I may do to you, Susan, I'll never lie to you. There's no point.'

She sat on the bed. 'What happened?'

He shrugged. 'I told you. Nothing dramatic. It just didn't make me happy so I got rid of it.'

'You make it sound like an abortion.'

'Of a sort.' Pope drained his Virgin Mary. 'Anyway, I can't sit here talking politics and pipe dreams all day, I've got a meeting at the Banco de Brasil. If you can be dressed in ten minutes, you can get a lift uptown in my car. Longer than ten minutes, though, and you can find your own way. Never forget, my dear; I am not here for your convenience – you are here for *mine*.'

She walked up the Avenida Presidente Vargas and cased the clothes-shop windows. There were lots of copies of Chanel and Vuitton, lots of acrylic and plastic, lots of bad seams and leather as over-tanned as the forty-year-olds on Copacabana beach. Rio seemed to specialize in what were politely known as 'fun clothes' and 'sports clothes'; only somewhere along the line fun and sports had become euphemisms for cheap and nasty. Even the familiar merchandise at Benetton and Fiorucci looked strange as though concocted by some cack-handed Martian with only a vague and grainy approximation on some distant TV screen to work from.

Still she bought, almost reflexively: I shop therefore I am. A tiger's-eye necklace at Sidi, silver earrings with green citrine centres at Prata Moderna and a gold ring set with a beautiful black tourmaline that screamed 'BULGARI!' but actually came from Balulac. A couple of pieces of basic black and white at the mercilessly monochrome Tutto Bianco, a backless and beaded red cocktail dress from Cenario & Figurino, a shiny black bikini from Cantao and

71

a dark green leather envelope briefcase from Victor Hugo, and she was done.

The people in the street looked easily as harassed as any other big-city lunch-hour shoppers, and she considered how silly it was that if a country had exceptionally clement weather its inhabitants were automatically described as 'vibrant', 'vivid' and 'vivacious'. Looking at the faces on the humid streets of uptown Rio, she could have shown any travelogue maker that living in a glorified sauna made you feel anything *but*.

In fact, if you took away the sun and substituted rain, Brazil wouldn't really be anything worth writing home about, she thought. With its flamboyant poverty and jerry-built skyscrapers, it was quite like Tower Hamlets with suntans. Not that she'd ever *been* to Tower Hamlets. She had never found poverty, either domestic or exotic, vicariously thrilling. It was too close for comfort.

Her disappointment mingled with and was finally swamped by her relief. Pope had slept in a different suite last night – not even adjoining; he said that would look 'tacky' – and read the business press all through breakfast. At four in the morning the phone had rung and she had waded thigh-high through sleep to answer it, fearful that it was the call to his room.

'Hello?'

'Still up at this hour? Can't sleep? Why not try masturbating?' Pope had suggested jovially before slamming his receiver down. It had taken her one and a half hours to get back to sleep. Otherwise he had behaved with the decorum of a duenna.

Glimpsing the window displays, feeling vaguely fractious and fretful, Susan Street suddenly became aware that she was being followed. In the same way that one can be in the same room as a sleeping person and know suddenly that they are awake although they don't move so much as an eyelash, she suddenly knew that she was being followed, halfway between a *sapataria* and a *supermercado*. A minute later she turned into a dark boutique and cannoned into a rail of cotton print dresses.

'*Deseja alguma coisa?*' said a short girl whose expression said her feet were killing her.

'Just looking, thanks.' She backed into the rear of the shop. Thirty seconds later he was framed in the doorway, a thin man of medium height in a dark suit, peering into the perennial dusk of the boutique. A minute later he was examining a rack of bikini briefs minutely, obviously too bent on his task to care about looking like a pervert. She slid out of the shop and into the *pastelaria* next door.

'*Ola, senhora!*' said a young man with beautiful teeth and bad breath. '*Bola de Berlin, pastel de nata, queque, bolo de coco, petit fours?*'

'That one, please.' She pointed to a meringue.

'Ah, *suspiro!*'

She fumbled with the unfamiliar *centavos*. 'I'm sorry, I

don't really . . .'

Laughing, he took some coins from her hand. By the quality of his laugher she guessed he was taking a little more than was absolutely necessary for his troubles. Brandishing a bloated paper bag at her, he grinned. '*Um suspiro!*'

Looking up through the window, she saw the man in the dark suit doing a bad job of inspecting of the cake display. Their eyes locked for a second before, both embarrassed, they looked away.

He didn't seem like your average kidnapper AWOL from the local goon squad; his suit was too expensive and shabby, his expression too worried and thoughtful. Was he an employee of Pope's, perhaps? Was Pope, for some crazy reason of his own, having her followed? She imagined how ridiculous her movements would look on a report: 'Suspect then purchased meringue.' No, 'Suspect then purchased *suspiro*.' It was ludicrous.

She stood in the doorway of the *pastelaria* looking at him challengingly. He stared grimly at the cakes as though they were long-lost cousins he was desperately trying to put a name to. But as she brushed past him, he turned. She could see that it was he who was the scared one.

'Wait. Please. You think I hurt you?' He spoke good English – better than Pope's she thought disloyally.

'Excuse me, please. You've got the wrong girl.' She walked.

He followed at her side. 'No, no. He hurt you. That Tobias Pope. You scared already – I see it in your eyes.'

She stumbled into a café.

He followed her. 'Please, miss. My card?'

A maniac with a calling card? Unlikely, to say the least. She took it wordlessly. Luis Montes, SEVERO A MENDES, an address in the business quarter and a phone number. 'My firm. Lawyers.'

She sat down and looked at him. 'For a lawyer, you're behaving very suspiciously, Senhor Montes. Did you want something?'

'Yes. Yes, I did.' He sat down awkwardly opposite her. '*Dois chas com leite*,' he said to the waitress with some authority. Turning back to Susan, his manner became desperate again. 'Please, yes. I would like to tell you about a girl I know. Knew. I want to tell you you remind me of her.'

'That's nice for you.'

Montes winced. 'No, it's not. It's not nice. No. You paler, a little thinner, a little older. But you have that same look as she had.' He hesitated for effect, a real lawyer. 'That look like someone has *bought* you.'

Enough was enough. She jumped up. 'Really? How very interesting. I think I'll go now, if you've finished. Have me followed and I'll have you arrested. You see, I'm a tourist, and therefore more important than you. Goodbye.'

'Wait!' He thrust a small snapshot at her. She saw a big, beautiful Latinate girl in a yellow sundress laughing over one bare shoulder. 'That's before she got the look. And before she died of course. A *minha filha*. My daughter.

Your friend killed her. Your *Pope*.'

'I don't believe you.' But she sat back down.

'It's true.' With one quick movement he leaned across the table and brushed the hair from her forehead. She jumped back and he recoiled with a loud hissing sound. 'You, too!'

The idea of being one of many girls scattered across several continents with SOLD tattooed on their faces did not appeal to Susan one little bit. Especially if some of them were dead.

'What happened?' she asked weakly.

'She was seventeen when she met Tobias Pope. Maybe you don't understand how it is for Latin American girl. No, you Inglesa, you probably understand these days. So near and yet so far. So rich and big, Estados Unidos. So much promises big fun. United States take and United States give. They God now.'

'That's a bit overwrought.'

'They *are*. You know what they can give. You young, pretty girl . . .' He laughed rudely. 'You no want Pope's beautiful young body.'

She couldn't deny *that*. 'Do you want to tell me about your daughter?'

'It's a short story. Short and sad. He gave her cocaine one carnival. Such a casual thing. Then away, back to work, other girls. But Cristina wanted more. She started to stay out at night. Clever girl, beautiful, studying history.

She became girl of cocaine *politico*, though – we have a big cocaine problem here now, stops over from Bolivia and Colombia. She died when gangs had a shootout.' He shrugged. 'Studying history, OK. But what use history against half an hour of ecstasy?'

'I'm very sorry.'

'Thank you. But I'm not sorry. Not any more. Just angry now.' He stood up, threw a handful of *centavos* on the table. 'One day I kill him. Not here, too easy to trace me. But in Europe, or Estados, I kill him and fade away.' He smiled like a real assassin. 'There, I'm just another wetback. Catch me if you can.' He put his palms flat on the flimsy table, which trembled under his hatred as he spoke pleasantly into her face. 'And maybe you'll call me and help me get up close, when he dumps you like he dumped my daughter, and you hate him. Maybe you already do. But you will soon. If he doesn't kill you first. *Adeus*.'

The soft evening breeze of Rio, almost as thick and sweet as the whipped cream which oozed from the melted meringue abandoned in Susan Street's suite, blew from the Atlantic Ocean across the beaches of Leme and Leblon, over the patio and through the French windows of Tobias Pope's bedroom on the Avenida Atlantica, taking with it like trailing bridesmaids the sound of the sea lapping at Copacabana and the distant hum from the samba contest in the stadium on Rua Maquis Sapucai marking the start of the carnival.

77

Pope sat with his back to the windows in a big leather armchair and looked up from the copy of *Fortune* in which he was reading about himself. He looked at Susan Street, who was lying on the bed in a knitted pale green two-piece by Rifat Ozbek which left her pale stomach and shoulders bare, reading a Kathy Acker novel.

'Lies, all lies,' he said.

'I'm sorry?'

'Think nothing of it. So you weren't impressed with Rio?'

'Not what I saw of it, no.'

'Maybe you'll be impressed by the carnival?'

'Maybe.'

'Or maybe it takes more than the futility rites of the poor dressed up for the leering Polaroids of the American-speaking world to impress you.'

'Might do.' She carefully noted the page number and closed the book. She felt the muscles in the soles of her feet cramp, a sure sign of wariness.

'How about a posse of pussy and a yard of cock?'

She turned over and sat up slowly. 'Sorry?'

'You heard.'

There was a knock on the door. Pope grinned broadly at her. 'Ah, good. The floorshow.'

He opened the door, and six young people, three boys, three girls, filed in. None of them was over twenty and none of them was over the moon. They leaned placidly against a wall in a row and looked calmly from Pope to Susan. One of the boys whispered something to another, who looked at her and nodded.

Tobias Pope stood in the middle of the room and clapped his hands. 'Your attention, ladies and gentlemen. Thank you. Now, what I wish is this. That, one by one, you will each step forward and explain in no more than three – that's *three*, *tres* – sentences who you are and why you are a whore. WHORE. I don't want to hear any lily-livered euphemisms like good-time girl, gigolo or poor deprived victim of exploitative economic system.' He clapped his hands again. 'Ladies first.'

A small girl in a white bikini stepped forward. 'My name is Maria. I am a whore because I have no education.' She looked at him uncertainly.

'A common tale of woe but a convincing one. Let this be a lesson to you. Next.'

A tall girl in a white beach dress stepped forward. 'My name is Rosana and I am a . . . whore because I have a sick mother and many small brothers and sisters.'

Tobias Pope blew a loud, lewd raspberry.

The third girl stepped forward. She wore black heels, black pedal-pushers, a black off-the-shoulder T-shirt and a black look. 'My name is my own business and I am a whore because it pays well. Just like every one of these chickenshits that's too scared to say so in case you send for a replacement.'

Pope threw back his head and laughed appreciatively. '*Brava, senhorita*! That's the spirit. I happen to know from your good supplier that you are popularly known as Thalia, but we'll let the pass.'

Thalia scowled.

He gestured at the three boys who lounged against the wall, grinning at Thalia's performance. 'You, you're all men and therefore anonymous. I will call you One, Two and Three. And I certainly don't want you to tell me why you're whores. You're whores because you're lazy and stupid, like all your *compadres*.'

They sniggered and nudged each other.

Susan looked at Thalia. If she had had the bad luck to be born poor and Brazilian, she might have been this girl. Thalia was slightly larger than life but only in all the right places, her sullen face full of a bitter intelligence. The girl, who had been glancing around the room sizing up various portable objects – lamps, radios, vases – suddenly caught Susan's eyes, and her stare was like three short sharp plunges of a knife in the face, breasts, groin. Susan blushed. Thalia looked again into her face and sneered.

'This is my friend Susan. She wishes to be fucked. By each of you, one at a time, and then *uma tortilla* as a grand finale. Queue up, please, no shoving.'

The Brazilians slouched into line. She could tell as a people they were unused to queuing as they grinned and pushed foolishly at each other. The boys at the front, impatient and eager, the girls at the back, Maria and Rosana examining each other's cheap costume jewellery and fingernails, comparing prices and varnish. They could have been waiting for a bus.

Thalia stood at the back, immobile, silent, still sneering. Looking at her, Susan felt suddenly frightened.

Pope walked along the line, handing condoms to the boys. 'Once only offer, never repeated. Next week you'll be back servicing sixty-year-old widows from Florida, so make the most of this. On the other hand, don't make too much of a meal of it if you can help it. There's no hidden camera here – no *maquina* – so no movie director is going to spot your hidden talent.' He looked at his Patek Phillipe. 'It's just turned seven now and I want dinner at eight. I am an old man and need my sleep.' He sat down in the leather armchair and looked again at his watch 'Ready, steady – GO!'

The first boy came towards her, unzipping his jeans. Her numbness became relief on two counts: he was both small and erect. The idea of either stimulating one of these strangers or trying to take a party-size penis filled her with dread. He was handsome, but not in a way that she liked; too smooth, too young.

He climbed on to the bed and kissed her, kneeling on all fours. Their teeth clinked and she turned her head in embarrassment, looking straight into the smiling face of Pope who had left his chair and was standing by the side of the bed with his arms folded. 'No sloppy stuff!' he called fussily, like an irked referee. 'Uck! Most unhygienic!'

The boy was kneeling up now, slipping the condom over his cock. Susan lay back weakly on the pillows and closed her eyes. He parted her legs and climbed between them, put his hand up her skirt and pulled her underpants down and off. He pulled her Ozbek skirt up and she felt every occupant of the room lean towards her with a low communal murmur of curiosity: a cross between people examining a piece of merchandise and people examining a car crash.

There were seven people looking at her exposed vagina. The idea made her want to crawl under the bed with embarrassment. But it also made her want to fuck like a rabbit.

The boy groped at her opening with his hand, positioned himself and pushed into her. Instinctively she tightened her muscles and he gasped with pleasure. A little intake of breath went up from the queue and she opened her eyes to look at them. Pope stood, his straight back to her, looking down between her legs. Maria had her hands on Rosana's shoulders and was standing on tiptoe. The two boys were erect inside their Levis.

Thalia was tapping her stilettoed foot on the floor, sneering. Susan held the boy tight as he moved back and forth. He was very young and enthusiastic, he didn't smell or crush her and he was as powerless as any girl in the face of the Yankee dollar; he might as well enjoy it. How easy it was to fuck someone you didn't know; much easier than kissing them, and infinitely easier than talking to them. She was just starting to feel the first pulses of pleasure when the boy gasped, buckled and collapsed on her, breathing like a spent sprinter.

Tobias Pope blew another raspberry. 'Pathetic! Next!'

Boy Two climbed on to the bed, rolling his friend off good-naturedly. He had fitted the condom as he walked to the bed and slipped into her like a well-oiled bolt. He was taller, a little older and a lot bigger; she was coming dangerously close to enjoying this and, in fact, dangerously close to coming. She closed her eyes and wrapped her arms around his neck.

He laughed softly in her ear. '*Ola!* He began to thrust, the culmination of each movement feeling like a question mark made flesh.

'BOR–ING!' decided Pope loudly. She could have crowned him. '*Do* something, boy! *Do something with her!* Strangle her, bite her, whistle Dixie if you must – *anything* to break the monotony!'

The boy grabbed her ankles and hoisted them up on to his shoulders: she readjusted her body, wriggling up on to him and groaning at the deepness of the penetration. She felt as though she were a red velvet sofa into whose plush depths the boy was sinking, never to return. Her hands gripped his hips, her dark hair spilled across the Porthault pillow, her narrow body heaved up against his and her large soft mouth stretched in a shiny and silent scream across her teeth, smearing them with Lancôme Brun Majeur lipstick.

Unaccustomed to both the position and the beauty and pleasure of his client, the second boy spilled his seed in record time.

The room was silent.

'*Como se chama?*' whispered the boy.

'I don't speak Portuguese,' she said, raising herself to press her clitoris against his bony body. She was desperate to come, at that stage where nothing in the world matters but that. The pressure was starting to get to her when Tobias Pope exploded.

'Jesus!' He raised a surprisingly small foot clad in a shoe that cost more than the Brazilian boy would earn in a year and kicked his behind as he crouched on all fours over Susan. The blow separated them and made them cry out. 'I've seen rabbits last longer! Rabbits with premature ejaculation problems! Get out, the pair of you, OUT!' He flung open the door and pushed them into the hallway. 'I'll settle with Rodriguez tomorrow – ten *centavos* the pair of you! Now SCOOT!' He slammed the door and mopped his brow. 'Christ, you can't get good help these days.' He clicked his fingers twice. 'Maria, Rosana, you're more men than they are, I bet. See what you can do with her.'

The girls jumped on to the bed, their expressions alert and curious.

'*Que quer?*' asked Maria politely.

'She means what would you like,' translated the tall girl.

'What?' Dazedly Susan raised herself up on her elbows and looked at them hungrily. 'Oh, anything. I don't know. What would you like to do?'

'FOR JESUS CHRIST'S SAKE!' yelled Pope. Maria and Rosana crossed themselves. 'Do that thing before I get the bellhop in to do it!'

Seizing a pillow and the initiative, Rosana slipped the Porthault under Susan's behind. 'Legs up, *por favor*.' Quick as a flash she rotated her body so that she knelt on all fours over Susan, her groin in her face.

Maria slid down the bed. 'Open legs, please.'

With her legs forming a perfect V – some sort of victory – Susan was set upon by the hot and avid mouths of Rosana and Maria, the one sucking and tugging at the clitoris with her lips and teeth until it swelled to three times its usual size, the other darting her long and expert tongue in and out. Sweating now, unbearably aroused, Susan put her arms up around Rosana's waist. 'Please, please, your dress,' she gasped. 'Please, I beg you, take everything off.'

Like formation strippers, the three of them straightened up in the same split-second to pull off their clothes – Maria the bikini, Rosana the dress, Susan the Ozbek top. Then without missing a beat they were back in that swamp of sucking again, and Susan felt as though she was being drawn down, down, down into a multi-mouth quicksand. The two girls were into their stride now, reaching a plateau beyond mere professional pride, working as one body with two heads, licking and plunging in and around her, the noise of the three liquid orifices filling the huge room more deafeningly than the most sophisticated sound system.

The audience reaction had changed from one of jaded contempt to one of tortuous expectation. Pope was still at the side of the bed but now bent double, his hands flat on the quilt as he peered at the junction of the three wet holes. Thalia and the boy had abandoned the desultory queue and stood on either side of him, their beautiful young faces looking over his shoulders like some grotesque perversion of a family portrait.

'Please.' Susan buried her face in Rosana's warm and salty stomach. 'Please let me. Please help me. I'm going to come.' She did.

The girls slumped, blind with sweat, against each other, two brown bodies and one white in a heap. A tic in Tobias Pope's temple made its presence felt.

'Get off her. Off her, you whores. I haven't had my money's worth yet.' He turned to the boy. 'You. Reclaim the dyke.'

The boy looked like Marlon Brando with the souvenirs of a bad skin, the scars and punctures that in moderation make a beautiful face even more heartbreaking. He turned his back to Pope and Thalia and stepped out of his jeans. Climbing on to the bed he swatted Rosana and Maria gently, like a lioness with pesky cubs. He covered Susan with his body where she lay panting on her stomach, lifted her hips and slipped her skirt off. 'Desculpe,' he said, taking one, two, three pillows from the head of the bed and putting them under her.

'What's happening?'

For answer he knelt behind her, took a buttock in each hand and thrust into her. 'No spik Inglês,' he apologized as he did so.

She screamed. He was huge. 'Please stop. Please.' He continued, unperturbed. She looked over her shoulder into his face, as clear-eyed and untroubled as a three-year-old watching its favourite TV show. Back and forth moved his hips, back and forth moved the huge thing inside her.

'You two!' Pope gestured frantically at the dazed girls on the bed. 'Suck! Suck her tits! PRONTO!'

They crawled clumsily up to the copulating pair and wriggled beneath Susan's straight arms. Lying on their backs they fumbled at her breasts, latching on to the nipples within seconds of each other and sucking greedily.

Susan looked down at them as the boy fucked her. Their eyes were closed and they looked almost happy. She felt a wave of fondness for these strangers who sucked at her, one who would die of AIDS within the year, one who would marry a hideous and humane Canadian chiropractor, have many children and cosmetic surgeries and be treated like a duchess till the end of her days.

The feeling in her nipples connected with her vagina. She looked over her shoulder and smiled at him; he smiled modestly back, proud of himself, a real pro. She touched her clitoris, and the boy behind her and the girls beneath her exploded in a moment of non-specific ecstasy. She threw back her head and howled.

They separated, shiny with sweat which made lewd noises as their skin unstuck. They smiled with embarrassment and avoided each other's eyes.

'OK.' Pope's voice flat. 'Order champagne whatever you want, wash and go. I'll be back in ten minutes I don't want to find anybody in this room who's the wrong side of beige.' He left.

Rosana, Maria and the boy looked questioningly at Susan. 'Please, the bathroom?'

'There.' She pointed.

The door closed behind the three.

Thalia walked to the foot of the bed. She folded her arms and one foot in its high heel tapped slowly on the floor. '*Desculpe* – excuse me, please. But haven't you forgotten something?'

'What? Please.' In her disarmed state, the fierce and beautiful girl in black frightened her.

'Yes, I remember. It's *me*. You've forgotten *me*.' The sadness of Thalia's voice was a thin disguise. 'You fucked all those people and you forgot about me. Poor little Thalia.' She sighed deeply. 'Always this is the way.'

'I'm sorry, but I can't think straight. I don't know what you want but if it's money I'm sure—'

'MONEY!' The girl was on the bed now, crouching over Susan's naked body. She held up her hand, and Susan cringed. 'See this?' She laughed shortly. 'No, baby, I'm not going to hurt you. I'm going to *love* you. Like *this*.'

Later Susan Street reflected that if a man had been a fly on the wall of the bedroom on the Avenida Atlantica that night, he would never again ask with a sneer what on earth lesbians did in bed. The sneer, and the smile, and the superiority, would have been wiped right off. Because a world away from Rosana and Maria and their delicate mouthwork, there was Thalia and her endless fury.

Already sore from the three boys, she couldn't help twisting and arching, couldn't help grabbing the girl and kissing her – Thalia viciously spat huge mouthfuls of saliva into her mouth as she did so – and couldn't help those words pouring out of her mouth, all four-letter and the most obscene one being LOVE, until Thalia pulled out in disgust.

'You. *You. You're* the whore. Not me. You know why? Because you *love* it. You don't have to do these things. I do. With your advantages I could have done – why, I could have done *anything*. You disgust me. You whore.' She stood over Susan on the bed and spat on her. 'And you know what's the worst thing? I could fall in love with a whore like you.'

* * *

She was still lying on the bed in a state of shock when Pope came back. It was still before nine and the noises of revelry from the city were getting louder.

'Enjoy it?'

'Yes, thank you.' She felt shattered. But would rather have flung herself from the balcony than let him know.

'Good for you.' He opened the wardrobe.

'Are we going to the carnival?'

'What?' He laughed. 'Drunkenness, drug abuse, stupid peasants in stupid costumes and street crime? If I want that I can go to the South Bronx or Brixton.' He looked at his watch. 'No, we've been good tourists – we've fucked the natives and helped the economy. Get dressed, we're going home.'

She sat in the aeroplane over London feeling used and shabby under the complexion-wrecking lights and thought about the weekend. So she'd slept with various swarthy types of either sex and come dangerously close to having her cervix split open by one of them . . . big deal. It had only been a Hispanic variation on her dark distant past. Then why did she feel so bad about it?

She ordered a split of Cristal and tried to shake the feeling. The really remarkable thing had been the Montes episode – what had *that* meant?

On an impulse she copied the number from his card into her Filofax and wrote by it LOUISA MOUNT. She tore the card into tiny pieces and put it under her seat. She knew Pope went through her things when she was sleeping and with a mind like his he could easily put one and one together and come up with Luis and Cristina Montes, some relation.

She didn't know why she was keeping the number. Maybe because after what she had been through in Rio, a man with a burning desire to wipe Tobias Pope from the face of the earth was the lifestyle accessory every clever girl needed this year.

FIVE

'Susan?' Bryan O'Brien queried. All eyes in the editorial meeting were on her. Someone sniggered.

'Oh, yes, Bryan?' She'd been thinking about Rio.

'I said great lead. Sex, miscegenation—' He turned to the most refined of the reporters, Charterhouse boy, and said in his broadest outback accent, 'That's inter-racial screwing for you Limey oiks – and money. Three kinds of dirt. Great.'

The assembled staff looked disappointed.

'Thank you, Bryan.' She shot a triumphant smile around the room and demurely lowered her eyes.

'Can you stay behind for a minute, Sue?' The hacks filed reluctantly out. When the door had closed behind the last one, he asked her, 'Have you heard about the Moorsom business?'

'Joe Moorsom? What business?'

'Dirty business, Sue. He plans to ask some questions in the House about Tobias buying out Tooth. You know, foreigners coming over here, taking our newspapers – good socialist internationalist stuff. Tobias finds him very irritating, Sue.'

'But it's not important, surely. What's a question in the House? It hasn't hurt Murdoch.'

'A piece of grit in the eye isn't important either, Sue. But it causes a hell of a lot of irritation and it can lead to something nasty if you don't get it out quick. Tobias seems to think Moorsom won't stop there, that he'll make a habit of it, cause some bad publicity. The thing is, Sue, I was talking to one of the lobby boys and they said you were friendly with Moorsom, oh, years ago, when you were still a reporter . . . ?' He looked at her expectantly.

'I don't particularly like the way the boys in the newsroom use the word friendly when it concerns a man and a woman, Bryan,' she said coldly. 'And I can assure you that there is not nor ever has been anything between Joe Moorsom and me.'

'OK, Sue.' He looked at her oddly. Damn, she'd gone too far. She left the office. He knew she was lying, she could tell. There was something between her and Joe Moorsom, something no one else shared. There was a fifteen-year-old rentboy with a scare thrown into him and a story to tell. *Rupert Grey was thirteen when his parents discovered he was 'queer', as his father put it. Till then, his parents had thought of him merely as 'theatrical'.*

But one day a note from the headmaster of Rupert's minor public school arrived, requesting the urgent attendance of Major and Mrs Grey. There they were horrified to hear that their son had been found below the assembly stage engaging in oral sex with a timid Chinese boy while above them the school choir performed the Saint Matthew Passion.

Rupert did not help his case by uttering a low highly audible moan of delight at the words 'oral sex'.

It was decided that he would be given one more chance to 'pull himself together'. He would attend counselling sessions twice a week and if he could rid himself of his 'perverse desires', the head told the shocked parents, the boy would have a good future. 'He is naturally bright, but lazy, and spends a good deal of his time showing off in front of the class.'

For the next two weeks Rupert found home life unbearable. Whereas before he had been allowed to lounge in his 'boudoir', free to enjoy 'the delicious view in the looking glass' undisturbed and read aloud choice passages of Wilde, Huysmans and E.M. Forster, he now found a concerned parental head popping around the door every ten minutes to see if 'Everything was right?'

'Mother, if you mean in your typically bourgeois way am I engaged in orgiastic delights with smooth-skinned China boys, sweat-oiled Negroes and hirsute Greeks, the answer is – only in the imagination. Now shut the door on your way out, there's a duck.'

One evening his father knocked on the door.

'Entre.'

His father entered, looking serious.

'Father, this is a rare treat! Why, if I'd known you were coming I'd have laid on some very tall blond Nazis for you to kill. Pray, take a pew.' Rupert gestured at a pile of silken cushions beneath a huge sepia poster of Rudolf Valentino.

'I'll stand, if you don't mind. Son, I think it's time we had a jaw. I know that you think I'm an old fuddy-duddy – I am, and proud of it. But I've had a lifetime in the army, and I've seen all sorts of men. You don't shock me. I've seen queers that would make your hair curl—'

'Please,' murmured Rupert.

'I know that you hate your mother and me but, you may laugh, we've only ever wanted the best for you. I've feared the worst about you for a while now. But your mother's a woman—'

'Lucky bitch,' the boy whispered under his breath, examining his fingernails. His nails, bare of varnish, looked positively, obscenely naked.

'—and you're breaking her heart. Mine went years ago. All I want to say is, try to understand. Your mother and I grew up in a different world. We didn't have the advantages youth have today, but it was a simple life, and a happy one. I sometimes feel sorry for young people nowadays, there are so many temptations—'

'Father, have you ever considered abandoning the army in order to set up a small petit-point sampler retail outlet? You've just managed to pack more clichés and homilies into that speech than an entire week's output of The Archers.'

'Listen, son. What I'm trying to say is, you're like an alien to us. We don't seem to be able to speak the same language. But maybe, just perhaps – well, together we can work this thing out. You're our son, queer or not, and we love you.' The major stood there, looking at his Hush Puppies.

Rupert flung himself backwards on to his satin quilt, hugged his knees and burst into peals of laughter. 'Cue the violins, bring out the onions – father and son embrace, mother weeps with happiness, celestial choirs sing and Douglas Sirk yells "PRINT!" – oh, Father, you're positively camp!'

The snooping of his parents, the sniggering at school – Rupert had adopted what he called the Law of Queens: 'Never complain, never explain' – and the desire for 'something grand and glamorous' all conspired to put Rupert on the last train to London one Monday night. Having forged his father's signature on a cheque and withdrawn five hundred pounds from the bank, his plan was to check into a West End hotel and 'pursue a stage career'. A gay London friend had promised to introduce him to the iconoclastic ballet dancer Sebastiane Boxer, who was widely believed to be more than a little interested in 'Young men with Talent'.

He spent his first week in London drunk on pink champagne. In the evenings, when his dreams of glory were not good enough company, he wandered along to Piccadilly to get 'a tasty takeaway'. On the eighth day one of them stole his cash and he was forced to do a runner from the hotel, leaving his *precious clothes behind to avoid detection. He went to a bar called Bette's to drown his sorrows at someone else's expense account and ended up in a transvestite squat in Spitalfields.*

After another two weeks, Sebastiane Boxer pronounced himself ready to see the boy. They met at his huge studio at St Katharine's Wharf, Boxer all charm as he promised the boy an audition. That night they slept together, though Rupert reflected that sleep was the last thing on Boxer's mind. He felt stiff in all the wrong places as he limbered up the morning after, watched silently and sullenly by the rest of the troupe.

'OK, Rupert, let's see if you're as good vertically as you are horizontally,' Boxer called from the stalls.

Rupert gave the cassette boy the nod, and the strains of Sheherazade filled the stage. But not for long. He was mid-jeté when there was a frantic signal from the stalls and the music was clicked off. Rupert fell to earth with a bump. He felt like Icarus.

'My, you dance just like Isadora Duncan!' said Boxer, striding on to the stage. 'Right after she broke her neck, that is.' He looked at the boy and shook his head kindly. 'You're a pretty child, Rupert, but you have about as much talent as my charlady. I suggest you go home and continue with your two times table.'

When he got back to the squat, the place was wrecked, the occupants evicted and the sad remains of his finery dumped in the street. Weeping, he cadged a coin from a passer-by and called his mother. She told him tearfully that his father had gone to the police over the forged cheque. Hanging up, he realized there was no going home.

Wandering through the rainy West End streets, he thought of death and, as he had done so many times in the past, pictured his funeral. Whereas in the past he had relished the idea – oh! The weeping parents and stunned schoolmates and extravagant sorrow of creative companions, not to mention the big black mammy singing heart-wrenching spirituals just like in Imitation Of Life – now it depressed him. Because now there was no one to weep for him. He had nothing but a badge saying 'THE FLEET'S IN' in his pocket when he entered Bette's that night. Not so long ago he'd been walking these streets full of hope and pink champagne with money in his pocket and a song in his heart – 'I Am What I Am' from La Cage Aux Folles, to be precise – on the lookout for a tasty takeaway boy. Now, as he walked into the bar, he realized that he would have to become one of these boys. Not forever, just until his career got off the ground and ascended the heavens, up where he belonged.

Joe Moorsom was something of a loner. His strict adherence to his socialist principles excluded him from the perks and privileges that others in his party indulged in without a care, such as pairing with Tory MPs to avoid attending votes, membership of all-party social clubs and the cheap and excellent alcohol provided the copious Commons bars.

His solitary nature extended even to his relationship with his wife and children. On weekends he returned to his northern constituency and his family, but invariably these days it ended in tears. She wanted more of his time, more of his attention.

'We hardly know you any more. You don't seem interested in the kids and you certainly aren't interested in me. What's happening to us, Joe? We seem like strangers to each other. I can't go on like this much longer.' These exchanges always fizzled out with a vague mutual agreement to talk about it 'next time'.

Like all solitary people Joe Moorsom had a secret. Publicly, there was the success story: the coalminer's son who became the youngest-ever official of the National Union of Miners; the education at Ruskin College, Oxford; the pretty daughter of the NUM; baron he married; the two highly photogenic children. He was only twenty-six when he won his seat in Parliament.

Now thirty-five, he was respected by those who didn't agree with him and loved by those who did for his blunt talk, his quick wit and his refusal to compromise his ideals. Much was made of his council flat in a hard-to-let highrise in the Elephant and Castle, a far cry from the regulation Labour grandee pied à terre in Pimlico. But in recent months his popularity had grown with the rise of public concern over child abuse; he was the chairman of the Child Protection Group and as the organization achieved a higher profile people stopped thinking of Joe Moorsom as just a plain-speaking breath of fresh air on Any Questions? More and more, it seemed very likely that he might be given a post in the next Labour government.

Privately, he considered his life an unqualified failure. All his life he had been haunted by the fact that, left to his own devices, he was profoundly homosexual.

Much as he loved the mining village he came from and despite the scores of speeches he had made on the inhumanity of smashing whole communities with pit closures, he knew that the kind, narrow-minded mining families, his own included, could never have accepted him as a practising homosexual in a month of May Days. It was only at Ruskin college that he dared be himself.

He was a Brasenose boy up from Harrow: privileged, right-wing and frivolous, everything Moorsom loathed. But the physical attraction made mincemeat of his ethics. After six idyllic months, though, the Brasenose boy transferred his lavish affections to the Old Etonian son of a West African chieftain.

At the age of twenty-one, at a TUC conference in Blackpool, he met Jill. She was working class, a socialist and very serious; everything Moorsom loved.

And every single time they made love, he had to do it from behind so that he could successfully convince himself that she was the Boy.

The night was wet and cold and the bar seemed warmer and more welcoming than usual. Recently Moorsom had taken to stopping in at Bette's most evenings just to nurse a beer and watch the boys. He never felt the need to approach any of them; just being there was enough.

As his reputation grew, pictures and pieces about Jill and the children were beginning to appear in more papers and magazines every month. He was camera-shy, at his best live at rallies, his second best on radio. But Jill had the homely glamour of the TV commercial's ideal wife, and the children were going from cuteness to beauty with no sign of an awkward adolescence. Not since the early days of the Kinnocks had there been such an attractive political family.

Of course he was pleased with the way things were going. But the attention his family was getting, and the good free publicity that resulted from it, made him feel even more of a hypocrite. What would these bedazzled journalists say if they knew that the dashing Joe Moorsom hadn't slept with his lovely wife more than ten times in the last two years?

He sighed into his beer and, looking up, saw the boy. He was sitting on a barstool wearing jeans and a leather jacket, his fine brown hair curling in a silky pageboy around his hollowed cheeks and his long fringe tickling his eyelids. He kept blowing it to keep it out of his eyes. Every time he did so, his raspberry-pink lips puckered and pouted alarmingly. He knew this, which is why he did not take the more convenient course of cutting an inch off his fringe. He was not pouting now, though, as he searched through his pockets.

'I know it's here somewhere,' he insisted to the barman, who was built like an Irish stevedore and dressed like an Italian starlet. The barman rested his chin on his hands and smiled sleepily. 'Can't you touch one of these gents for it? Losing our knack, are we?'

'It's just cheap plonk, for God's sake! You'd think it was Krug the way you're carrying on!'

The boy, as Moorsom had known he would, had the loud, proud, spoiled voice of a Southern Counties only son. He was looking around the bar now, and his eyes alighted on Joe's. He smiled.

Joe looked away.

The boy slipped off his stool and came over. 'I thought I'd better say aloha' – he smiled – 'because you look like the strong and silent type. Look, I'm dreadfully sorry to bother you but I stupidly came out without my credit cards and that terrible old cow behind the bar won't let me have it on tick. Could I borrow the money from you? Cross my heart you'll get it back.' He could have been the Brasenose boy's younger brother.

'What are you drinking?' Moorsom muttered.

'Pink champagne, please,' said the boy quickly. He called across the room, 'A bottle of your best pink, my good man,' and accompanied the request with a triumphant middle finger sticking up out of his right fist.

'I can't stay,' Moorsom blurted. He took out two ten pound notes and put them on the table. 'Enjoy your drink.'

'Are you for real?' Rupert's eyes widened. What a find – a shy one. He seemed a little common and Northern, but he thought nothing of giving twenty quid to a complete stranger, so he must be a live one. Probably one of those screamingly repressed self-made Northern businessmen with a wife and two veg. A sugar daddy! – how incredibly camp. And fortuitous. 'Look, don't go for a minute.' He put his hand on Moorsom's arm and smiled up at him the way he had seen Lana Turner do so many times on rainy BBC2 Hollywood matinée afternoons. 'They say drinking alone is the first step towards alcoholism. You wouldn't like my liver on your conscience, would you? Just think of the little thing, all pink and pristine. Just say the word and you can save it.' He blew his fringe out of his eyes, with all the puckering and pouting that entailed. 'Please.'

Moorsom stared helplessly at the boy. All these years of working for other people, marrying for other people, living for other people. Didn't he have a right to have something for himself? As he sat down his voice was weary. 'OK.' But he felt as though a huge weight had been lifted from the back of his neck.

At first Rupert refused to believe that Moorsom lived in the Elephant and Castle. He thought it was a rich man's little joke. By the time they were crossing Blackfriars Bridge, he believed him. He pouted in the cab, he sulked in the lift and when he saw the size and spartan interior design of the flat he broke into a loud wail of anguish and fled into the bathroom.

But when he came out he was smiling, and holding an open copy of the Sunday Best. 'What an amazing coincidence! I'm in showbiz, too!'

Moorsom looked resignedly at the centrespread. There, in glorious Technicolor hypocrisy, stood himself, Jill, Debbie and Michael, lined up and smiling proudly in their modest Northern semi. 'JOE MOORSOM – MARXIST WITH A MORTGAGE, REBEL WITH A CAUSE' blared the headline.

He had cringed at the headline the first time he saw it, too, when Sue had shown him the layout. But she had laughed at him patiently. 'It's what our readers want from their politicians, Joe. To their mind anyone with a mortgage and 2.5 children couldn't possibly be an enemy of the people.' She rustled the layout importantly and impatiently, but he could see she was hurt. She had been pleased with herself when she had shown it to him. 'Look, if you don't like it just say the word and I'll write a piece which says you eat small children for breakfast, want to publicly disembowel the royal family next time Labour win power and believe that Britain should sign the Warsaw Pact. I'm really sorry if you think I've done some smarmy PR job, but I thought your real interest was changing things. And you can't change things unless you're in the mainstream. And that means photographs of the kiddies, and the wife, and the house, and all that irrelevant garbage. I'm sorry, but I didn't make the rules. I'm just trying to help you because I think the things you believe in are the right things.'

'Sue, I'm sorry. I'm just an old hippie.'

She laughed at that, the idea was so ridiculous.

'It's great – it really is. It's just hard for me to think of myself as this person.'

She was a clever girl, and well thought of as a journalist, so he let it go – what did he know?

Now he knew his feelings of dread had been justified as Rupert gazed calculatingly at the paper. 'How old is little Michael?' he asked dreamily.

'Twelve.'

'Oh, isn't that nice? In a couple of years he'll be the right age for you to . . .'

Moorsom lashed out at him and was surprised to feel his wrist caught in a thin iron grip. 'I am a trained ballet dancer,' Rupert hissed. 'My body is a deadly weapon. Rough stuff comes extra.'

'Extra?' Moorsom slumped back in his chair, rubbing his wrist.

'Au naturellement. You didn't think we were going to the chapel and going to get married, did you, dear boy? Oh no. You're a Labour MP, it says here, and you care about poor people and the redistribution of wealth. Well, I'm one and I want some of yours.' Rupert jumped on to the bed, bounced and flung out his arms. 'Now come here and show me the honourable member.'

He looked so beautiful, and so familiar; the breathing image of the boy whose face Moorsom had carried in his mind for the past seventeen years. He sat on the bed. 'I want to ask you one question and I want you to answer me truthfully. How old are you?'

'Old enough.'

'Seriously.'

'I'm eighteen.'

'It's still illegal.'

'So is everything delicious.' Rupert smiled at him. 'Now you have to answer me honestly. Tell me what you'd like.'

'Just . . . I feel awkward saying it.'

'Go on, silly.'

'Just . . . act as if you love me.'

Rupert began to unbutton the man's shirt. 'Love comes extra,' he said.

Sexual enchantment doesn't affect only the lives of those experiencing it. It affected Joe Moorsom's secretary and researchers, with whom he now flirted mercilessly. It affected his wife and children, on whom he now lavished long-distance affection. And it affected Susan Street when she received a huge bunch of orchids at work one Tuesday morning with a card saying, 'LUNCH! CANCEL EVERYTHING! JOE' and felt obliged to forgo lunch at L'Escargot with a notoriously entertaining and bitchy actress in favour of a working-man's café in Farringdon – the only place Joe could go to eat without suffering the indigestion of guilt.

'What's happened?' she asked, poking moodily at a fried egg.

'The big one, I'm afraid.' He laughed modestly.

She sprayed tea all over her egg. 'You've been given a place in the Shadow Cabinet!'

'What a one-track mind you have, Susan!' he said impatiently. Couldn't she tell? Wasn't it obvious? 'I've fallen in love.' He lowered his voice. 'He's wonderful, Susan.'

'And you're telling a hack?' She was genuinely alarmed.

'No, Susan,' he said patiently. 'I'm telling you. As a friend.'

She shook her head and pushed her plate away. 'Oh, Joe. Oh, no.'

He was red now, with anger and embarrassment. 'Susan, I really thought I could tell you. We've had a few evenings when you've got drunk and told me about your . . . past, some of

the things you got up to. I really thought you'd understand.
There's no one else I can tell. I come from a mining village.
I'm married to an NUM woman, I'm sponsored by the NUM.
Don't you see how impossible things are for me?'

'I'm sorry, Joe – I'm really happy for you. I'm just worried.
With everything that's happening for you right now . . .'

'I appreciate your concern,' he said coldly.

The lunch ended in less than ten minutes and he disappeared
quickly, leaving Susan to pay the meagre bill. Which was
unusual, because he always paid his half, insisting that there
was no such thing as a free lunch.

She wondered how he had come by the misapprehension that
there was such a thing as free fuck.

One person unaffected by the sexual enchantment of Joe
Moorsom was Rupert Grey. After the initial relief of not being
destitute and prostitute had faded, and after a week lying in bed
reading Smash Hits, Rupert was bored. He was not allowed
to answer the phone. He was never taken anywhere. Joe was
starting to look less like a sugar daddy and more like a jailer.
It was worse than home sweet home.

'But you're in showbusiness!' he protested when Joe
suggested yet another evening nursing a king prawn marsala
in front of EastEnders. 'Show people don't live like this! They
lead grand and glamorous lives!'

'Rupert, I am not in showbusiness. I am a politician. A
Labour politician.'

'You get on TV, don't you?'

'Now and then.'

'Then you're in showbiz. Like Robin Day.'

'Rupert, if I wanted to live in the way you suggest, which I don't, I couldn't. I don't even take all of my salary. I draw a miner's wage and give the rest back to the party.'

Rupert threw back his head and screamed with frustration. 'You SUCKER!' That night in bed he said he had a headache.

'I want to go one of those restaurants I'm always reading about,' he announced the next day. 'Langan's, Lockets, the Gay Hussar. He tittered. 'I especially like the sound of the Gay Hussar.'

'Rupert, I don't GO to those places.'

'Then maybe I'll find myself someone who does.'

'Please don't say things like that, angel. Oh look, my speech.'

Rupert turned moodily towards the TV. There was a news film of Joe Moorsom taken two nights ago in Cleveland.

'Society can no longer expect the under-funded and over-stretched social services to save children from abuse and exploitation – society must take a long hard look at itself. Silence is no option – only an aid and a comfort to the great sickness within ourselves. The great threat to our children today is no longer the anonymous man with the bag of sweets but the silent mother, the sick father and the scheming relation. For too many of this supposedly civilized nation's children the place where they should be protected and precious is a place of torment. If the torture of children *happened in Latin America, we would call it fascism; if it happens here, we call it home life. But our houses cannot be home while children are being tortured in them. Only the truth shall make our children free – and only their freedom will give us the right to call ourselves a civilized country once more. Thank you.'*

'Lovely speech, darling,' said Rupert over the wild applause.

'Thanks.'

'Angel?'

'Yes?'

'How much do you think the papers would pay for a story informing them that the nation's most prominent protector of children from sexual abuse is fucking a fourteen-year-old?'

'But you told me—'

'I was lying,' the boy answered happily. 'But even if I was eighteen, it would still be illegal.'

'Illegal, but not obscene.'

'OH! So I'm obscene, am I!'

Joe Moorsom looked at the boy he loved standing there in pink ankle-socks and a turquoise satin turban with a fake emerald jammed into his navel and thought that, yet again, honesty was probably not the best policy. 'No, of course not.'

'Thanks a lot.' The boy looked at him coldly. 'Listen, Joe, it's been a lark. But I don't think we're compatible. I can't waste the best years of my life in a council flat on the fourteenth floor. I think I should move out quite soon.'

'Rupert!' Moorsom caught him by the wrists. 'Don't say that!'

'Shall if I want!' The boy lit a Sobranie. 'Though of course, I shall need some help.'

'What do you mean?'

'Money, silly!'

'A loan?'

'Oh, no. That's all cold and formal and nasty. No, I shall want palimony.'

'But I've only known you for three weeks!'

'Ah, yes. But to quote your good self, they've been the happiest weeks of your life. We're talking quality of time here, not silly old quantity.'

'Palimony . . .'

'Just think of it as wealth redistribution, JoJo.'

The palimony demands grew day by day, fuelled equally by Rupert's wild imagination and greed. The combination proved lethal. Rupert refused to believe that anyone who appeared on TV was not immensely rich. At first he would just chant at Moorsom, 'A flat in Cheyne Walk – a charge account at Fortnum's – a Gaultier suit—' and then the little yellow sticky notes started going up:

'A CRATE OF PINK CHAMPAGNE EVERY DAY FOR THE REST OF MY LIFE'

'MY PHOTOGRAPH TAKEN BY ROBERT MAPPLE-THORPE'

One day his secretary answered his phone only to nod and turn to Moorsom with a cryptic message. 'It was someone called Rupee. He said it rhymed with whoopee and he said you'd understand. The message is, "One large Borzoi, male, dyed puce".'

It was this indiscretion which made Moorsom realize that a halt had to be called to the proceedings. That evening he confronted the boy. 'Rupert, I have no money. If I did, I'd gladly give it you. But these demands have got to stop.'

'Really?' There was a new note of contempt, class-based contempt, Moorsom couldn't help feeling, in the boy's voice. 'Well, listen to me, my honourable little member, and listen closely because I don't intend to repeat it. I'll tell you what's got to stop, and that's this horrid deceitful stinginess. I'll do without the presents – to judge from that awful tie you're wearing your taste is all in your mouth anyhow – but I want my palimony. I want fifty thousand pounds, JoJo – that's five oh comma oh oh oh – and I want it soon, while I'm young enough to enjoy it – before my fifteenth birthday. You can take it from the miner's slush fund or the blind pit ponies' poor-box or you can do more TV – I don't care where it comes from. But if doesn't come soon, your lovely wife and wonderful kiddies are going to see their honourable member splashed all over the front pages one Sunday.' He smirked, enjoying the look of stunned horror on the man's face. 'Won't that make them sick up their Shreddies?'

'You were right,' he told her grimly, looking into his Scotch. 'He's threatening me. Fifty thousand or he'll sell his story.'

'Fifty! What does he think you are, a chat-show host?'

'He doesn't live in the real world, Sue. It's not his fault. It's that awful soulless middle-class public-school upbringing—'

'Oh, for God's sake, stop making party political broadcasts, Joe! There are a million like him in this city from every walk of life. And stop making excuses for the little tart. He's a con man, pure and simple.'

Moorsom was silent. To her horror she saw a tear fall into his empty glass. 'I love him, Sue.'

'Your wife's going to love him, too, isn't she? Not to mention the NUM. Why, they'll probably sit him on the front float at the next Miners' Gala and crown him Queen of the May. After they've finished lynching you, that is.' She gnashed her teeth. 'Look at what you've put in jeopardy, just for some diseased little slut with a tight asshole.'

'If you're going to be obscene there's no point in going on with this,' he said primly. 'I thought that maybe you'd be able to think of some way out, that's all.'

She drained her vodka martini and chewed on the lemon twist for a moment. 'Send him to my office,' she said finally. 'Around four, when everyone's at lunch, tomorrow. He's young enough to throw a scare into . . .'

'Yes, he's very young—'

'—but old enough to know better,' she finished firmly.

Susan sat behind her desk in her best Nicole Farhi houndstooth suit and looked at the boy very seriously as he came in. She rose and shook his hand solemnly. Around her computers clicked and clattered and by the way he looked around she could tell he already felt out of his depth. Not without reason, he considered newspapers a sort of showbusiness, and showbusiness was what awed him above all. It was a cinch.

In a quiet but deadly serious voice, she told him about the libel laws of the country and how no newspaper would touch his story. She made most of this up. Then she told him how judges especially disliked blackmail because many of them were homosexual too and dreaded the day they might be put in the same position by some greedy little boy. To ensure against this, they were fond of making an example of every unfortunate would-be young blackmailer who appeared before them. She threw in the Freemasons for good measure and Rupert's eyes widened. It always worked.

Having prepared the groundwork, Susan lingered over the entrée. Had he read any books or articles about what went on in juvenile detention centres? Well, it wasn't a Derek Jarman wet dream of endless communal showers and pillow fights, she could tell him that much. Yes, she reflected, it wasn't so much what those places had that was scary, as what they didn't have. No personal effects and little luxuries. No Godiva chocolates. No Perrier. No toilets in the cells, just slop buckets. No shampoo, just soap. By the time she moved on to the severe dearth of mirrors, Rupert had covered his ears and was repeating over and over in a robotic voice that he wanted to go home. She had to call a security guard to help him down the stairs and out of the building.

* * *

That had been three years ago. The boy would be still well under the age of consent. She knew his name and his face and it wouldn't be too hard to trace him with strategic use of the rentboy community and a cheque book.

She didn't even have to do that – just have a word in Joe's ear, call in her favour. He owed her one.

If she could persuade Moorsom to drop the matter she could advance herself immeasurably in Pope's eyes, show him she was an operator, like him, and worthy of his respect. She could probably bring the editorship a step closer and maybe stop these ridiculous tasks.

But it was *blackmail* – and such a lousy thing to do to a good man. What *could* she do?

The phone rang.

'Sue, it's a man. He won't give me his name. He says,' Kathy laughed, 'he says he's one of your victims. Shall I put him through?'

'Go ahead, Kathy.'

'Susan Street?'

'Speaking.'

'You listen, Susan Street, and you listen good. As good as you listened to that lying black whore. You've picked the wrong man, girly. I know things about you, Miss Street-Walker, things you wouldn't want printed in your precious paper. Things you're very likely to see on the front page of some other rag in the very near future.'

The French-Yorkshire accent was unmistakable. *Sacré bleu* bah gum indeed! He could see into the dark heart of international finance and he knew where the body was buried. Why shouldn't he be able to see into her life too?

She felt a feeling she was unfamiliar with. Fear.

SIX

The beautiful Danish waitress gave them a special big smile because Susan Street was well known as a girl who tipped as big as she talked and drank as hard as she worked. The smile caused Zero to choke on one of the sweet, sticky, lurid drinks her working-class girlhood had left her with a taste for and then to sit up straight in her seat, holding her hands out in front of her like paws, panting.

The waitress laughed – crazy English – and Liam, the much-loved manager of the Groucho Club, wagged a stern finger at the begging blonde as he passed by on his rounds.

'So—' Zero lounged back on the sofa, nursing her Midori melon liqueur. 'What's the latest in the glamorous life of the dyke I'd most like to stick my finger into?'

'Very funny.' Susan smoothed the skirt of her royal blue Christian Lacroix suit and wondered what Zero would make of Thalia. Mincemeat, probably. 'Well, it's going OK. I've shown you my little . . . adornment.' She touched her fringe. 'And Rio was – well – it was an orgy, I guess. No more, no less.'

'How many foreign bodies?'

'Six.'

'That's not an orgy, that's a dinner party. It can't be an orgy till it reaches two figures.'

'*You'd* know.'

'So how do you feel?'

'I feel . . . that's a good question. I suppose I feel . . . *strong*.'

'Not depressed, disgusted, all those wimpy things women are meant to feel when some man done misuse them?'

'Do me a favour – I don't suffer from female trouble. But I do feel just a little trepidation about what he's going to hatch out next. I can't imagine where we go from here – goldfish?'

'I see a vision.' Zero stared into her Midori. 'You will be blindfolded and taken to a basement in Bayswater. You will be bound hand and foot. And you will be powerless to resist as a beautiful blonde from Tiger Bay wearing a twelve-inch dildo makes mad passionate love to you.'

'You wish.'

'I *know*. I got the gift of prophecy from my old pagan granny, look you.'

'Dream on, baby.' Susan drained her glass. 'So how's the brilliant career of the demon lover. Struck out with anyone but me yet?'

'You're kidding. I never met a girl I didn't like. Even the ones that may look like complete dogs at first always turn out to have something perfect about them on closer inspection – even if it's their eyebrows or their knees. I got this new one, a performance artist from New York; she's forty and looks twelve. The entire right-hand side of her body is tattooed with the Stars and Stripes. It's a statement. I'm crazy for her; I adore American women. It's true what that writer said – they're a third sex.'

'Two is too many for me.'

'So how's the girl in *your* life?'

'Say what?'

'*Matthew*.'

'Oh, he's fine. I suppose. We never really talk. Sometimes I insult him. Sometimes he lectures me. But it's all one-way traffic. There is one thing – sometimes he catches me in the bathroom before work. His new thing is to walk around with a hard on and nothing else on; I don't know what this is supposed to make me do – jump on him in sheer animal lust, I guess. But it only has the effect of making me take him even less seriously – men look even more ridiculous with their clothes off. Last time, I couldn't stop myself; I looked straight at it and said, "That reminds me – we're out of button mushrooms." '

Zero laughed. 'When *I* used to go with men and they were hung like hamsters, I'd say, "I didn't know men had clitori!" when they took their trews off.'

'Another good one is, "What's wrong, don't you find me attractive?" when they're bursting with pride over the size of the thing.'

They fell against each other, giggling. 'Designer dykes,' the man at the next table whispered grimly to his friend. 'This city is full of them all of a sudden. In five years, it'll be just as bad as Paris.'

'Talking of cock, you know who's coming over soon?' asked Zero. 'Pope Junior. That gorgeous little Rachel had to book the flight. I heard on the grapevine he is absolutely hideola – even for a man. You know the type – makes Phil Collins look like Mel Gibson. You can tell he's Pope's son, eh bach?'

Susan sighed and signalled to the waitress, who was leaning on the bar and casing Zero. Looked like the demon lover of the valleys had scored again. 'Another ugly American – *just* what the world needs now.'

'Mmmm?' Zero had been flicking through Susan's credit cards, as was her habit each time they met, looking for new affectations to taunt her with, and had found instead her donor card. 'Look, look – it says here that any part of your body can be used by someone else after you're dead.' Looking at Susan wide-eyed, she pouted. 'Which bit can I use?'

It was seven-thirty on a Friday evening as she tried yet again to compose a short headline for a new survey which showed that eighty-three per cent of British women found men respectful, committed and caring.

They obviously hadn't had the pleasure of Tobias Pope. She sighed, decided on something horribly banal and looked up.

Pope was standing in the doorway of her office, wearing a camel-hair coat and carrying a silver-headed walking cane, smiling sardonically. She gaped at him.

'Don't look so thrilled, you ungrateful little slut,' he whispered as he shook her hand heartily. There were others still around.

'But it's not . . .'

'Don't worry, I haven't got a treat in store for you. This is just a social call. I happened to be in town on business.'

'Funny business.'

'Television business.'

'That's nice.' She looked at him warily.

'We're going to see a girl at her flat, and then we're having dinner at Langan's, and then we're going to see a pop group go through their paces. How does that grab you?'

'Great.' She yawned.

'Your enthusiasm kills me. Now, who's this penny-ante little politico we've got to wipe off the board?'

Susan recognized the girl who opened the door of the Lowndes Square flat straight away. Lady Caroline Malaise; vaguely aristocratic, probably somewhat royal, she had starred in a clutch of soft-focus, semi-commercial soft-porn films some years ago, always as a gently born young

121

Englishwoman copiously shedding clothes and virginity in various leafy dells, wooden baths and minstrel galleries. Her resemblance to a blonder, more luminous Princess Diana had driven the foreign paparazzi, particularly the Italians, mad. That was when the photographs of her and Pope, forever leaving Annabel's and the Clermont, had been in all the papers. Very little had been seen of her since and, opening the door, she seemed smaller and thinner than her likeness.

But, Susan had learned, so were most people. Apart from Tobias Pope.

Brisk introductions were made and the driver was briefed. During pre-dinner drinks, Susan noticed that Caroline had an odd eye. She tried to stop herself from looking at it but was irresistibly drawn. A couple of times Pope caught her staring, and smiled in a manner best described as unwholesome. The third time, he threw back his head and laughed.

'Show Miss Street your eye, Caroline.'

To Susan's horror the girl lowered her head, poked at her eye and wordlessly extended it on her palm across the table. The lid closed over the socket and Susan's stomach lurched.

'Thank you, my dear. Performed with exactly the insouciant *sang froid* that made you famous, albeit briefly.' He turned to Susan. 'Several years ago I was dining with Caroline in St James's and a young fan, a fan of her tasteful art films no doubt, winked at her. Being relatively free of airs and graces for one of her caste, she winked back. And no doubt the young fan in question went home and had many happy wet dreams at the thought of it.' He sighed deeply. 'But unfortunately, later that evening, back at Caro's flat, I was a little clumsy with the champagne we were having as a nightcap. The cork, you know. Took the poor girl's eye out. Accident, of course, but rather lyrically Biblical, don't you think? An eye for an eye . . .'

Her oysters lay untouched in front of her. A wife in a clinic, Cristina Montes dead, Caroline Malaise eyeless in Langan's and herself sitting there like a lemon with SOLD tattooed on her face – Tobias Pope was certainly the answer to a maiden's prayer, you had to say that for him. She couldn't eat, didn't eat, begging off a main course by pleading a late and large lunch. But no one was fooled. She was grateful when they paid the bill and piled into the car.

'Which band are we seeing?' she asked Pope.

Caroline answered. 'My little sister, Candida, and her shower, worse luck. They're called Fuck U, I'm afraid. That's like in U and non-U.'

'They're obnoxious young aristos with more money than sense and more fingers than braincells,' cut in Pope. 'Still I think they have a gimmick. People are sick of yobs. They like having their noses rubbed in the dirt by their betters. Why do you think they elected your good leader?'

'Oh, Toby, Mrs Thatcher's not an aristocrat. That's the whole point.' Caroline laughed fondly.

'Ah, yes. I understand the difference. That's why she rules the country while you are engaged in the important business of sticking your trust fund in your arm.'

Caroline bit her lip.

Susan was not overfond of clubs – she had gone to too many while she was knocking around with the god-like Gary pride – and she was relieved when they were whisked backstage and settled sidestage by one of the boys at the door. Within minutes four young men in dinner jackets led by a girl in a pink Lindka Cierach ball dress were striding purposefully towards them.

The girl had long, brazen blonde curls and a cleavage the colour of bread-and-butter pudding. She looked as though she had been fed intravenously on English nursery food for most of her young life. 'Hello, babes. Hello, Tobes.' She stared rudely at Susan. 'Don't think I know you.'

'Umm . . . Susie Street,' mumbled Caroline.

'Oh, rilly! Are you anything to do with Lulu and Mumu Street? Great fun at their place in Gloucestershire last month! Didn't see *you* there though.'

'Candida, Susan is not a Gloucestershire Street. She is a wrong side of the Street.' Tobias smirked.

'Oh, rilly?' She giggled. 'I don't think you'll like our songs much, Susie!'

'Tell Susie what they're called, Candy.'

'Well, there's, "We're All Going On A Peasant Shoot", "The Porsche Will Always Be With Us", "Let Them Eat

Humble Pie" . . . lots and lots, rilly. And every one a number one, right, Tobes?'

'I hope so.'

'Kids!' A young man in his early thirties with slicked-down hair, a briefcase and a cellular phone hanging from his ear like some exotic Yoruba adornment buzzed up to them. 'On in five minutes, right?'

'OK, Gaz.'

'Don't sweat it, Gaz, right?'

'Hello, Mr Pope. Glad you could make it.'

'Your pleasure, Gary. Gary Prince, you know Caroline . . . and this is Susan Street.'

'Pleased to meet you, Susan.' He shook her hand formally, trying to work out who she was and how useful she could be.

Susan Street stared. It was Gary Pride, the virgin's friend! And he genuinely didn't recognize her!

She'd heard he'd had ECT. But he seemed OK, apart from a ferocious tic and the fact that his memory didn't appear to go further back than the day before yesterday.

The parade passed by. Pope turned to Susan. 'You used to write about this awful noise, didn't you? Watch this lot, and tell me if they've got anything. *I* don't know. Actually, don't bother. I'm buying them for the way they look and where they are in Debrett, not what they sound like. The audience I've got in mind never listen to anything but the sound of their own voices anyhow. You've heard of rich Americans buying titles? Well, I'm the rich American and they're the titles.'

'What exactly do you want them for?'

'For my little place in Sun City. That brave and independent homeland has many things, including ceaseless sunshine and more darkies than you can shake a stick at, but it doesn't have a glut of Peerage berks. And there's nothing the new rich love more than seeing the old rich cavorting for their pleasure.'

The band were onstage. 'Thank you, oiks!' The crowd cheered. 'Our first number is called "Revolt into Style". ONETWOTHREEFOUR!'

Well the B boys are as happy as Larry
Cos they're all going to the Café de Paris
To protect your heap you don't need Mace
Just let peasants read *The Face!*

Pope laughed. 'WHAT DO YOU THINK?'

'VERY NICE.'

'SUSAN, YOU'RE SUCH AN OLD FASHIONED LITTLE MERITOCRAT!'

Caroline smiled vaguely and tugged at Pope's sleeve as the volume of the band was mixed down a fraction. 'Toby, what time is it?'

'It's five minutes later than when you last asked me. And two hours till your next medication. Please try and control yourself, my dear – use a little bit of that stiff upper lip that made your people great. And don't interrupt my conversations with Miss Street again or I'll have your other eye out and give them to her as earrings.'

Caroline snivelled.

'God, I hate these women,' he whispered. 'Upper-class women, they're either like horses or rag dolls. This one's a doll with its wind-up gone wrong, Junior out there is a prancing pony. I much prefer women like you. If there *are* any others like you.'

'But I'm pretty malleable too, aren't I?' She wondered what he was up to, and why he was flattering her. Or was he just telling the truth? She *was* pretty fucking special, when you came down to it, especially compared with these privileged pains.

'Malleable, you!' He laughed at the idea.

'I do what you want, don't I?'

'Oh no. You do as I *say*. But you do as you *want*. Otherwise you wouldn't do it. Watching you go through your paces is like watching a beautifully oiled machine go through its programme. I noticed that at the tattooist's, and more so in Rio. You've got guts. My kind of girl. I've been thinking about you since Brazil, and I like what I've seen.' He turned his head abruptly. 'Well, shall I sign this shower or not?'

She didn't know. She was too busy fighting the insane temptation to reach out and touch his hand. 'Whatever you want,' she said slowly.

* * *

The sun shone brightly on South Africa House as the five member of Fuck U lined up to sign the contracts laid out on trestle tables. The press photographers were out in full force. Police held back lines of angry young demonstrators, radiant in their righteousness, and among them Susan saw Joe Moorsom, standing silently with a banner which read POPE=APARTHEID. She sat with Caroline in the limousine, watching through smoked windows.

Suddenly a fracas erupted from *within* the cordoned space. It was Gary Prince, born-again businessman, reverting to type and screaming 'Fuck you! FUCK YOU!'

'Yes, that's the name!' mocked one of the band boys. 'Keep it up, Gazza! The more publicity the better! Remember the Sex Pistols!'

'Fuck you! I've been conned, you bastards!'

'These young people need a chaperon no longer, Mr Prince,' intoned Tobias. 'From now on, they have me. I shall look after them as though they were my own.'

Caroline laughed. 'Have you met his son?'

'Next week.'

'Have *you* got a treat in store.'

'I'm their manager! I got a contract!'

'No you haven't, Gaz,' said Candida contemptuously.

'A gentleman's word is his bond! You said so, Nick!'

'But only if he's talking to another *gentleman*, Gaz!'

'Officer, please take this man away. He's bothering my artistes.'

'I'll 'ave you, Pope! You've picked the wrong man, sonny!'

'Officer, please take this down in your notebook. This gentleman appears to be threatening me with violence.'

Susan watched the police take Gary Pride away. It took five of them, he was so angry.

She turned to comment on this to Caroline and saw her staring straight at Pope, her good eye so dead and livid with loathing that it was indistingishable from the false one.

She turned back to the street and watched as Pope shepherded his latest acquisitions into limousines. Would he have them tattooed, too? Would he kill any of them, or just dump them? Whatever, a lot of people already appeared to have both the motive and desire to wish Pope dead.

She wondered if she would ever be one of them.

Or was she already?

The hallway was full of red roses when she got home from work, and she sighed because she knew they were from Matthew. Matthew *always* sent red roses, which showed such a chronic lack of irony and imagination that it was like walking around with a sign on your back saying I AM A SENTIMENTAL SAP. Charles had always sent daisies and orchids mixed, which she supposed was a knowing nod to her youth and decadence while Zero, when she remembered, favoured lurid red tulips – ripe, open and unmistakable in their insinuation.

'Do you send them to all your girls?' Susan asked her.

'Only the ones that won't sleep with me.' Zero batted her long eyelashes innocently.

But *roses*. She sighed again. These days every thing about Matthew made her sigh, from the noise he made eating his Wheati-Chomps (not to mention the grotesque glee – which she had once found so adorable – he invariably displayed upon finding the free green plastic battleship within) to the amount of money he earned – pathetic.

For a long time now she had been earning more than twice as much as him, a fact which, especially considering her gender and origins, never failed to amaze and delight her – and which, when intoxicated by drink or success, she never failed to tell him about.

'You know the Speak Your Weight machine?' Matthew said one night after a particularly verbose bit of boasting on her part. 'You're like a Speak Your Salary machine.'

Jealous jerk. Yes, taunting a man about the money he made was the Nineties' equivalent of teasing him about the size of his penis, she decided – it hit him where he lived. And the penis-tease wasn't *half* as effective since those killjoy sexologists had come up with the glad tidings that penis size was unrelated to providing pleasure. Though personally, Susan believed that *that* one should be taken with a good-sized Siberian salt-mine: the only girls *she'd* known who didn't like a big one were the girls who didn't particularly like sex. They probably liked tiny ones because it made it that much easier to pretend the dirty deed wasn't happening.

But no one, in the Nineties, could pretend that a small salary was as sexy as a big one.

Matthew, even, didn't have a good answer. Usually he tried the strong, silent and superior act but once in a while he would rally with a lame comeback. 'Isn't it true, Susan, that *anyone* can make a lot of money in this society if they're prepared to sell out?'

'Ah, Matthew. The Sell Out. That popular fallacy put about by failures. No, dear, *not* anyone can sell out. Only the chosen few ever get the opportunity, because you can't sell out unless you have something that someone is prepared to pay a high price for. Show me someone who hasn't sold out and I'll show someone who hasn't got anything anyone wants to buy.'

'It's people like you who are destroying the National Health Service!' he shrilled before slamming the door – a sound which more and more had replaced the full stop as the culmination of their conversations.

But after a spot of deep breathing and shallow thinking he was back with a smug smirk and a second wind. 'You're so mercenary, Susan. Yet I thought you were a feminist.'

'Oh, I am, Matthew.' She stared at him blankly, already anticipating his new line of attack and relishing her counter-thrust.

'Well, correct me if I'm wrong, but I thought feminism

was about creating a more *humane* society. Not a more mercenary and brutal competitive one.' I've put in my thumb and pulled out a plum, you bitch, said his smile. Top *that*.

She shrugged and narrowed her eyes, looking at him lazily, ready to pounce. 'Oh, I don't know. I like to think feminism's a broad church. For instance, there are Christians who burn crosses on Negro lawns in the southern states of the USA and there are Christians who follow Karl Marx in Latin America. The only thing they have in common is that they are Christians. Feminism is like that now. There are moustachioed milch-cows who sit in the mud around airbases insisting that women are peaceful and loving and nurturing and that all the trouble in the world is caused by men – an idea of women very compatible, don't you think, with that of the Victorians, who idealized women as angels of the hearth? Angel of the airbase is just as constricting and stifling the way I look at it.'

'Yes, but—'

'And what will I get, pray, if I *am* nuturing and passive – my reward in heaven? No go, Jack. No – the reason for the emergence of free-market feminism in the Eighties is the fact that to be ruthless, competitive and individualistic is the most rebellious thing a girl can do; it denies every theory from right and left, about our weakness. Quite frankly, if any well-meaning Earth Mother tells me that because of the shape of my genitalia I am automatically nuturing and caring, I'm going to take her face off with a Sabatier filleting knife to prove her wrong.'

'Didn't you used to be a socialist?' he said accusingly.

'Certainly. Before I woke up to the fact that socialism has become a male weapon to divert women's energies from feminism. Who's more frightening to men, and free – Mrs Thatcher or Mrs Kinnock? Is *that* socialist woman these days – jam tomorrow, so long as *you* pick the fruit and stand by your man? Then give me the free market any time – I'll take my chances and find my own way, thank you very much. And I'll get there a long time before these women who shout so loud about feminism and waste all their energies working for socialism. For *men*.'

He stood looking at her, shaking his head. 'It's very frightening, the way you talk these days, Susan. It's like hearing one of those crazy Olympic athletes who'd do anything, take any drug, just so they can *win*. Winning is all that matters to you.'

She laughed. He sounded like some neurotic wife of a hotshot executive in an American soap opera. 'That's silly. I *never* think about winning. I never *plan* any of my career. It just *happens*. Things just come to me.'

'I know.' He nodded. 'You never think about winning because it doesn't even occur to you that there's any other option. Don't you see how scary that is in a human being?'

She shrugged. 'No, not really.'

'Do you know what Napoleon said?'

133

'Not tonight, Josephine?'

'Napoleon said, "I have no ambition." And in a way, he was right. Because Napoleon *was* ambition. He and you didn't choose or think about it – you *are* ambition.' He finished with a flourish and stood looking at her proudly, no doubt expecting her to fall to her knees and thank him for revealing her innermost desires to her at last.

Instead she puckered up her luscious lips and blew an enormous raspberry.

Her laughter had echoed after his Bruegelian scream as he ran from the room in furious frustration.

Now she picked up the florist's card from the telephone table. SORRY ABOUT THIS MORNING. LOVE, MATTIE.

Mattie! She was going to throw up.

They were at that stage of a relationship where monogamy is shading slowly but surely into celibacy, and with this development go a million reasons to argue about everything but the real thing. This morning there had been no decaffeinated coffee for Matthew's breakfast, which signified, according to that indecipherable male logic, that she didn't love him. Well, she didn't – but the lack of coffee had nothing to do with that. It had to do with the fact that neither of them had the time to go to the supermarket any more.

She had watched, both amused and appalled, as he ranted, raved, went red in the face and finally lay down flat on his back on the floor and did his deep-breathing exercises 'in order to keep my temper'. Keep his temper! – Talk about bolting the stable door after the horse had hoofed it.

What could she do about Matthew? She hated the idea of being alone, but wasn't this worse? They hadn't slept together in months; no wonder she was such a sitting duck for Tobias Pope and his perverted plans for her. Sitting on the stairs she shivered as she remembered Rio, and then the phone rang. 'Hello?'

'Hello? Miss Street-Walker?'

She gasped. Lejeune. 'How did you get my number?' They were in the book under Matthew's name, and the office would never be so irresponsible.

'The same way I get everything, Miss Street-Walker. With my Gift.' He sounded very pleased with his gift, she thought, as indeed he had every reason to be. But the smug malice in his voice and the degree of fear she felt made her angry.

'The same gift that tells you how to play the stock market, you mean? Is that the one?'

'One and the same.'

God, but he rubbed her up the wrong way. 'Excuse me, Mr Lejeune, but is this the same famous gift that isn't strong enough to tell you when a tart's recording your sordid little orgasms for posterity and the front page with an obvious little machine under the bed?'

He didn't like that. There was an intake of breath, then

a forced relaxation. 'A little oversight, lass. But I'll tell you one thing . . .'

'What?' she sneered shakily.

'It's strong enough to pass through time zones undiluted. Did you have a nice time in Rio?'

'I haven't ever been to Rio,' she said quickly.

He laughed horribly. 'Silly, silly, Miss Street-Walker. Your passport could tell another story. And so could my Gift. Don't die of ignorance, will you? I've got lots of treats in store for you. And give my regards to the boyfriend – I'll have a big surprise for you both soon.'

The phone went dead. She sat down slowly on the stairs, stared at the flowers that filled the hall and felt as though she was at her own funeral.

SEVEN

'You should hear Washington Brown sing! Well, you will, in a matter of hours, I guess! He'll be squealing like a stuck pig when I cut him loose – black pudding!' Pope chuckled at his subtle witticism.

'Washington Brown is a legend,' said Susan primly from where she sat at the window of the hotel penthouse suite which overlooked the Pope Fun Complex of Sun City. 'You know, Mr Pope, something I can't work out is that when white South Africans are questioned about whether they really have any right to be on this continent, they rhapsodize about how they love the country, how it's the most beautiful, unspoiled heaven on earth. So what do they do with paradise? Build Las Vegas in the middle of it!' She gestured down at the complex of nightclubs and casinos. 'If this is what they want, couldn't they just move to Paris or London or Nevada, where they'd have all the sleaze they could shoot up? And let the real South Africans get on with it?'

'You have the logic of the global village idiot, my dear. The world turns and civilization, lemming-like, must have its say and its way.' He threw down the room-service menu he had been studying. 'God, these people are hicks. They still drink French wine!'

'Don't you like them? The whites?'

He made a face. 'Give me credit for some finer feelings, madam. They are quite possibly the most despicable white race on earth. They're hideous, for a start – they look like those inbred retards you have the misfortune to see around the Mississippi Delta. Their women are *useless* as sex partners, put completely beyond the pale by that *disgusting* accent, which must be the ugliest ever to torment the human ear. When God made the Boer, he was firing on three cannons. Why couldn't he have slapped the British or the Italians down here, a white race with some grace or humour? At least they might have stood a chance of getting some part of the civilized world on their side against darkie. As it is, your Southern and Western African darkie is a charming chap, and the women are delightful – beautiful legs. Yes, one day they'll give these hicks what for. I only hope I've shut up shop by then.'

'But if you dislike the whites here, why do you do business with them?'

He smiled at her as if she were a beloved backward child. 'It's called money, my dear.'

'But of course.' She felt stupid, to be caught talking to him as though he was a normal human being.

'Get up to North Africa, on the other hand, and the women make appalling sex partners – vile legs and moustaches that any self-respecting sailor would kill for.'

Susan couldn't help laughing at the matter-of-fact grumpiness of his voice and the depravity of his words. He looked at her, startled, then smiled. 'What's so funny?'

'You are! You're such a swinger!'

'Well, listen to the toast of the *favelas*!'

She fell silent. It was the first time he had referred to Rio since London. She remembered that Tobias Pope liked to mix pleasure with business, and that once again she was the bait.

'Talking of rough trade, you should hear my new boy. Two years ago he was a struggling blood bro from the south side of Chi. I do believe he sang on one of those "I hate Sun City" records. Now he's found God and cocaine and an expensive *Ebony* model and he's going to sign with me here for a cool million.'

'What about Caroline's little sister and her crew?'

'Oh, just a little support act. Not the real thing. People come here to see great *black* singers, like Washington. They *adore* Washington. Or they did, until very recently. Always leave them wanting more . . .' He laughed at her, not unaffectionately. 'What's that sour little mouth on you? It looks just like a little cat's asshole.'

'I just think it's a bit much, that's all – to say these people *adore* a black man, whereas when they go home from their dirty weekends they'd *spit* on him if he so much as tried to use the front door.'

'Well, you'll be able to demonstrate your great love for our black brothers very soon, won't you, dearest?'

Tobias Pope bent over his papers with a secret smile.

Susan sat at the window and thought about Washington Brown while Pope's lawyers worked in another room to write him off the map. One of the biggest stars of the Seventies, white powders and white wives had made a mess of him. Now in his mid-forties, he was about to be dumped for an unmarked if unremarkable young lightweight who made more money endorsing breakfast cereal than he did singing.

He was understandably bitter and unmistakably here, standing in the doorway between two white men half his age and swaying like a boxer in his tropic-weight beige suit. They dropped him like laundry as they passed with Pope into the boardroom.

She stared at him. He had been big before her time, but she had almost comprehended what he meant from the old footage she had seen of him and the old records which, like any lonely, horny teen, she had sought out. Now he was overweight, bleary-eyed, with bad skin and a sour smell. It was the smell of withered success. In the morning, before the shower, she smelled the ghost of it on herself.

He scowled at her. 'How long your boyfriend gonna be?'

'I'm not sure.'

'Hey, you English.' He really relaxed. She saw the muscles move forward, then backward, in his arms. 'Hey, I always liked England. I like the people, I like the clubs. I especially like Branston pickle. You know Branston pickle?'

'Not socially.'

'Yeah, I like those English clubs – and the English girls! You sure mix a lot in England. Well, not you personally, I mean, I don't *know* you. But English girls sure do mix a lot in them clubs. You look at a white girl where I come from, she thinks Black Power's gonna rape her grammaw!' He cracked up.

'Mr Brown . . .' She felt very shy and awkward, and hoped desperately that she wouldn't be required to sleep with Washington Brown. Not only was he very probably terminally jaded by now and murder to arouse, but he had once been her hero. And it was always a terrible mistake to sleep with your heroes. 'I know it's a boring thing to say and you must have heard it a million times this week, but I loved your records when I was growing up.'

'Aw, thanks.' He looked both abashed and calculating. 'You tol' your boyfriend that?'

'He's not my boyfriend, he's my boss.'

'Yea, he's my boss too.' Washington Brown examined his immaculate nails. 'And he screws me, so I reckoned he was prob'ly screwing you as well.'

'No.'

There was a sticky silence. She could tell he didn't believe her.

'You read this book *Revolutionary Suicide?*' he finally asked her, rifling in his briefcase and shoving at her a hardback book bearing a photograph of a handsome light-skinned black man called Huey Newton.

'No, I'm afraid not.'

'Yeah, I'm afraid not, too. I'm afraid not I didn't read it fifteen years ago, when it might have done me some good.' He sulked. 'Happen I might not have ended up here in this shithole, getting dumped on by Whitey in his wisdom.'

She didn't know what to say. Finally she opened her mouth, and put her foot in it. 'I did admire Angela Davis, though. For keeping her own name, as much as anything. Imagine answering to Angela Davis, when all your friends were going back to their roots and changing their names to Shotzome Burundi!' Her laughter was too loud, amplified by her nerves. He looked at her with blank scorn. 'Apparently Chaka Khan's real name is Yvette Williams,' she finished lamely.

'Oh, Washington!' The youngest lawyer put his head around the boardroom door. 'We're ready for you now!'

'Revolutionary suicide,' muttered Washington Brown,

shambling to his feet. 'How about a bit of revolutionary assassination?'

'Do you mind if I call you Boy?' said Tobias Pope to the beautiful young black man who stood naked before him.

'Sir, for what you're paying you can call me girl. That goes for my brother too.'

Pope looked across the room to where the brother stood fastidiously hanging up a white suit. 'Identical twin?'

'Yes, but without a hard on. He was a minute earlier, so I'm an inch bigger. Fair do's.'

Pope laughed and slapped the man on the back.

'Gad, I like the African! Tell me, how long before you kick the stinking boring Dutch out?'

The man's face went stiff. 'I have no interest in politics.'

'I understand. But not a day too soon, eh?'

'Business will always be good for me, sir.'

'I don't doubt it.' Pope cast a professional eye over the man. 'And the lady, sir?'

'Lady?'

'The lady I am here to visit.'

'Oh *that* lady!'

A prim expression sat strangely on a six-foot-two naked black body.

'I am sure she *is* a lady. And a beautiful lady at that.'

'She's a girl, a pretty girl. Nice, too, and smart. English. You like the English?'

'A great people,' said the man solemnly. His brother crossed the room to join them, flashing a shy smile and a huge penis. 'You can call him Boy too, if you want.'

Pope laughed. 'OK, Boys One and Two. Follow me.'

Susan Street lay spreadeagled on the bed. She had tied one on and been tied up by an obliging aide of Pope's. She had drunk so many Bellinis at dinner she'd lost count. Now she blinked rapidly. 'Oh, hello, Mr Pope. And hello you, too, whoever you are. You know it's just like they say, I'm seeing double. There's two big—'

'Silence, imbecile. No, you are not seeing double, though that's a miracle considering the amount of that disgusting orange concoction you put away over dinner. Meet Boy One and Boy Two.'

'Oh, hello.'

'I'm pleased to make your acquaintance, miss.' Boy One walked around the bed. 'But what is this? You are bound?'

'Don't you approve?' asked Pope from the doorway.

'But no. How is the lady to express her sexuality when so restricted?'

Pope sniggered. 'You've got women's lib here too, eh? You poor bastards. On top of everything else!'

'It is not enhancing of a woman's natural beauty, these . . . *fetters*.'

'I get the message.' Pope strode over to the bed and untied her swiftly. 'I thought you might appreciate the irony, but obviously that only grows on three square meals a day and adult suffrage. OK, do your worst, both of you. Don't forget your tackle.'

'What would the lady wish?'

'The lady's not footing the bill, I am. And I wish both of you, with the lady, one after another.'

The first man said a few cryptic foreign words to his brother and they both looked slyly from Pope to Susan. Together they moved towards the bed, fitting short white condoms over long black penises. They reminded her of the magic wands of childhood, the black length and the white tip. Magic wands, indeed! She giggled and close her eyes.

They lay down beside her. Four hands stroked her head, her face, her breasts, stomach, thighs; it was like being with an octopus who had learned its strokes at Madame Claude's. She was coaxed like modelling clay and rolled over on top of the silent twin.

'Get up,' said his brother. 'Kneel over him.'

She straightened dizzily over his groin; his brother gripped the huge erect penis and probed her with it. She winced.

'It's OK. Relax.' He moved his brother's cock exploratively over her whole genitalia; she pushed reflexively back and then with one long, smooth, silent whoosh! like a firework leaving a milk bottle and slipping up into infinity, he was inside her – all the way up to her ribcage, it felt like.

'Stiff upper lip, girl!' commanded Pope. He was sitting

on the bed beside them with his arms folded, looking very pleased with himself.

'Sure you don't want to change places?' she quipped.

'I wouldn't trust myself not to fall head over heels in love with both of these fine fellows. Now stop talking and get going. Good God, girl.'

She moved on top of the twin, gingerly and with some trepidation. She had never been comfortable this way, and his bigness left her very little room to manoeuvre. She closed her eyes and rotated her hips and was beginning to feel the stirrings of something when the twin spoke in brief and rapid African.

'Excuse me a minute, sir,' said his brother. 'He's not used to this position. He's got to stop or he'll come.'

Tobias Pope clapped his hand to his head. 'Where, oh where, is a race which lives up to its advance publicity in bed? OK, take a break.' He was already on the phone. 'I want Krug, apple pie, and I want it pronto, Tonto.'

'Working for the Yankee dollar,' the talking twin whispered in her ear.

Susan laughed weakly. 'Do you come here often?'

'This is the first time I've had the pleasure to come to this particular suite. But generally, I've been in more hotel rooms than the Gideon Bible.'

'What's your name?'

'Warren.'

'I bet it's not.'

'It will do. You couldn't pronounce the name I was given.'

'Sorry to break up the *tête à tête*, children,' called Tobias Pope as a knock came at the door. 'But here's the chuck wagon.'

A trolley bearing half a dozen bottles of Krug on ice and a huge apple pie on a silver salver was pushed into the room by an elderly black man. Susan and the silent twin still crouched on the bed, looking like a particularly advanced Allen Jones coffee table. Without a glance at them he wheeled the trolley to the bed and stood looking at his feet.

Pope pushed some coinage carelessly into his hand and he left the room, still looking at the ground. Susan felt her face burn with non-specific shame.

'OK, break,' Pope ordered.

Warren lifted Susan slowly and expertly off his brother and sat her on the bed. His brother sat up and began to rub her shoulders.

'Thanks, that's just what I need.'

He flashed her a brilliant smile.

Warren walked to the trolley. 'Oh, champers, lovely.'

Pope looked at him, amused. 'Don't wait to be asked, do you?'

'Ask and you shall get, sir. That's the Bible.'

'It sounds more like Dale Carnegie. Damn, no glasses.' Pope looked around the room, and a sly smile crossed his face when he looked at Susan. 'Miss Street, can you stand on your head?'

'I suppose so,' she said dubiously.

'Right, go and stand on your head over there – you can use the wall as support.'

'But I want my champagne!' She'd been drunk and she'd been sober; drunk was better.

'You'll get your champagne, madam, and sooner than you think.' He popped the first cork expertly and handed the bottle to Warren, who raised it to his lips. Pope put a hand gently on his bare, glossy arm.

'Warren. How do you ever hope to find the lifestyle you seek, which was no doubt inspired by bad American soap operas, while you still lap from the bottle like a kitchen toto? Use a vessel, for goodness sake.'

'But there are no glasses . . .' Warren looked yearningly at the Krug, beginning to suspect that it had only been brought up here to torment him.

Pope gestured towards Susan; Warren turned to look at her and smiled. He found the combination of comedy and eroticism – her narrow, luminous body with her dark hair fanning out over the red carpet and her breasts falling into her wide-eyed, determined face as she watched them solemnly – lovable rather than arousing. 'Hey,' he said.

'Hey you.'

Tobias Pope leaned close to him. 'One thing you must learn, dear boy, is that champagne tastes best with fish. That's why it's synonymous with smoked salmon. And what do we have here?' He pointed at Susan. 'A living, breathing side of the stuff.' He put his mouth so near Warren's ear that he could taste his tangerine-scented pomade. 'Champagne tastes best out of cunt. That's the most essential thing you've got to learn about life. That, and the sayings of Karl Marx.'

Warren laughed and spoke to his brother who took hold of Susan's feet and spread them. Opening her with one hand, his tongue fitting into the gap between his front teeth as he concentrated on the delicate task, Warren poured.

She closed her eyes against the slight burning sensation. It made as much sense as anything else that had happened since that death in the Brighton bedroom. She felt liquid trickle icily down her stomach and visualized it forming stalagmites – stalactites? – on her nipples. She was full, and the twin held her firmly as Warren bent down to drink.

Pope stood smirking at them as Warren straightened up. 'A pretentious little bouquet?'

'Delicious!' He courteously grabbed Susan's feet and gestured to his brother. More Krug was poured, more lips sucked at her.

'A bold little vintage, I should think,' said Pope. 'Stroppy, assertive, with just a hint of . . . subservience.'

'You wish some, sir?'

'I'm allergic.'

'Oh, how dreadful,' Warren said happily, taking a swig from a fresh bottle while confidently supporting her with one hand.

'I don't think much of your brother's table manners. Look at him, going at the poor girl like a piglet coming off a hunger strike at its trough. You can drop her now – I think we've all had enough.'

Warren carefully let go of her feet, propping her against the wall; she slid down it, collapsing inelegantly and causing champagne to spray out of her. The three men looked at her as she lay there: the twins still had their erections and Pope still had his smirk. Which was probably as near as he ever got to having an erection, she thought moodily.

'Do you fancy another dip, gentlemen?'

Warren spoke to his brother and then to Susan with a smile. 'Kneel, please.'

The silent twin knelt behind her, entering her champagne-drenched insides easily this time. Warren held her by the hair and guided her mouth to him.

She gagged and spat. 'Yeucch! The lubricant on it – it's like fish oil!'

'I wouldn't have thought you'd object to that after that little performance you gave in Rio, my dear.'

'Mr Pope, I really can't—' She screwed up her face in disgust.

'Look at this, you boys, will you? This is a real comment on the morals of the modern girl. They don't mind putting a foot of throbbing meat in their throats even if they did only shake hands with its owner half an hour ago and have never been formally introduced. But a little bit of aesthetically displeasing rubber and – oh! How could you ask this of me?' He looked at Warren. 'OK, I'm speaking to you man to man now. Well, man to boy. You have a clean bill of health in your public parts?'

Warren drew himself up to his full height and gave Pope a look which expressed all the wisdom, sorrow and indignation of his people. 'Sir. How can you ask me that? I would rather you had cut off my right hand.'

'OK, I take it back.'

'Cut off my right hand and thrown it to the dogs—'

'Don't pile it on, boy. Well – I like you and I trust your boss; take the damn thing off. What Susan wants Susan must have.'

While Susan couldn't exactly say she *wanted* the best part of a foot of African cock rammed down her throat, Warren was a sweet kid and she might as well make the best of it. His brother knelt up to get a better look, holding her firmly and pumping professionally, and she felt pleasure stir and build.

Considering how difficult it is for just two people to achieve a simultaneous orgasm, it was either true love or a tribute to the twins' expertise that the three of them began to climax at the same moment.

'Good, good!' Tobias Pope over the three-part harmony of their groans. 'Now pull it out, boy! Shoot! Shoot in her face!'

As champagne trickled out of her insides, and sperm trickled out of her mouth, Susan Street couldn't help reflecting, even as she arched and throbbed in the throes of her orgasm, that the world was turning upside down.

EIGHT

'Sorry about the time, Bryan,' said Susan automatically as she stepped calmly into the editorial meeting three-quarters of an hour late. 'Only Zero needed a little pep talk.'

'Say no more, Sue. We're only happy to have you back from a taxi ride with Zero Blondell in one piece.'

'She thinks we don't—' she said, and gasped as she looked at the most beautiful thing she had ever seen. It wore a dark grey business suit, and she was about to register its skin as olive when she realized that olives were either black or green and this skin was the palest beige. Its hair was black, a very Seventies cut which had once been seriously long and still didn't have the heart to be short, curling over the collar of its white shirt. It wore a black knitted tie, which she immediately visualized gagging her.

Insomuch as the beautiful thing resembled anything it was Michael Douglas, though the Michael Douglas of the small screen rather than Cinemascope, being no older than thirty-three. When it smiled its teeth were discoloured and cracked; she wanted to run her tongue over them, read their secrets like Braille.

'Sue, this is David Weiss. At long last.'

It was obvious from Bryan's tone that she should know who David Weiss was. The name rang a bell; was he some hotshot financial hack, perhaps? He held out his hand and said '*Hi*' in a low voice. Weiss, as in Vice Squad: how appropriate. He was American; he had to be financial. *Best* readers were very big on being advised what to do with their money; David Weiss was obviously Bryan O'Brien's answer to Bob Beckman.

'Hello.' She shook his hand. 'Nice to have you with us.'

'It's nice to be here.' He was looking at her in a way that made her stomach do things it could have got an Olympic gold medal for if it had been doing them on a high board.

The editorial went by in a blur. She kept looking at him; not his face, she knew that now, but his body, his thighs, his groin. She had to know what he had in there, then she could think about something else. But right now it was impossible. Looking at his groin for the nth time she felt his eyes on her and looked up. He wasn't even smiling, just staring at her in a way that made her saliva glands flood as if she had just smelled a steak after a six-week diet.

When Bryan O'Brien announced, 'It's a wrap,' she was on her feet and out of his office in a shot, almost running until she came out on to the second-floor landing of the *Best* building. She leaned against the wall for a moment before starting down the steps to the toilets. Her clitoris was going to burn a hole in her Norma Kamali bodysuit if she didn't detonate it soon.

As she put her hand on the door, she felt a hand on her shoulder.

'Excuse me – Susan?'

She looked up into the face of David Weiss. 'Do you want something?'

'Yes. The same thing as you.'

With a sharp intake of breath she caught him by the tie and literally dragged him into the toilets. They were empty. 'Quick, quick,' she gasped, and they staggered like drunks into the nearest cubicle, locking the door.

Pressing against each other they kissed frantically. Then she freed her hands to undo her bodysuit between her legs. She ripped off her tights, kicked off her shoes and stood looking at him, panting.

'Susan, will you do me a favour?'

'Anything.' She meant it.

'Take my cock out. I've had an erection ever since you walked in that door, and it's killing me.'

'I'd much rather it was killing me,' she said, and they kissed bluntly and impatiently as she opened his trousers

155

and took it out inch by inch – not believing that there could be yet more and more of it. It must be a trick, like those long strings of coloured kerchiefs conjurers kid children with; she felt the same wonder now as she handled it. It was like a cosh wrapped in plush pink velvet: ten inches easily rising from thin, furry thighs. She bent to kiss it.

'There's no room for that. There's no time.' His voice was husky. 'Get over that toilet.'

It was, as Susan told a sulky and disgusted Zero later that week, the way all those surreptitious whispers tell you sex is meant to be, before you get old enough to know better and expect less. You know those mash books where women turn into wild animals because they love fucking so much, and go off their heads if they have to go without it? It was like that. (Zero had groaned.) Whereas we know that, in reality, most men are so useless (Zero had brightened considerably here) that most women find sex marginally less pleasurable than waxing their legs. But this was back to those adolescent basics; back to heat and lust, before the romance industry gets its claws into you and makes you think you want sweet words and soft lighting. The lighting here was fluorescent and terminally unflattering, and the words were 'You cunt', 'You whore' and 'I'm coming, you bitch, squeeze it!' but it was perfect sex: the beauty of the man, the intensity of the desire, the purity of the act. It was, Susan said later, the Big Thing at last. And she wasn't just talking about his cock.

They separated and stood panting against opposite walls

of the cubicle. They looked at each other and laughed and David Weiss said, 'Gee, whoever thought up the name casual sex for sex between strangers was way off. I can't remember sex that uncasual.'

'Me neither. And there's nothing more casual than the type of sex you get in a long relationship that's gone bad – that take it or leave it, like it or lump it sex.'

'Say, you're wise as well as beautiful. As John Wayne was always saying to those Tartar princesses.'

Again they laughed, darting glances of shy and amazed delight at each other as they got back into their clothes. When she was dressed he took her face in his hands, looked into her eyes and smiled. 'Isn't this weird, us hitting it off like this? I thought you wouldn't give me the time of day.'

She laughed 'To be honest, I didn't even know Bryan had hired you. I'm hopeless on that side of things.'

He wrinkled his brow. 'Say what?'

'Numbers. I get vertigo.'

'Susan – sorry, who do you think I am?'

'A financial journalist.'

He shook his head. 'Susan – I'm David Weiss.'

'I know. I think I've heard of you.'

'No, you don't understand. I use my mother's name. Because I fell out with my father. He brought me here by way of patching things up. My father is Tobias Pope.'

* * *

The rest of the afternoon passed in a daze, like when you get drunk at lunchtime. She even had that coppery taste in her mouth, the one that doubles for both fear and hangover and now, it would seem, love. She kept sending Kathy out for Crest, Amplex and Listerine, but nothing could budge it. The novelists told you about lack of sleep and appetite, but that was acceptable because they made you look and feel so dramatic, consumptive, *romantic*. What the novelists didn't tell you was that love gave you halitosis, just when you least needed it.

He had the office next to hers, with the same glass partitioned door; she kept finding excuses to walk past it. He had the staff in one by one – Bryan, Oliver, Max, the subs, the reporters. But not her.

Around five-thirty she passed his door yet again and this time he had Zero with him. The atmosphere of ill-will that radiated from the girl was so strong that it seemed to seep under the door like a camp dry-ice dangerous chemical in a Fifties sci-fi film. Zero sat bolt upright, her tail pushed comically to one side sticking straight out from her chair, staring at David Weiss solemnly. Susan could see from her profile that she wasn't even pouting. What on earth could he be saying to make Zero lose her pout?

Susan was furiously and furtively flossing her teeth when the door swung open and there stood Zero, staring at her accusingly. '*Bora da*, baby doll,' she said quietly.

'Come in, Zero. Shut the door. Why don't you put your feet up and tell me a few lies about people?'

'Don't know what you mean.' She closed the door and leaned against it.

'Why did you tell me David Weiss was a dog, Zero?'

'Because I knew you'd want to fuck him the minute you saw him. I was just trying to put off the awful hour of reckoning, wasn't I? Have you to myself a bit longer.'

'Don't be silly,' said Susan weakly.

Zero spat on the floor and they both peered at it, glistening insolently, quite impressed but somewhat unsure of just what the gesture signified. Then Zero wrenched open the door and turned to go.

'Wait! I mean – what did he say to you? If there's any misunderstanding of your position here, I'll go now and tell him just how important your—'

'Sorry,' sneered Zero, 'but I can't help you there, bach. If you must know, he told me the usual. That I had a singular talent. That he understood that working on a tabloid with all its limitations might sometimes be problematic for me. That he sympathized, he really did. But if ever there was anyway he could be supportive, please let him know. I told him I didn't have a hernia, thank you very much, and he just looked at me with those *stupid* brown eyes like a cow who's been goosed. Then he bunged me a rise – five thou p.a. And said didn't I find it very time-consuming, answering all my own fanmail, and wouldn't I like my own secretary? Only if she's got an honours degree in cunnilingus, I said. That shut him up.' Zero made an obscene gesture with her wrist. 'What a fucking *girlie* – I expected him to ask did I have painful periods next, and would I like a hot water bottle on the firm.'

'Men can't win with you, can they, Zero? They act lousy and they're pigs. They act properly and they're girlies. Exactly what do you want from men?'

'Well, for a start, I want them to keep out of my way. That includes Yank bigshots who throw around salaries and sympathy as though they were stockings and chewing gum. Then eventually I'd like their complete and total extinction. But I'll settle for a cull, so long as I can have a club of my own. Did you know there are fifty thousand spare men in London alone? If they were seals we'd be allowed to cull them. And men aren't half as pretty. Or smart.'

'Go away, Zero. I'm not in the mood.'

'You're not in the mood for anything, are you, girlie?' snarled Zero, leaning across the desk, 'Except ten inches of kosher beef served hot up the ass.'

'That's sounds like fun,' said David Weiss from the doorway. 'Where do I join the queue?'

They watched Zero flounce away, her wired tail appearing to give them the finger.

'What a very attractive and angry young woman she is,' said David Weiss. 'A very clever young woman too – I've been reading her column these past months. She's gay, isn't she?'

'Not right now she isn't. She is a lesbian, though.'

'I don't blame her. If I was a girl, I'd be a lesbian too.' He smiled at her. 'What on earth could anyone see in a man?'

'You'd be surprised.'

'Do you want to come back to my hotel with me?'

'More than anything else in the world.'

'Let's go.'

Susan had always imagined that people's sexual natures were nothing more than extensions of their personalities. Thus Gary Pride had been clueless and clumsy in bed, Charles had been courteous and energetic and Matthew had been sensitive and persevering. Zero would be arrogant, adolescent and lascivious while Tobias Pope, God forbid she should ever get a chance to confirm it, would be superior, sadistic and cold.

David was different. In two hours they had done it five times, each time with more brutality on his part, and she was sore all over, inside and out. But now he had her wrapped in blankets and drinking hot chocolate laced with *crème de cacao* as he fussed around the room, opening windows in preparation for smoking a cigarette. 'You're sure you don't mind?' he asked for the third time.

'Of course not.'

He smiled down at her and threw himself headlong on to the bed like a puppy ready for play, sucking on his Camel. 'It's a filthy habit, I'm going to give it up.'

'I hope that's the *only* filthy habit you're going to give up.'

'Sure thing.' He stroked her hair, then drew back. 'Jesus. What's that? That thing on your forehead?'

She thought on her feet. 'Well, you've found it; my guilty secret. I had it done one night, oh, years ago, just before I joined the *Best*. In a fit of half-assed rebellion about selling out, I don't know.' How Matthew would laugh!

'You poor kid.' He smoothed her fringe down over it. 'Did it hurt?'

'I was too drunk to feel it. It's just embarrassing now. But it would look even worse if I had it removed – a big, raw scar. As it is I can keep it covered.'

'Gee.' He looked at her sorrowfully, then gestured hugely and vaguely around the room, laughing. 'Will you look at this? This a.m. I was the new nerd in town, getting hit on by the cabbies and losing my way and worrying about whether I could do my job. Now I'm in bed with a beautiful English broad, and I've got a job, an office, everything!'

He seemed so happy that it scared her. If he was as happy as she was, then there was so much to lose. 'Are you serious? I mean, seriously so pleased?'

He looked at her as if she had just announced that she was Queen Marie of Rumania. '*Serious* I'm serious. Aren't you happy about this too? Don't tell me you're one of these broads who thinks it's a sign of peasant stock to show their feelings and play games all the time.'

'No, I hate that.'

'Those manipulation games are very big in New York, and they're for penny-ante people who don't feel they've been dealt a good hand in life. They're the people who keep you waiting for hours to see if you'll wait for them. That's how they prove their worth to themselves – it's a sure sign of an inadequate.'

'I hate that too – it's really Seventies. I always come on time.' Well, she would from now on.

'So I noticed.' He closed his eyes and snuggled up to her. 'Stroke my balls. Just for a minute.' He wriggled and purred.

Touching him, she laughed. She had always found testicles the ugliest items in the history of the world, like figs covered in fungus; it was strange to be with a man whose body seemed as familiar and unrepellent to her as her own. 'It's strange, we come from such different worlds, and we're strangers – but we seem so much alike.'

'We're twins, maybe – Siamese twins. Separated at birth by some hotshot smartass surgeon. Boy, did we show him.'

She was starting to feel tired. 'Can I . . . am I staying?'

He sat up and looked at her, shocked. 'Oh, no. How could you think that? This is the scene where I call you a cab and call you Suzanne.' He punched her arm lightly. 'Of *course* you're staying, dummy.'

'Can I take a shower?'

'Want me to help?'

'No, stay where you are. I'll only be ten minutes.'

'Sure.' He grabbed the remote control and went at the TV like a teenager.

She went into the bathroom and turned on the shower, stepping under it. But it was cold, and the shock of it made her gasp, revving up her recent memory as it hit her breasts. She stepped back, breathing heavily; just one more time, he wouldn't mind. She knew him by now. He'd love it.

She padded quietly into the living room just in time to hear him say, 'I miss you.'

But she'd only been gone a minute . . .

'Of course I do, Meesh. Yes, Bunny. Talk to you tomorrow. Bye.' The receiver clicked.

'Who's Bunny?' she asked quietly.

He wheeled around, naked and guilty. 'Susan . . .'

'Who's Bunny?'

'It's my . . . it's a girl in New York. Her name's Michèle – Michèle Levin.'

'I see. Do you have a photograph of her?'

He shot her a worried look, took his wallet from the trousers on the floor and handed her a colour snapshot of a girl. She had straight blonde hair of the type that American Jewish girls seem to grow spontaneously when their father's income reaches the million mark, a ski tan, a sweet, insecure smile and a slight cast in one eye.

Calmly, Susan ripped it once, twice, three times and threw the pieces up into the air. They fluttered ineffectually to the floor as though trying to look inconspicuous, like

164

children on a staircase trying not to make their parents' loud row worse. 'Confetti for our wedding,' she said. 'Cross-eyed fucking *cow*.'

He hung his head.

'Can I ask you a question?'

'Shoot,' he said defeatedly.

'Is it a normal part of your love play to fuck this sweet young thing in lavatories?'

'Of course not.' He seemed genuinely shocked. 'It's not that sort of relationship.'

'Then what sort of relationship is it?' she snorted. 'Platonic?'

'No . . . we've known each other a long time, you see, since we were kids. We lived on these neighbouring estates in Connecticut in the summer. We're sort of . . . unofficially engaged.'

'I see. How old is she?'

'Twenty-six.'

The same age. 'May I ask you, do you often accost strangers and fuck them standing up in public places?'

'You're the first.'

'Oh my, I'm honoured. She gets your fraternity pin, I get a quick one in the toilets. The *staff* toilets. *Your* staff toilets. God, fucking the help – how Victorian can you get?' She turned away and picked her dress up from the floor.

'Susan.' He came up behind her and tried to touch her. She shook him off. 'I'm so sorry. I didn't mean to lead you on. But the way you were looking at me in O'Brien's office . . . I thought you wanted to as much as I did.'

'So it's my fault?'

'It's no one's fault.'

'Oh, no. I beg to differ. It's *someone's* fault, you shit-eating prick.' He looked at her, appalled. 'There. I bet *she* doesn't talk like that, does she?'

He laughed softly. 'Michèle speaks six languages and she can't get mad in any of them.'

She wanted to throw up. She felt like a hooker in a hotel room hearing a client talk about his wife. Any moment now he'd get out the pictures of the 2.5 babies.

'Her family are rich, of course.'

'Her father has a bank . . .' He shrugged apologetically, as though her father had syphilis.

'But of course.' Susan Street from Nowhere-on-Sea. What a fool she had been. 'I see.'

'Susan—'

'Keep it, David. Save your breath for lying to your dumb doormat girlfriend, not me.' She squirmed into her Kamali body, Alaïa dress and Emma Hope heels and picked up her briefcase. 'Here's where you call me the cab and call me Suzanne.' She walked to the door. 'But hold the ten bucks. Put it towards an eye-straightening op for Bunny Money.' She opened the door, went out and looked back over her shoulder at him. 'Because I don't need it. I'm on your father's payroll, remember. He can tip me better than you could ever dream of in your wildest, wettest dreams.' She closed the door, banged on it with her fist and screamed loud enough for the late swimmers in the hotel basement pool to hear, 'AND HE'S A BETTER FUCK, TOO!'

She fell into the lift, out of the lift, into a cab and out of a cab. Then she fell heavily against the doorbell. It kept playing the first three bars of Dire Straits' 'Sultans of Swing', over and over – Matthew's idea of fun. What a fucking irritating wimp he was, with that med-stude humour doctors never grow out of. At that moment, she hated Dire Straits, doctors and rich, handsome, young Americans more than she had ever believed possible.

'Susan! What the – where are your keys?'

'Can't find them,' she mumbled, pushing past him and bolting up the stairs.

'What's that smell? Where have you been?'

'It's sick. With Zero.' She ran into the bathroom, locked the door and leapt out of her dress. Throwing it into the bath, she grabbed a box of matches, lit one and threw it and its unfulfilled comrades into the tub too. Seven hundred pounds' worth of smoke filled the room. She opened the window and leaned out, gulping the air, tears rushing down her face. Smoke gets in your eyes, she thought vaguely.

'Susan?' He was banging on the door. 'What's that smell? What's going on? What's happening to us? We've got to talk!'

167

'Just go away, Matthew. I'm sick. You can't help me. I'm sick.'

'I'm sick of you!' she heard him yell before he burst into tears. She turned on the taps, fell to the floor and curled up on the bathroom mat. She dreamed about hearts, bleeding, running around the office of the *Best* like chickens with their heads cut off.

The next day she lay on the floor staring at the ceiling until she heard Matthew's Renault pull away. Then she got up and looked at herself in the mirror. She looked old. She cleared the designer ashes from the bath, cleaned it, poured half a bottle of Badedas into the water and lay there, concentrating on keeping her mind blank. When it didn't work she slipped down under the foam and stayed there until her lungs felt they might burst.

Her instinct to survive pushed her up to the surface, as it always had in even deeper and hotter water than this. She rinsed herself, dried, dressed and took a taxi to the *Best*.

It was half past one when she arrived and, as she had anticipated, the usually busy office was doing its daily midday impersonation of a high-technology ghost town, a *Marie Celeste* furnished by Amstrad. She wandered through the open-plan room listlessly.

As she neared her office, she became aware that she was not alone. She could hear the unmistakable sound of copious computers going through their sleek, sinister paces and of tickertape spilling from mechanical mouths – and it was coming from her office. She ran to the door, pressed her face against the glass and gasped.

Tape lay strewn across desks. Computers flickered insinuatingly. Even as she opened the door, the clatter began to cease. Soon everything was silent and she stood in the middle of the room, looking round in a daze.

A computer in the far corner caught her eye. It beeped, flickered, and was blank. Then, for a split-second, it flashed her a message.

HAVE A NICE DAY, LOVE, CONSTANTINE.

NINE

Susan was listening to *Question Time* and looking at the frantic jumping pulse at her wrist when Oliver Fane put his head around the door. He was smiling broadly, so obviously he had some bad news for her.

'Ah, Sue . . . I've just been in with the jolly swagman. He's got his billabongs in a bit of a twist, it seems, what with your pal Moorsom and his enquiring mind. Apparently he wants to see you ASAP.'

'Thanks, Oliver.'

'My pleasure.'

'Sue . . . ! Sit down.'

'Hello, Bryan.'

He nodded at the radio. 'D'ja just hear that?'

'Yes.'

'It's not good copy, is it, Sue?'

'Not really, Bryan.'

'It's not good copy at all.'

'It's just a question in the House, Bryan—'

He held up a hand. 'Sue, we've had this conversation before, I seem to remember. The point is that this *would* seem like a minor irritant to you and me because we're minor players and haven't got much to lose.' Speak for yourself, Abo. 'But to a man like Pope, with so very much to lose, this sounds like the opening shot in a major offensive. All this talk about South African gold and the American stranglehold; it's not exactly good publicity, Sue. There's a very xenophobic streak on both the left and right in this country, an all-party thing like hanging – except the MPs go for this as well. Especially when it comes to so-called foreigners buying up previously British media interests. It's not just the *Best* and the publishing company – Tobias has great plans for your little island. Cable TV, films, the whole works.'

'I'm aware of that, Bryan.'

'I just got off the blower to him, Sue. D'ja know what he said? He said, "Tell that stuck-up little chit that if she doesn't put the screws on her boyfriend fast, I might get sick of taking stick from that half-assed little island of hers. And if I do, there isn't going to be a paper for her to be editor of." Is that clear?'

'Crystal.'

'He means it, Sue. It's not bluff. Face it, the world's his oyster and good old Blighty's hardly the pearl. He could be doing his business' – and here Susan noted grimly and inwardly that this was also a metaphor for the process of elimination – 'in Oz, or Nippon, or Lat Am. He's doing this country a favour by doing business here.'

'It's a sort of Marshall Plan for millionaires, Bryan, isn't it?'

He sighed. 'Sometimes you're a bit too clever for your own good, Sue.'

She wondered if there was an equivalent phrase in any language other than English; probably not.

'The thing is, I've been talking to a member of the staff who shall be nameless—'

'—nameless and blameless, Sue. Company loyalty, that's what Oliver's got.'

'Really? I thought they called it rimming.'

'One and the same, aren't they?' He sighed. 'Look, Oliver's been talking and he says you and Moorsom were *very* close – not just lunch, but orchids. Men don't send orchids to casual acquaintances. Oliver says you were confidantes, probably lovers. What's it to be, Sue? And make it the truth.'

She looked at her hands, thin and white with torn cuticles and red knuckles. She could use a hand job. Rephrase that. 'We were confidantes. He felt pretty isolated at Westminster, as I did here. We came from similar backgrounds.' She looked at Bryan half-beseechingly, half-defiantly. In the past, reference to her working-class origins had made a lot of people back down, gagged by guilt. Flexing her roots, Zero called it. Bryan O'Brien wasn't so soft.

He sighed. 'Don't try that, love. I was brought up on a sheep station in bleeding Wagga Wagga. When I used to play with me John Bull printing set, they thought I was going queer and took me to the sawbones for an anal examination.' His face went hard. 'Confidantes.'

'Yes.'

OK. I'm not asking you to tell me anything. But I'm going to tell you something, and if you've ever been told anything remotely like it before, I want you to nod. OK?'

'OK.'

'Oliver says there are a few Moorsom stories on the statutory rapevine. True or false?'

'True.'

'Tarts, isn't it? Male or female? How much under-age?'

'I can't think under pressure, Bryan.'

'Then you're in the wrong game, love.' He picked up his phone, called his secretary's number. 'Yas, step inside for a mo, and bring your pad.' He looked at Susan dismissively. 'Maybe a day off will refresh your memory, Sue. And remind you how it feels to be unemployed.'

In her room she grabbed her raincoat and her leather envelope and then just stood there, poleaxed. What was she supposed to do now? Get on to Joe? Threaten him? Get hold of Rupert? Pay him? Resign?

'Hello,' said David Weiss from the doorway. He came in and closed the door.

She didn't even feel upset, she was too preoccupied. Love was a luxury, but her career was real life. 'Hello.'

'Susan, I want to explain.'

She sighed. 'Don't bother, David. You wouldn't be able to find the words and I wouldn't be able to find the time. And I shouldn't have to remind you of this, as you're the boss, but it's very unprofessional to talk over personal matters in office hours. Amateurish, some would say. Typical of an overgrown little rich boy who's never had to hold down a job on merit and graft in his life, some would say.' She picked up some papers from her desk and rustled them vaguely. 'Go away, I've got a problem.'

He didn't go away. He sat on the edge of her desk and looked at her. 'Two heads are better than one.'

'Yeah, but go and tell that to some poor bastard with two heads.'

They laughed. She sat down in her chair. 'Since you're interested, and as you're the boss, I'll tell you what it is. I've got a career/conscience dichotomy.'

'A dichotomy sounds like some sort of surgery Zero would have.'

'Cute. Well, this is just a normal, everyday case of putative blackmail. A while ago Mr X tried to blackmail Mr Y and I stopped him. But now I'm being asked to blackmail Mr Y with help from Mr X so that Mr Y will stop asking sticky question in the House about the intentions, honourable or otherwise, of your sweet silver-haired old pappy. *Comprendez?*'

'Joe Moorsom?' David's brown eyes looked even more bovinely startled. 'You've been told to blackmail him?'

'Oh, I don't know. Greymail, maybe. Maybe I've been on the purple press too long; I call pressure blackmail and sex love.' He looked at the floor. 'The thing is, it's not just a second-league celeb and a twenty-two-year-old rentboy we're talking about here. The boy was fourteen years old at the time. Chronologically. Spiritually he qualifies for a free bus-pass. And Moorsom, I don't know if you know this, made his name speaking out against the abuse of children – especially sexual. He's sponsored by a very traditional union and he has a wife and two children who are adored by press and public. He's very good at his job and the next step is a position in the Shadow Cabinet. It all adds up to such an awful lot to lose that I guess Bryan thinks he'll back off at the first hint of it all coming tumbling down. And of course, as his friend, I'm supposed to drop the hint. Like BO.'

'And you find that immoral?' he asked seriously.

She looked at him sharply. 'Get serious. I don't speak American. I don't know what immoral means, unless you're talking about war and starvation. I just think it's a bad career move. He's my friend. And he's going places.'

He thought conspicuously. 'Listen, you're right about

observing office hours. But can you meet me for a drink after work?'

'Isn't Bunny in town?'

'No. And neither is my father, so we'll both be free, won't we? Can you?'

'OK. The Kremlin Club, you know it?'

'I joined last week, but I haven't been there yet.'

'Have you got a treat in store.'

The Kremlin Club served only vodka – twenty-two types. The menu was written in Cyrillic script. The waitresses wore high boots, grey uniforms and Red Army caps. The Red Army Choir sang rousing patriotic songs. And no one on less than 50K a year was allowed to join.

'This is a great place,' said David appreciatively, looking around. 'We have nothing like this in New York. It's a very European sense of irreverence. I can dig it.'

Susan sniggered into her Stolichnaya. Why did every American, no matter how young or beautiful or rich or clever, speak as though they'd gone into a coma in 1973 and only just woken up? They dug things, had hassles and downers and then got mellow, whereas English people liked things, got busy and sad and then cheered up. It was a perfectly adequate language. She supposed that their massacre of it was some sort of misguided attempt at establishing linguistic independence; they were still-bridling from being a colony, as young West Indians born in SW2 learn to talk the pidgin patois of islands they have never seen as an act of self-definition.

His corny speech made her feel better. David Weiss wasn't such a bargain, despite his looks, money and ten inches of the best kosher salami this side of Bloom's deli. 'Were you ever a hippie?' she asked him accusingly.

'I'm only thirty, for Christ's sake!'

'Come on. The Sixties lasted well into the Seventies in your neck of the woods.'

'Well, I did have a pair of Frye boots.'

'Oh, God.' She wriggled down in her chair and glared at him across the hammer-and-sickle-shaped table. 'I'm not with you.'

He laughed, then frowned. 'Susan, we've got to talk.'

'That's another Americanism. It means – we've got to analyse.'

'What's wrong with that?'

She shrugged. 'I don't go in for public navel-gazing. Svetlana, you can put another double in there when you're ready.'

He waited until the waitress had brought fresh drinks, then leaned across the table. The red metal tip of the sickle seemed about to run him through; he didn't seem to notice, he was so serious. 'I think that what happened between us could use a little analysis.'

'I don't.' She stirred her vodka with her finger. 'But then I'm an analysis-retentive.' She sniggered at her pun. 'OK, you want an analysis of what happened between us. Here it is: you're a very good fuck.'

'I don't mean we have to talk about what went on in bed. I mean we have to talk about what happened afterwards.'

'Do you by any chance mean your long-distance swooning and spooning with a certain boss-eyed rich bitch?'

'Don't.'

'I must say, she has a very smooth upper lip – going by your photograph, that is. But then, they get electrolysis on their thirteenth birthdays, don't they? Like English girls get ponies?'

He shook his head wonderingly. 'Susan, this isn't worthy of you. You're acting like a *bitch*.'

'Oh, really? Isn't it funny that when a woman acts like a human being, when she shows anger, pain and ambition, they call her a female dog? Female dogs don't act that way. Men do, though. *People* do.'

He raised his hands, palms towards her. 'Listen, if you're going to get into some militant feminist thing—'

'Feminist? Because I'm annoyed that you misled me? I think you'll find that an aversion to being conned far pre-dates feminism. I think you'll find that men have it, too.'

'Susan, Susan.' He caught her hand. 'Why are we talking about men and women when we should be talking about *us*?'

'To ignore what men have done to women since the dawn of time is to forget your history. And to forget your past

179

is to become a slave to the future.' She hiccuped, pulling her hand away and signalling to Svetlana, who was really a Beck from Bushey called Belinda Bellman. Susan didn't know quite what she meant, but she liked the sentiment and the way it sounded. She was nearing that stage of drunkenness when anything, even the Shipping Forecast – German Bites Pharaohs: Silly – seems profound. 'You lied to me,' she accused, pointing a shaky finger at him.

'I didn't lie to you at all. I didn't say I didn't have a girlfriend back in New York. If you think back, you'll remember it was *you* who dragged *me* into that john.'

'And you fought me off like a crazy thing, as I remember. Five times in two hours.'

He sighed wearily. 'Of course I didn't fight you off. You're a beautiful girl.'

'Is that the only reason you slept with me? Because I was beautiful and there? Like climbing a mountain?'

'It's a new town to me. I was lonely.'

'Do you love me?' she pleaded.

'Susan, I adore you.'

'But do you *love* me?'

'Susan, I don't even *know* you. I met you yesterday. What do you want me to say?'

'Lie to me. Why stop now?' She looked into her glass. 'Tell me about your girlfriend.'

'Why do girls always say that?'

'You tell me, Dr Freud.'

'OK.' He took a long pull at his strawberry vodka (the big girl). 'She's twenty-six. I've known her since we were in our early teens. She went to Bennington and she majored in English. She speaks six languages and she's a sculptor. She likes sushi, skiing and Sade. She's a very nice girl.'

'Is she good in bed?'

'What?'

'You heard.'

'I don't think I'm going to answer that.'

'That means no.'

'It means nothing of the sort.'

'It means no. OK, so she's bad in bed. Which is convenient for you. Because it gives you an excuse to put it about all you want and still you can say to yourself, "Oh, it's just sex with these others. It doesn't threaten what I have with her." Isn't that what you think?'

He nodded.

'God, men are predictable. David, sex is the biggest threat there is to *everything*. It's brought down governments and empires. It can surely send your little lovenest in the sky crashing down to earth. David, sex isn't going to the prom – sex was *never* safe. The only safe sex there is is masturbation. When there's more than one person in the bed, sex is always potentially dangerous. It was believing that sex *could* be safe, that it could be used as a playpen like those stupid American fruits thought, that made it literally fatal.'

'I don't understand.'

'Don't you? Don't you understand what I mean? I've got a sexually transmitted disease.'

His eyes were enormous. 'What?'

'It's called love. I love you.' She was drunk now, on her own lack of shame as much as Stolichnaya.

He looked as if herpes might be a preferable option. 'I'm not sure if that's a good idea.'

'Well, I'm sorry, I'll ask you first next time. But answer me something. Do you love your girlfriend?'

'Yes,' he said quietly.

'No, you don't. Because if you did, you wouldn't sleep with anyone else. It's simple as ABC.'

'Are you telling me I'm the only man you sleep with?'

'Since I met you? Yes.'

'Are you going to stop sleeping with my father?'

She hesitated. 'That depends.'

'On what?'

She wavered. 'Lots of things.' Why on earth had she told such a stupid lie in the first place? To hurt him, of course. It hardly added to her youthful glamour to appear to be fucking a white-haired senile delinquent.

'Let me ask *you* something, for a change.' His face looked different; he was angry. She had hit him in a soft spot, the mental equivalent of his testes, his Achilles ache, with that analysis of his half-hearted love for Michèle Levin. 'You put out for me, and for my father, and for that guy who died. Do

182

you always put out just for the top guy at the newspaper? Or do you fuck the messenger boys between main courses?'

She looked right back at him. 'Well, as rule I look after numero uno. But I made an exception for you. It's a long time since I fucked a messenger boy, and as I remember they're lively little things. And take away the influential parent and what are you? Not much more than a messenger boy in an Armani suit.'

He got to his feet, not easy considering the shape of the table. 'I've had it with you. You are a manipulative—'

'That's a very Seventies word,' she told him calmly.

'A manipulative, calculating, cruel girl. I'd call you worse names, but you'd probably have an orgasm right here.' He signalled to Svetlana who was loitering with intent to sell the story to *Private Eye*. 'I think it's so incredible the way you're sitting there lecturing me about love, and my love for a good and honest woman at that, when you fucked that last guy to death, you're fucking my father to an early grave and you probably still fuck that guy you live with when you can't get to sleep and you can't be bothered to jerk off.'

He was beautiful when he was angry. She felt her groin contract; she rubbed her thighs together and almost spasmed with desire. 'Wait.' She put a hand on his. He shook it off. 'Do you want to fuck?'

He looked at her, his eyes blazing. 'Where?'

'There's an alley—'

'OK.'

Up the alley beside the Kremlin Club, she picked her way on high heels until they came to an alcove where rubbish was dumped by neighbourhood bars and restaurants. She could see his angry, beautiful face in the moonlight. 'Here,' she said.

He pointed at a dustbin. 'Get over that trash.'

She stepped out of her shoes and tights, and laid them on top of her briefcase. She bent over the dustbin, holding on to it. He stepped up behind her, opened her thighs and entered her immediately. He jabbed deep, hurting her and meaning to, a dozen or so times before stopping, ejaculating and withdrawing so fast that she cried out.

She turned and smiled at him. He was wiping his cock on her tights. They had cost fifty-two pounds from Fogal of New Bond Street. Never mind, she would claim a new pair on expenses. She could just see Max's face as he read her weekly claim sheet: 'New pair of Fogal tights to replace ones ruined by boss's sperm.' She laughed.

'Is it like that with her?'

'No.' He zipped himself up and threw her tights down. 'That's why I love her.' He walked away in the moonlight without looking back.

'Hello, stranger,' Susan said as Joe Moorsom slid on to the stool beside her at Annie's Bar with a wary smile. Stranger was right; it had been three years since they had last met. At first she had been hurt by his avoidance, but she was sensitive enough to understand that he had been severely shaken by what they had gone through together. It was like being in a car crash; you just wanted to walk away from it.

He had talked about it on the phone soon afterwards. 'I feel dreadful, Sue,' he had said. 'I can't help it. I'm a socialist, I believe in treating people as I would wish to be treated. And we bullied him, just because we're adults and professionals and know how to throw a scare, and he's just a defenceless boy.'

'Joe, are we talking about the same person? Because your little friend was about as defenceless as a cruise missile crossed with Barbra Streisand.'

'There must have been a better way,' he said stubbornly.

'Yes. It's called garrotting.'

Since then his career had ascended uninterrupted by any whiff of sell-out or scandal. The mood of 'affluent altruism' predicted by the market researchers to be the political wave of the Nineties made him even more of a cinch for the next Cabinet. At thirty-nine he had the harassed good looks of a man with too many responsibilities for his years, which only served to make him more respected. Only a few people knew that the look was the look of a man with a secret and a fear.

Within a year of their collusion, Susan was kicked upstairs and made an editor. They had both been busy people, though not too busy to talk on the phone every six weeks or so. But the calls had stopped the day Pope bought the *Best*.

'Hello.' He smiled tightly. 'Though I shouldn't really be talking to you.'

She couldn't believe his cheek. 'I'm still the same person, Joe. Are you any less of a socialist because the man who's your leader now is more right-wing than the man you were voted in under?'

He shook his head irritably. 'It's not the same.'

'He's your boss.'

'I answer only to the people,' he said pompously.

'And they're a hard jury, aren't they, Joe?'

He looked at her sharply. 'Well, Sue, what can I do for you?'

'You can let me buy you a drink.'

'I'm on duty.'

'How's Jill?'

'Fine.'

'And the kids?'

'Great.'

'They must be teenagers now.'

He looked at her hard. 'That's right.'

'Talking of whom, did you ever hear from our mutual friend again?'

'No. Never.' He looked at his hands. 'We scared him all right. Much more than was necessary. I still think about it.'

You still think about *him*, you mean. 'He'd be . . . seventeen now?'

'Yes. Why?'

'Joe,' She sipped her vodkatini. 'People are talking. My editor, the reporters. They're scared of what you're doing, the questions in this place, and they're asking around the grapevine about you. They don't know his name and age yet, but rentboys are not known for their loyalty—'

'—any more than journalists.'

'—or politicans. If someone hangs around enough bars flashing enough notes, sooner or later someone's going to come along who knows someone whose BF slept with that divine butch NUM politico. And the hack will cross his palm with a piece of silver or a Gold American Express card and he'll lead him straight to Rupert Grey. And Joe, you know Pope. This, with your record on child abuse, is a gift to him.' She drained her glass.

Joe Moorsom laughed softly. Then he shook his head and looked at her with loathing. 'And you're the gift wrapping, aren't you? You're the one they sent along to put the pressure on with a pretty please and a bit of harmless flirtation.' He whistled. 'God, I knew women could be crafty bitches. But you really take the prize, Susan.'

Scratch a fag and find a misogynist, Zero often said; like Gertrude Stein, she was a lesbian who believed that male homosexuals were male first and homosexual second, and thus worthy of loathing: 'They're all woman-haters.'

'But that's like saying that all lesbians are man-haters!'

'Of course they are – why on earth do you think we

only sleep with women?' Zero looked at her as if she was a cretin. 'We vote with our cunts. But the difference is that it's fair to hate men and unfair to hate women. It's like blacks and whites. Blacks are quite right to hate whites, after all they've put them through. But if a white hates blacks, there's something wrong with them. Nessy pa?'

Susan could never think of a good argument against this point. Looking at Joe Moorsom's sneering face and hearing him spit 'women' as though he was talking about syphilitic mass murderers, she resolved never to bother to try to think of one again.

'Just stop that right now,' she hissed. 'I don't know whether it's escaped your notice, but you're in this mess because of what some scheming little boy did to you – not your wife, not your mother and certainly not me. Not even really the Best or Tobias X. Pope. This started with a fag.' She decided their friendship was history now anyway and hit him with her worst shot. 'Two fags, counting you. And I really resent having my gender used against me when this whole situation arose because, yet again, some man was led by his cock and didn't give a damn about how many people would be hurt by his sordid little bout of sexual incontinence.' She stood up.

'And I resent having my sexuality used against me,' he hissed, sliding off his barstool to face her. They sounded like two rattlesnakes on the verge of divorce. 'Especially by the type of newspaper which thinks that morals is a surname common in Latin America and little else. I think you can find your own way out. Just leave by St Stephen's Gate and follow the gutter and the stench. Eventually you'll get back to your paper.'

'So you won't co-operate?'

'I'll co-operate with whoever wants to destroy your newspaper, Susan, that's who I'll co-operate with. I'll nail your boss if I have to lose my career, my wife and my deposit in the process. I'm not some naive little rentboy you can throw a scare into, remember.' He banged on the bar and called to the barman, 'Another vodka for the lady. Better make it a double.' Lowering his voice he leaned close. 'You're going to need a little Russian courage to go back and explain to your boss what a cock-up you made of your nasty little mission. Goodbye.'

She awoke that night from a troubled sleep to hear the black Braun alarm clock beside her bed doing what came naturally. She peered at the dial: just after 3 a.m. This couldn't be so – the clock had never contradicted its daily time-set once in the five years she had owned it.

'What?' she heard Matthew moaning. 'Whassat?'

As she groped for the clock, the burglar alarm screeched. Matthew sat bolt upright. 'Shit!' He ran downstairs as she fumbled with the clock. It wouldn't stop. Yet it wasn't stuck.

'It must be stuck!' she heard Matthew yell. She ran to the window and leaned out; other people in the quiet square were doing the same, throwing down ice-cold early morning oaths like buckets of water on a rogue tom-cat. Behind her the telephone rang, adding a third voice to the shrill duet. She picked it up.

'Are you sitting comfortably?' a familiar voice purred. 'Then I'll begin.' There was a laugh, and a click.

Down in the street, the horn on Matthew's Renault and the alarm on its door started up in unison and earnest. Her head seemed full of white noise, ready to burst; tinnitus with a production job courtesy of Phil Spector's Wall of Sound. She lay down, pulled a pillow over her head and screamed.

The model looked like a beautiful Martian but she was, Susan quickly discovered, the only human being in the place.

The place was a secluded Scottish castle which looked like an extortionate Hollywood stage set for a sword and sorcery epic but was, in fact, a health farm. She had called in sick at work and fled there the morning after Lejeune's latest assault, fearing for her composure. She had had to use her press connections to pull strings, since the establishment only took twenty-four clients at any one time, and now here she was on the fifth day of her week, sitting by the indoor pool with the model.

Six foot one, with albino hair and matching pink eyes courtesy of contact lenses, she was known professionally as the Mouse. She was the thinnest girl Susan had ever seen, so much so that the translucent skin of her twenty-two-year-old face was pulled tight over her bones to an extent normally only seen in severe cases of face-lifting.

She had come to the castle on the insistence of her agency, who had driven her there both physically and metaphorically by threatening to strike her off their books. They were the best, and Mouse had been used to the best ever since she abandoned Arkansas and the given name Clare for London and fame at the age of eighteen. She had complied, and here she was; not to lose weight, of course, but to lose a career-menacing habit comprised of narcotics and a taste for the lowlife.

Now Mouse swished her hand in the water and pulled out a bottle of Krug. 'Nearly cold enough, fuck it. This last old rich guy I had, he was *such* a wine snob, and *so* possessive. "Let it breathe, Jean-Pierre" he'd say to the waiter. Shame he didn't feel the need to let *me* do the same . . .'

She had been in residence for a week when Susan arrived and had already made waves in more places than the hydropool: with her stubborn refusal to join any of the exercise classes, her loud screams of anguish and confusion whenever a suntan in any shade or form was mentioned, the chaos she had caused when persuaded to try her hand at archery, her habit of streaking naked through the leisure craft classes shrieking 'WOOOOOOOH! I GOTTA WEAVE A BASKET!'

and her ceaseless demands for sweet foods from kitchens 'which make the soup line during the Depression look like the horn of Cornucopia,' she told Susan with some feeling (her father was a history professor and the Mouse had a good education and brain, which she concealed the way less modern and gifted girls concealed spots). She had been discovered on the second morning of her stay scratching at the kitchen doors and begging, 'Cheesecake, cheesecake!'

Susan, venturing out from her room after a good night's sleep, had found the Mouse in the indoor pool. After five self-conscious minutes the Mouse had swum over with a long, lean, lazy crawl; she swam as though she was modelling the new Gaultier but was in fact naked. She cased Susan's off-the-shoulder black swimsuit before venturing an opinion. 'Montana?'

'Yes.' Susan smiled encouragingly. She was pleased for a chance to talk to this strange creature she recognized from the covers of *Marie Claire* and *The Face*.

'Guess where I got this?' The Mouse heaved herself up out of the water, exposing her long ribcage, and fell back giggling and splashing. 'ARKANSAS!'

'Could they do me one the same?'

'Hey, you've got a great shape. You've got a *shape*, period, which is more than I do!' The Mouse trod water for probably the first time in her life. 'So why aren't you out showing it off in one of those cute little tennis dresses? Or golfing slacks? Or playing croquet in a Chanel two-piece? Or jogging? Or doing yoga, or aerobics, or cycling, or clay pigeon shooting? Or availing yourself of any one of the facilities we'll have to hand over an arm and a leg for when we finally get sprung?'

'I can't stand physical jerks. In more ways than one.'

'Hey, great!' Mouse peered at Susan. 'Are you here to lose weight?'

'Only in the purse.'

'I figured that. What you here for?'

'Tired and emotional.'

'Me too.' The Mouse swam beside her. 'This health stuff is a load of garbage. I never looked better than I did when I was twenty and I was taking two grams of coke a week, smoking horse three times a day, getting four hours' sleep a night and having the crap kicked out of me every ten days by this fantastic spade I was fucking. I swear, I've never looked or felt better. But then I went crazy. Since then I've become versed in moderation.' She giggled. 'Only one gram a week!'

As a veteran, the Mouse had taken Susan under her spindly wing. They went for all-body massages – 'Get off of my case and on to my face,' the Mouse told a beautiful but gay masseur when he lectured her about her spine – and to the tennis courts to sneer at the hearties – 'Hey, baby, want to lose ten pounds of ugly fat? Cut your head off!' Now they had been corralled into the indoor, ozone-purified pool, where drink seemed a small concession towards keeping them quiet.

Mouse pulled the Krug's cork with her perfect Arkansas teeth. 'Jeez, but I'll be glad to go home on Sunday. You too I bet. Promise you'll call me?'

'Of course.'

'I swear, I didn't know what I was letting myself in for. I visualized Disneyland with enemas. Horny masseurs. Dyke sessions in the sauna. All this place has given me is a raving case of alcoholism, on top of everything I came here to be cured of.' She swigged hard and passed the bottle to Susan.

Susan drank. 'You remind me of a friend of mine. Called Zero.'

'Zero Blondell!'

'The same.'

'Christ! – *that* one. A man with a twat – the deadliest combination on the planet. I had a fling with her – oh, a couple of years ago. I was just coming out of this relationship with this guy who'd only go with girls who wore Little Black Dresses and nothing else. When he promised to shower me with the perfect adornments for the LBD, I visualized a wagonload of square-cut diamonds. But what he meant was a black eye every Friday. Said it completed the LBD like nothing else on earth. Look at Anouk Aimée in *La Dolce Vita*. Boy, do I know how to bring out the worst in a boy . . . '

So said Mouse. She was beautiful, clever, fun, but Susan was left cold by her pink eyes and *ennui*. She wanted to be alone for a while, and thought she might as well utilize a few of the castle's resources before she went home, so she stood up and, knowing the answer, said, 'I'm going to take a sauna. Coming?'

As she had known, Mouse shook her albino crop violently. 'Uh uh. It's more than my job's worth.'

'I'll see you in about half an hour then. Will you still be there?'

'Sure thing.' The Mouse reached into the pool for a second bottle. 'In the zone called prone.'

The third sauna Susan tried was empty, and she peeled off her swimming costume and sank down on a bench with a sigh of relief. She lay down, closed her eyes and let her mind float up, up and away like a helium balloon cut loose at last. David, Pope, the paper, especially Lejeune – she left them all behind, earthbound, gaping up at her as she melted away into the shimmering heat like a mirage. She fell asleep with a smile on her face.

She was aware something was wrong even before she was awake: she knew in that half-conscious state that usually ends with a sharp start and waking. This time the start never came; instead she felt herself dip idly and shallowly into consciousness, sampling it as though she was testing bath water with her elbow. She was just about to give up waking or taking a bath as a bad job and go back to sleep when something inside her screamed: WAKE UP.

With an effort she pulled herself into a sitting position and almost fell off the bench with dizziness. It was the heat: the sauna was hotter than Rio, hotter than Sun City. The sweat on her body had ceased to bead, and now slathered her with a greasy second skin, making her think of the stuff cross-Channel swimmers covered themselves in.

She stood up and staggered to the door, colours dancing before her in changing formations as though she had kaleidoscopes pressed to both eyes. She clutched at the door handle as if it was David Weiss's schlong, and tugged.

Nothing happened.

She tugged again, this time with both hands. The effort made her head feel as though it was about to implode.

Still nothing happened.

'Help!' she called weakly. Then louder: 'Help!'

It was useless. The walls of the sauna were thick and sound-proofed. She sank to the floor, stunned and shaking in spite of the heat. She felt herself start to black out. She closed her eyes . . .

'Susan! Susan!' The thick wooden door pushed painfully against her naked body, and a gust of what seemed like fantastically icy air hit her on the shoulder. 'For Christ's sake, girl, watchoo playing at? Shit! What's going on in there? Susan?'

'Mouse . . .' With a massive effort, she rolled over on to her back. The door opened a few inches wider and the skeletal Mouse slipped through the gap. Then she was in the sauna room, crouching on her heels and shaking Susan by the shoulders.

'Jesus, Susan! You trying to add yourself to the Marks & Spencer range of pre-cooked gourmet goodies or something? Hack Bonne Femme? Come *on*, girl – on your feet and get *out* of here!'

'Can't,' she croaked.

'Ok. Just keep still. You're taking a free ride.' Grabbing her by the feet, the Mouse pulled her out of the room, dropped her and looked around frantically. 'Water. Water. Gotta get your body temperature down. I got it! The hydropool – gotta get you in the hydropool!' She pulled Susan down a narrow corridor and into a room blue with Italian ceramic tiles, a sunken bath full of swirling white water in the middle of the floor. Depositing Susan by its edge, she climbed down into the pool herself and then reached out and took the half-conscious girl in her arms, easing her into the cool water, holding her there as she floated on her back.

After a while Susan opened her eyes.

'You OK?' whispered Mouse, sounding scared for the first time.

'Think so. Feel a bit sick. A bit dizzy.'

'At least you've cooled down a bit. Christ, you should have seen the colour you were! Like a lobster being boiled alive. I saw one once in France. What the Sam Hill were you playing at in there?'

'The door wouldn't open.'

'Bullsheet. It opened for me, and Schwarzenegger I'm not.'

Susan cased the concave Americaine. 'Thanks, Mouse. You saved my life.'

'I saved your *ass*, girl. But you'd have done the same for me. Listen, you feeling better? Can you stay here alone for a minute?'

'Yes.'

'You're still a funny colour. But hang loose, I'm gonna go get one of the screws – they'll know what to do. If this was the US, you could sue them puce for locking you in that hellhole, for sure. Here, hold on to the sides – that's it.'

'Hurry up, won't you?'

'Sure thing. *Uno momento*, love-bucket.' The Mouse slithered and skidded out of the pool room, still naked.

Susan floated on her back, hands on the sides of the hydro, her mind slowly grinding back into action. Door sstuck sometimes. That was all. Accident.

The water, which had been burbling gently, seemed to grow a little fiercer.

She must have touched a switch. She groped along the poolside to reset it.

Her hand met smooth tiles. The water began to spill over the sides of the bath as its heaving increased.

Her hand slipped from the rim of the hydropool and she felt herself being pulled down into the cold blue bubbling cauldron that the bath had suddenly become. She opened her mouth to scream, and swallowed chlorinated water.

Her curriculum vitae flashed before her eyes: *The Beat*, *Parvenu*, the reporter's job on the *Sunday Best*, the deputy editorship. Then she swallowed more water, and that was all she knew.

When she awoke some dyke nurse was kneading away at her breasts as if trying for the blue ribbon at some pastry chef competition and Mouse was trying to put cocaine up her nose through a ballpoint-pen holder.

Alarmed by both activities, she came to her senses rather more quickly than was usual, wrenched herself away sharpish and sat up, blinking around her.

'It's alive!' shrieked Mouse indelicately.

'Miss Street! You gave us quite a fright!' scolded the nurse, who was in actuality nothing more depraved than a God-fearing Scots grandmother with no desire to see a death on the premises.

'Not half so much as your killer jacuzzi gave me.' She put her head in her hands, her elbows on her knees.

'You must have passed out,' said Mouse, 'and gone under. I shouldn't have left you while you were so faint from the heat. I already told Mrs Moran about the sauna.'

'Yes, Miss Street – you must let us extend to you a further week, gratis, to compensate for your nasty experience,' said the nurse, ever mindful of bad publicity.

She opened her mouth, ready to tell them how the water had suddenly seemed to turn on her. Then she thought better of it. They'd say that the heat had turned her head; that she'd imagined it. She stood up wearily. 'Thanks, Mrs Moran, but no thanks. I won't be staying my full week as it is. I'll be going back to London tomorrow.'

There was no point in staying any longer than necessary, she thought to herself as she went to her room to pack. Because, she was starting to realize, the number of miles she put between herself and Constantine Lejeune didn't matter. She could run, but she couldn't hide; not from a man with a thousand eyes, and twice as many torments in store.

TEN

Matthew Stockbridge wore a blue tracksuit and an expression usually kept in a jar by the bedsides of the terminally ill. Which was, nevertheless, very suitable to the occasion. 'We've got to talk about our relationship,' he said.

'What's wrong, run out of patients?' Susan quipped weakly.

'Very funny.' He looked at her sternly. She sat at the kitchen table in a loose, long black T-shirt, her legs bare, her dark hair piled up, with a black Winchester Filofax and a black Harper House Dayrunner in front of her. The Filofax, bought five years ago, was going to the big brasserie in the sky; the Dayrunner had cost more than twice as much and was less than half as common. It was also made of something she didn't even want to think about.

But trust Doctor Death to get his caring sharing oar in. 'What's *this* made of?' he said with distaste, holding it up between thumb and forefinger.

She stood up and snatched it from him. 'How should I know? A laid-off steel worker. An unwaged minority person. A member of the Fabian Society. Or one of your fucking patients. There. That's the Susan you like to think you know and love, isn't it?' She sat down and continued copying numbers into it.

He chuckled, pleased with her performance and his own sense of superiority. 'You've turned into a real little yuppie monster, haven't you? The Filofax that ate the world.'

She sighed and threw down her Mont Blanc. 'Yuppie. That *has* to be the *laziest* word, used by the most bog-standard of people, since *charismatic*. You know who's called a yuppie these days? Anyone under fifty with their own teeth and a roof over their head on more than ten G p.a. It's become completely meaningless, Matthew. I'm surprised you still use it.' She scored one, and continued with her Bs: Bracewell, Brampton, Brody, Broughton, Blondell.

'We've got to talk,' he repeated.

'Who's stopping you?'

'Susan.' He put his hand on hers, stopping her from writing. 'We can't talk while you're copying out your Filofax.'

She sighed. 'Matthew. Every evening for the next two and half weeks, I have dinner with some hack, some money man or some poncey author whose poxy book we're thinking of bidding for for reasons beyond my comprehension. On Sundays and Mondays I need to sleep and I can't stand to either write or think; I do that all week. Now, my Filofax is embarrassing me to the point where I can't bear to get it out in public – I feel disgusting, like a flasher. I feel soiled. I see people looking at me with pity and contempt. I *have* to spend my one free evening re-doing it. Now at this rate, I estimate that I'm free for lunch in the year 2000. Shall I book you a window then, or would you like to talk now? I *can* do two things at once, I assure you – I spend my days doing five things at once. Why, I can probably write, talk and chew gum at the same time. What do you say?'

He stuck out his jaw – what there was of it. 'The day I buy a Filofax, I give up.'

'Matthew, you gave up years ago. That's why you're still on twenty thousand a year.'

He looked at her bitterly. 'Do you know what's wrong with women today?'

'No, but I'm sitting comfortably, and I'm sure you're going to tell me.'

'They're turning into the sort of people men were before they got wise. They're making all the mistakes men used to: treating the opposite sex like shit, working themselves into the ground in pursuit of fame and fortune, completely losing sight of the spiritual side of life and the eternal values, and sacrificing everything on the altar of success.' He stopped, panting. 'That's what's wrong with women today.'

'Really?' She looked at him very coldly for a long time. She heard more and more of this New Man-ifesto these days, and she liked it less on each hearing. It was called moving the goalposts in any language, and it stank of personal grudge and moral duplicity. She smiled, sugar and strychnine, and said softly, 'Well, you lot shouldn't have made it look like such fun, should you?'

'What do you mean?'

'I mean I didn't see men running home in droves from offices at lunchtime and banging on the doors of their houses shouting to their wives that they'd seen the light and from now on wanted to express their spirituality through the creative medium of dusting. No, they were out having five-martini lunches and shagging their secretaries. You lot loved the marketplace just fine until we got interested too – then you throw up your lilywhite hands and tell us how dreadful it is. Too late, buster! This fucking concern is just *another way of telling women what to do*. Well, don't worry about us. Yes some of us will get ulcers, and some of us will crack up, and some of us will screw up our domestic situations, and some of us will end up at forty with a cat and cook-in-the-bag cod in parsley sauce dinner for one and wonder if it was worth it. But more women will be happy, and more women will be fulfilled than ever before in the history of frigging personkind! Because IT WAS OUR CHOICE! We had the freedom to choose not to swallow the shit you offered to choose us tied up with a Valentine's heart. You think women were happy before? Contented with their lot? Isn't it funny, then, that for the first time in recorded history, the incidence of mental illness and suicide amongst men has overtaken that of women? All those happy housewives, why were they cracking up left, right and centre? Who's stuffing Valium? Not me – some Godforsaken housewife, that's who! And you see them! So don't stand there preaching at me that having a career may be damaging to your health!'

'Have you quite finished?'

'Almost. Try this. Try saying *blacks* instead of *women*. Try telling blacks they shouldn't go after material success because, oh, I've been there and it's all empty and meaningless! You see how phoney that sounds? It's called *keeping the niggers down*. And you're not doing that to me, or to any other woman!' She finished at a yell. He looked at her, amazed. 'So there,' she said weakly. She wasn't in the habit of revealing this much of herself to Matthew. She felt almost naked. It was definitely the most she'd said to him in a good three years.

He looked at her, amazed. 'I didn't realize you felt so strongly about feminism, Susan.'

'You don't realize how I feel about anything.' Tears of self-pity caressed her kohl. 'No one does.'

'You're never here for more than fifteen minutes in a row. What am I supposed to do? Buy his and hers cellphones and talk about our relationship on our way to work and squash?'

'That would be better than *this*.'

He threw open the fridge. 'Look, Susan. Look at this. This is emblematic of our whole relationship. Tell me what you see.'

She stood up and peered. 'I see two lemons, a bottle of Chablis and some penicillin.'

'That penicillin is houmous, Susan. Bought two weeks ago at M&S. It's the only food we've had in the house for the duration. The rest has been tandoori takeaways for me and expense account for you. It's got to stop, Susan.'

'But why, Matthew? Why is a relationship based on how many hours one or another of the parties spends slaving over a hot stove? You're not just being emblematic here. You're being fucking medieval, boy.'

'Susan, Susan.' He sank to his knees on the other side of the table. I don't want a housewife. I want *you*. Can't you be a career girl *and* my Susan?'

'No, baby, no. I can't be your Susan. I can't be anyone's Susan any more, not even my own. I'm Susan Street, and I belong to no one and everyone.' She thought about what she'd said; it was probably meaningless, but it sounded good. Sort of like late-period Marilyn Monroe. She shook herself. 'Why don't you go and put some Jellybean on?'

She heard him in the next room, mumbling and fumbling with the sound system. Eventually Adele Bertei's achingly beautiful voice slunk into the room and wrapped itself around her like a cat's cradle made of silk.

She heard Matthew moaning as the sublime dance track faded. If it wasn't white, male and answered to the name of Knopfler, he wasn't interested. How could she possibly be expected to perform sexual acts with a man who liked Dire Straits? It was perverted and unnatural.

At the back of her Dayrunner, she found a bridge score-card. Could she . . . ? No, he'd never pry. He might be a doctor but he had ethics, poor bastard.

She wrote TASKS at the top and 1 2 3 4 5 6 down the side. Then she wrote:

1. KING'S CROSS. Tattoo.
2. RIO. Three girls, three boys.
3. SUN CITY. Two men.

Three down, three to go – not bad for a girl from Nowhere-on-Sea who was neither nowhere or at sea where many better born or bred girls would have been carted off to the funny farm by now. Break her, would he? She laughed out loud.

Matthew came back into the kitchen and stared at her like Gary Cooper in *High Noon*.

'Would you kill Katharine Hamnett?' she asked him conversationally, scanning her Hs.

'Would I what?'

'Kill Katharine Hamnett. Is she a dead number, do you think? You know – Stay Alive In 85. On The Breadline In 89? Over And Done In 91?' She giggled. 'A dead insert, or what?'

He shook his head wonderingly. 'Susan, all day I am faced with people who may die if I don't make the right decision. Your toughest decision today has been whether or not to tear a name from your Filofax. Is it any wonder we can't talk any more?'

'So what do you want me to be?' she sneered. 'A *nurse?* So you can overwork and underpay me and condescend to me when in actual fact I'm carrying twice as much responsibility as you? You've read one too many hospital romances, Matthew.' She laid down her pen. 'Let's stop talking in Want Ads. You're not annoyed because I do a more flighty job than you. You're annoyed because I earn more than you.' She began to count down silently: five, four, three, two—

'That's it!' Matthew screeched, banging his fist on the table and running for the door. 'I've had it! You ALWAYS say that! This time I've had it!' The door slammed, and he flashed in a blur of blue tracksuit past the window. She laughed, and started on the Js.

Susan sat at a window table within the cool monochrome depths of Le Caprice and watched with fascinated horror as Caroline Malaise pushed and pulled at her heart-shaped steak tartare.

'Look at that,' she said. 'Toby sent me one on my twenty-first. With a man from Securicor. It was Valentine's Day . . .'

'Yes?' Susan had never had a happy relationship with meat and, with this one act, she was to remain a vegetarian for the rest of her life.

'Yes. He said, "It's all meat, Caroline." And I do see his point. Your heart *is* a piece of meat, isn't it? Wouldn't you rather someone was straight with you rather than try and kid you your heart was made of Belgian chocolate?'

'Actually, I think I'm going to have to be boring and go for the Belgian chocolate. How's Candida?'

'Not doing too well, poor thing.' Caroline spoke about her sister as though she was a herbaceous border. 'Toby's record company majordomo has decided they're a novelty act, and a bad one, and he's put them on "ice", I believe is the term. It means he won't release their records but neither can anyone else. If you want my honest actual, they were silly to let Gary go. *Obviously* Toby's going to get the best deal for himself, isn't he? But I do think it's rather mean. Candida's only a sprog. She's *spitting* blood, apparently. Do *anything* to get back at him.' She picked an orchid from the table and began to tear it with the precision of a shredder and the passion of a psychopath. 'Susie, who's Joey Moorsom?'

'He's an MP. Labour. Why?' She was only marginally less surprised than if Caroline had asked her who the president of North Yemen was.

'Toby's not very fond of him, is he? Why?'

'He doesn't think Tobias should be allowed to buy into media here. What with Sun City and all.'

'Well.' The steak tartare and Caroline's fork were doing a very good impression of a fast day at Pamplona. 'I do see his point. Don't you?' She sighed. 'An American just bought my pa's place in Somerset. These fantastic old people we've looked after for years in the cottages . . . out they go. He's building what they call a *theme* park.' Caroline looked up and her eyes were full of tears, or Badoit, or the Napa Valley Chardonnay they'd drunk with their sorrel soup. 'Out goes Nanna, and in comes a killer shark. Toby says I'm being silly. What d'you think, Susie?'

'That certainly sounds like the American way.'

'Toby said it's called progress. Progress! That sounds like the name of a stream engine . . . ! What time is it, Susie?'

'Quarter to two.'

'Oh.' Caroline brightened. 'My medicine. I'll just be a minute.'

Like an optical illusion by *Vogue*, the slender blonde in the brown wool was replaced by a tarantula in tulle, its dark red hair cut in an ear-length power bob, its green eyes glinting with gossip and greed.

'Hello, Ingrid,' said Susan resignedly.

'Hello darling. Having a Hers lunch?'

'Looks like it, doesn't it?'

'It most certainly does. I also have sightings of you with Susie Douglas at the Kremlin, Lynne Franks at the Western

World and that awful little bleached blonde clit-licker at the Groucho. What have they got, darling, that I don't?'

Apart from brains, looks and talent? Not a lot. She shrugged. 'Oh, Ingrid . . . all business.'

'Funny business, if I know that little clit-tickler.' Ingrid leaned ravenously across the table. 'Who's the blonde? Not Caroline Malaise?'

'Yes.' She saw Caroline come up behind Ingrid to her table.

'Really! How d'you know her?'

'I'm Toby's London girl,' said Caroline, smiling down at Ingrid as if she was a long-lost, much-loved Nanna. Obviously her medicine had hit the spot. 'Well, I was until he met Susie. He wants us to be *friends*, I think.' She giggled. 'I think it's called the Pasha Syndrome. All the world's a harem.'

Susan looked down at her plate in mute horror.

'Can you join us?' Caroline was saying to Ingrid. 'Sorry, I don't know your name. But you have beautiful hair.' She traced the line of Ingrid's bob to her cheek and giggled. 'Do you remember what colour it said on the packet?' The narcotics were having a disastrous effect on her inhibitions which, to judge by the eagerness with which she had shed her clothes for the moving camera during her brief career, had been subterranean to start with.

'I'd love to.' Ingrid grabbed a chair in a split-second and sat there between them, grinning triumphantly from one to another. Yes, the bush telegraph of the media was going

211

to have a pretty busy afternoon once Ingrid got back to the *Commentator* office. 'But I can only stay two ticks. I'm with a fascinating man.' She giggled. 'I think you know him, Sue. Well, he knows *you*.'

'Oh, who's that?'

'Over there at the corner table.' Ingrid turned back to Caroline and started talking to her about polo. Who was she kidding? Caroline was such a very urban Sloane that the only polo she knew about was a mint with a hole in it.

Susan looked across the room. The man was about forty, sipping red wine and smiling at her. He was handsome, if you liked small, greasy Latinos with skin that made the Rocky Mountains look like chiffon velvet and teeth like fluorescent strip lighting. As he held her eyes, he raised his right hand and, still smiling, drew his forefinger across his throat.

It was Constantine Lejeune.

ELEVEN

'Let me get this straight.' Zero bounced excitedly on a banquette at the Vendome. 'Pope's got Joe Moorsom, *and* Gary Pride, *and* Caroline Malaise and her sister and her band, *and* Washington Brown on his case, all wanting him looking like twelve tins of cat food. And you've got Constantine Lejeune on yours who's now teamed up with that superannuated debutwat Irving. And now your old pal Moorsom's sore at you, and so are Bryan and the boss because you couldn't get round Moorsom for them. And to complicate matters, you're in *lurrrve* with the kosher sausage, who won't play ball because he's got this girl in New York who makes Mother Theresa look like La Cicciolina.' She shook her head sympathetically, but couldn't control a smile like a bacon slicer. 'What a fucking old mess you've got yourself into, bach.'

'I need a Negroni.' Susan looked around for a waitress.

'I need a Negress.' Zero giggled.

Susan hadn't seen her so happy in weeks. 'Thanks for the sympathy, Zere.'

'Sorry.'

'Well, what can I do?'

'For a start, quit hanging out with heteros. They're nothing but trouble. For now – forget the fuck and the faggot, they'll keep. Lejeune's your big problem. Do you have any more stuff you can counter him with?'

'No, we used everything Serena gave us. The sex *and* the stock market.'

'What exactly are you frightened he'll do?'

'Something much bigger and nastier than alarms and computers going bleep in the night. Psychic things.'

Zero made a noise.

'I *saw* it, Zere, you didn't. He can *do* those things.'

'Bollocks.'

Susan hesitated. 'But it's something else. I'm afraid he'll cook something up with Ingrid.'

'Come *on*. "Girl Wonder In Sex Slave Seven In A Bed Romp With Pope". It's a great headline, but it's hardly the *Commentator*'s cup of Earl Grey.' Zero sniggered. 'They're not the *Best*, you know.'

'Everyone's going downmarket, Zero – downmarket forces. The fact that I stitched him up, and that Ingrid wants to wipe me off the board, and that even the alleged qualities are starting to carry scandal now, even if it *is* about Claus von Bulow and Robert Chambers – they just *might*. He's Tobias Pope, not some scream idol. If it got out that he'd had me tattooed, and taken me to SOUTH AFRICA, and watched me in bed with prostitutes of every conceivable colour and gender . . .' Susan shook her head desperately. 'Don't you understand what that would mean to my *career*? I'd be a bimbo, a laughing stock. I wouldn't stand a *chance* of getting the editorship. I'd be lucky to get a job as a researcher, after that.'

'Pope would still give you the job. He wouldn't care what some toffee-nosed Sunday paper thought.'

'It wouldn't end there; everyone would be on it like a duck on dough-boys. And you know what a fuss the government are making about the morality factor when it comes to handing out the cable franchises. The electorate are already terrified that their children are going to be force-fed hard-core porn at the touch of a switch. The government is hardly going to think it's a vote-catcher to hand one out to a man whose leisure hours are largely concerned with setting up those very same hardcore scenes in the flesh. And if he can't get his cable, he'll be off. He'll sell the *Best*, and I'll be out on the street.' She drained her Negroni.

Zero was silent for a moment. 'What's Lejeune been doing since we ran Serena's story?'

'He's been lying low. Cancelled his public appearances, radio show, TV spots. He's planning something, Zere.'

'Planning be buggered. He's keeping out of his adoring public's way. You know that crowd he attracts – all those skinheads and international Zionist conspiracy freaks. They'd have his guts for garters.' She darted a worried glance at Susan. 'You don't think he'd get together with Moorsom?'

'But Joe's a Labour MP, and Lejeune's a racist.'

'Bach, don't you remember the anti-Common Market campaign? Power and Benn on the same platform?'

'Face it, there's nothing I can do to Lejeune. He's got me.'

'Then you'll just have to concentrate on sorting Moorsom out. You've got something on *him*. Seventeen years old, camp as a row of tents and answers to the name of Rupert.'

'It's sordid, Zere . . . even if I could *find* him, which I doubt, I don't know if I want to . . .'

'Pull yourself together, girl. Do you really want Pope to think you can't pick off a backbencher? After all you've been through? Do you think he's going to give the editor's chair to someone with such a weak stomach? You've been through a mutilation and two orgies for this job – are you going to buckle at the knees because some malicious fag says "Boo!" to you?'

Susan looked at her empty glass. 'But how would I find Rupert Grey?'

'I've found him for you already.' Zero smirked. 'I danced with a girl who's danced with a boy who's danced with Rupert Grey. He hangs out in a pub in Meard Street called

Ye Old Troute. For the price of a glass of pink champagne, he can be yours. Or anyone's.'

'Shan't,' said Rupert Grey, blowing sullenly at his fringe. He liked that word, almost as much as 'Don't', 'Won't' and 'Can't'. Between them, they had more or less made up his side of the seven-minute conversation Susan had been having with him in the early evening smog of Ye Olde Troute.

After three years of waking up in strange beds with even stranger men, Rupert Grey looked remarkably fresh. The hair was still silky, the figure – Rupert would always have a figure rather than a body or a physique – still lithe, the pout still holding up admirably. Well, he was still only seventeen.

'Please,' said Susan again.

'No. I won't help you. You were mean to me when I was all alone in the world. Why should I trust you now?'

'I'll pay you,' she offered eagerly.

'Money means nothing. You can cancel the cheque.'

'Cash.'

'You can mark the notes and do me for blackmail.' His pout trembled bravely. 'Those judges are hard on blackmailers, because so many of them are in compromising positions. They'll make an example of me, to put people off.' He looked at her accusingly. 'There's no conditioner in prison. You *told* me.'

She cursed herself for laying on the Draconian conditions for personal grooming in reform school so thick. There was no way Rupert Grey was going to risk being separated from his Vidal Sassoon Deep Heat Protein Treatment sachets, not for any six-figure sum no matter how you arranged the digits. 'OK,' she said resignedly, gathering up her things.

'Wait.' Rupert stopped her. 'There might be something you can do for me.'

'Name it.'

'You're powerful, aren't you? People come to you, wanting your paper to write about their artistes. Record company people and PR people, they want to be in with you. They take notice of you. If you say jump, they jump.' He looked her in the eyes, and his were as a straightforward as child's.

'So what do you want from these people?'

'I want to be a *staaaar*.' He said it as though it was the most beautiful word in the world, better than love, money or buggery. She thought it was probably the first sincere, painfully simple thing he had said in his life.

'I'm not sure I can make you a star, Rupert. I haven't had much experience at being a Svengali.'

He shook his pageboy impatiently. 'I'm not asking you to *make* me a star. No one *makes anyone* a star. A star is a star. All you have to do is introduce me to someone who can see my potential – I'll do the rest. And then no one will be able to touch me. You can't touch a star without burning your fingers, even if they're on the end of the long arm of the law. And then, if you want me to reveal how I was used by that man Moorsom, *la publicité* can only be good. It's a great angle, isn't it? – youth, beauty and innocence used and abused and thrown to one side by some famous old creep old enough to be my grandfather – why, I'll be the male Mandy Smith!'

Only marginally more feminine, Susan thought. 'But what sort of star do you want to be, Rupert? What can you do?'

'I can sing.' He pouted. 'I can sing at least as well as Boy Georgina, or that old tart Marilyn, or Jimmy Somerville. It's all done in the studio anyway, isn't it? Everyone knows that.'

'I suppose you're right,' said Susan wearily. 'OK. I'll see what I can do. What's your number?'

'I'm not telling *you*. I don't trust you yet. You can find me here most Mondays. I think of it as my office.'

'OK.' She gathered up her things and slid off her barstool. Who could she have a word with, who specialized in Svengalidom? Lynne Franks? Simon Napier–Bell? Vivienne Westwood? No, they all had bigger fish in small ponds to fry. This wasn't going to be as easy as Rupert made it sound.

In the street, she looked up at the ornately painted sign that marked Ye Old Troute. And as if by free association, a name from the past sprang into her mind and on to her lips in tandem

'Gary Pride!'

* * *

Since losing Fuck U to Tobias Pope outside South Africa House, Gary Pride had made a partial recovery and a modest name for himself as manager of two acts; a band called U.S.S.A. who claimed to be the first Russo-American band in the world, playing something they called Glasnost Rock which featured electric guitars and balalaikas and lots of songs about fighting the Muslim hordes. Then there was a French lesbian torch singer, sleek in the way that only French lesbians could be, who called herself Donna and did a beautiful version of 'My Girl'. They were all very attractive and got a good many covers of the style magazines between them, not to mention a lot of modelling work and free entry to nightclubs. In fact, they had everything but The Hit. Try as he might, Gary Pride could not get his charges into the charts. If he couldn't get into the Top Fifty, he was very unlikely to be able to get into the Groucho Club and, sure enough, Susan came through the revolving door to find him sulking in reception and arguing with the receptionist about his phone.

'Sorry, you'll have to leave it here.'

'Tell 'er, will you?'

'Sorry, Gary, it's against house rules. They'll look after it for you.'

'You'd let a lame man take in his crutch, or a man with a bad ticker take in his pacemaker, wouldn't you?'

'Yes, of course.'

'Well, that's what this is!' He brandished the ugly phone dramatically. 'My life-support machine!'

Susan cast an apologetic and despairing look at the receptionist. 'Gary, the club's really filling up now. If we don't bag a sofa soon, we'll have to sit in Siberia. Sara will mind your phone for you. Come on.'

The thought of Siberia scared the image-conscious Gary Pride (she couldn't get used to thinking of him as Gary Prince) like nothing else, and he quickly abandoned his phone and skipped smartly into the club. 'Well?' he glowered at her once they were seated. She could tell he still didn't remember he'd had her technical virginity all those years ago in that frenzied night of boredom; his memory of her went back no further than a few months ago and her role as Tobias Pope's London bird.

'Well, it's like this. I need your help.'

'Help? Help *you*?' He laughed in a manner he probably thought of as hollow. 'That's a good one.'

'If you can help me, I may be able to get your band back for you. I know for a fact that Mr Pope isn't terribly interested in them any more.'

'Is that a fact?' He looked suspicious, but interested.

'They're on ice, I believe it's called. He won't put out any of their product, and he won't let them go. When the contract runs out, they'll be only too pleased to return to you with their amps between their legs.'

'Iced, are they?' He laughed uproariously. 'That's a good one!'

His vocabulary was certainly a lot more down to earth these days, she thought – no more talk about parfait knights and buffalo dignity. ECT, it can cure your purple prose. 'Well, do you want them back?'

'Wouldn't mind. On their knees, though; *I'm* the boss this time.'

'But of course.'

He sighed. 'OK. What do *you want* out of this?'

She opened her leather folder. 'Nothing much. Nothing out of your line of work. There's this young singer I know, called Rupert.' She handed him two eight-by-ten black and white glossies. He took them wordlessly. He studied with impressive professional detachment the studies of Rupert's pale young face cupped coolly in one hand, and Rupert's slender body clad in tennis whites with what looked like a year's supply of the Queen's Club spare ball stuffed into his crotch. 'He sings as well,' she said sarcastically.

'Mmmm.' He didn't notice. 'How old?'

'Seventeen.'

'Yeah? Queer as a nine-bob note, of course.'

'Of course.'

'No sweat. In fact it could be a plus.' He thought about it. 'A queer, eh? I could use a cute young queer. Fresh meat – that first batch of gender benders are starting to look well dodgy. They'll never see twenty-two again, that's for sure. Seventeen, right . . . ? Below the age of queer consent, if I'm not mistaken.' He closed his eyes. 'Do you know a song called "Too Young"?'

She dredged into her distant youth. 'Donny Osmond?'

'Thassit . . . but that was the cover version. Some letter-sweater jock did it in the Fifties first. "*They try to tell us weee're too young! Too young to reeely beee in looove!*"' sang Gary Pride. His voice hadn't improved, and Susan knew sorrow as the club turned to look at them with interest and concern. 'Geddit?' he asked her excitedly.

'Very nice.'

'Nice! It's fucking brilliant! I get my cred and eat it! See, everyone will twig that he's singing about being too young to be buggered, so I get my cred and the fag market. And they've got a fuck of a lot of readies going begging. But on the other hand, the song doesn't *mention* bending, blowing or buggery so they can't ban it, so I get my airplay and my teenies. I'm telling you, with this kid I've got every angle covered.' He looked proudly at the close-up of Rupert. 'All the guys want to fuck him, all the girls want to convert him, all the mothers want to give him a good square meal and all the fathers want to lynch him. My little cash-cow!' He lifted the closeup to his lips and in full view of the interested patrons gave it a loud, smacking kiss. 'Nothing can stop us!'

* * *

'What's your mother like?' asked Susan as David Weiss got up from his big bed at Claridge's and started opening windows prior to committing postcoital pollution.

'Maxine – she's beautiful, cultured, crazy as a loon, just your average German–Jewish New York Princess who happened to marry a complete and total bastard.' He drew deeply on his Camel. 'You know she's in the Sunny von Bulow Clinic?'

'Yes, what is it? Drugs or drink?'

He cast her an offended look. 'Neither. Nervous exhaustion. There's nothing wrong with Maxine that a divorce wouldn't put right.'

'Then why doesn't she?'

'It's not that simple. He won't. There are shares . . . things of hers tied up in Pope Communications. He's got her stitched up, I'm afraid.' He looked at her. 'I joined the company because I thought it was time I knew a little bit about it all.'

'What were you in before?'

'I was with a publishing company.'

'Did you like that?'

'It was OK. Some cousins of my mother owned it. Leopold and Lehman.'

'You mean this is the *second* family business you've been in? God, you're really straining at the leash to do your own thing, aren't you?' It sounded so mean. 'I'm sorry.'

'That's OK.' He threw himself on to the bed and lay on his back, smoking and looking up at the ceiling.

She couldn't resist a final jab. 'What happens when you get tired of newspapers? Will you go and work for Mr Levin's merchant bank? The son-in-law also rises?'

He ignored her.

'Do you see your mother often?'

'I used to, when I was in New York. She's about an hour upstate.' He put out his cigarette. 'I saw her last weekend, actually.'

'You were in New York last weekend?'

'Yes.'

She rolled over on to her stomach. 'Did you see *her*?'

'Michèle? Of course I did. She's my girlfriend.'

'Did you sleep with her?'

He sighed. '*Susan*. You're acting like a sixteen-year-old. Of *course* I slept with her. She's my *girlfriend*.'

'I see.'

'Hey, come on.' His voice was cajoling. 'Don't spoil what we've got.'

'What *have* we got?' she muttered into the pillow.

'We've got the most incredible physical thing for each other I've ever had in my life. Isn't that enough?'

'No.'

'Hey, come on—' He reached to touch her shoulder and she flinched away from him. 'Hey.' He turned on the spotlight over the bed and traced the red welts his belt had

225

left on her back. He was instantly re-aroused, and, leaning down, whispered in her ear, 'Say please.'

She rolled over, jack-knifed her knees and kicked him away with such force that he fell sprawling on to the floor. Then she jumped to her feet, ran into the bathroom and locked the door.

'Susan, for Christ's sake come out of there!'

'Go away!'

'Come out of there and talk this thing over!'

'NO!'

'Come out right now or I'm getting dressed and going out.'

She unlocked the door, pushed past him and slunk back to bed. 'Well?'

'*Now* what are you getting so upset about?' He sat down beside her. 'You *know* about Michèle now. Of *course* I have to see her when I'm in town.'

'I want—'

'Go on,' he encouraged.

Incredible; she'd got into bed with a big sexy Jew and woken up on a psychiatrist's couch with a solicitous trick-cyclist. She took a deep breath. 'I want to know why you love *her* and not me if this really is the best physical thing you've ever had.'

He sighed. 'Susan, sex and love aren't the same.'

'Who says?'

'Really, Susan.'

'All right – not always. I know that. But sometimes they are.'

He shook his head. 'This isn't love.'

'Why? Because the sex is too good?'

She'd hit a nerve; he looked at her, shocked. Then he smiled. 'Yeah, a bit, I guess. Maybe you're right. But I just don't and can't associate this kind of sex with marriage and kids and settling down.'

'Isn't that weird? – I couldn't dream of marrying anyone I *didn't* have this sort of sex with. Taking the dirt out of sex seems to me as self-defeating as taking the taste out of food.'

'You're a modern girl, Susan. You're in a freefall and all you feel is a sense of your freedom. I'm in that freefall too and all I feel is the lack of ground under my feet. I have to feel there's something secure in my life. And ever since I've known Michèle she's seemed to me to be the one pure thing in a world of revisions and corruption. I need the vision of that thing to keep me going. It's nothing personal against you.'

'I see. So if I hadn't let you fuck me the first time I met you, or whip me, or come in my mouth, or do it to me over a trash can, there is a chance you could have fallen in love with me?'

He frowned. 'It's not that simple, Susan. I don't see women as either virgins or whores; I just don't see how real life can live alongside this sort of sex. Something's got to give. Besides, if I dumped Michèle after all these years, and with her believing we'd get married some day, what sort of man would I be?' He laughed. 'My father's son, that's who.'

She thought about Tobias Pope and his ugly, blunt, completely cliché-free way of looking at the world. It was strange; she'd been whoring for him with strangers just because she wanted the editor job, and yet when they weren't in a sexual arena he spoke to her frankly, conspiratorially and with a certain degree of respect. She slept with David out love, and he treated her like a cross between a fallen woman and a child. She thought that maybe a touch more of his father in him wouldn't go amiss.

'OK, I give up.' She closed her eyes. 'I give up. It's like arguing with a Catholic over the Virgin Mary. But will you remember one thing?'

He laughed. 'What's that?'

'When Bunny falls off her pedestal, I'm next in line.'

'Susan, the only reason I'd put you on a pedestal would be so I could look up your skirt.' He climbed on top of her.

When Susan met Rupert Grey at Ye Olde Troute the next Monday and told him the news, giving him Gary Pride's card with a personal message scrawled on it – 'Hi kid! Call soonest and let's make lots of money! Love on ya. Gaz' – as proof, his eyes shone, his lips parted and in his head she could tell that he was hearing angel choirs choreographed by Douglas Sirk. He supped from his bar stool and faced her with all the single-minded spirituality of Jeanne d'Arc going to the stake.

'I'm ready,' he said.

'Hello, Susan. It's Ingrid.'

The voice was cool, collected and verging on contempt-uous. Where were the five wet kisses which usually heralded Ingrid's calls? She had always hated them; now their absence seemed ominous. 'Hello, Ingrid.'

'Dinner tonight, darling?'

'What? Sorry – you know how it is. I have to book at least two weeks in advance. How about drinks on the twelfth?'

'No – dinner tonight.'

'I'm sorry, Ingrid, that's impossible.'

'OK. Is it still hurting you, is that why you need an early night?'

'I'm sorry, I don't understand. Is what hurting me?'

'Your tattoo. Doesn't it give you terrible headaches, being in such a sensitive area?'

'I don't know what you're talking about.'

'You most certainly do. Dinner now?'

'No.'

'OK. That suits me. I've got a new friend. And it's more than my life's worth to ignore him. My life and our diary column. The best mole we've ever had. You wouldn't believe the things he feeds me. Why – sometimes I think he must be telepathic.'

Well, here it was. Her worst fears being used on her like an electric cattle-prod by someone who had every reason to want her wiped off the board. 'Really?'

'Yes. Well, I'm sorry you're tied up tonight. I'll go out with my new friend instead. I'm afraid we do talk about you an awful lot! If your ears burn, you'll know who it is!'

'Thanks.'

'By the way, Susan, do you have a b/w photo of yourself? A recent one?'

Her stomach did a triple back somersault without a safety net. 'No, I don't. Why?'

'Oh – just for our files. You never know these days when any of us will hit the headlines!'

'I'm sorry.'

'Well, never mind. Maybe I'll send one of our snappers out to catch you unawares! Posed shots are so stiff, don't you think? Our diary page has a strict policy of not using them these days. Spontaneous shots are so much more . . . revealing.'

There was a man's laugh on the line. For the first time Susan became aware of an extension.

'Whatever you want,' she said slowly and deliberately. 'I'm ready.'

'Good. Ciao, babes.'

Then everyone hung up.

TWELVE

'To people who are neither, the words rich and fashionable go together like a horse and carriage, or divorce and marriage,' said Tobias Pope to Susan Street's back as she gazed beyond the glass wall of his East River penthouse to the Manhattan skyline in the late morning sun. She was weak in the presence of such beauty and wished she was King Kong so she could scale it, pull it down, leave her mark. She wished he'd shut up and leave her alone with this skyline, which was more beautiful and more inclined to make you believe in God than all the fields and trees and mountains and rivers, all the so-called natural wonders of the world put together. Nearer, my God, to thee, on top of the Woolworth Gothic.

'But unless you leave out showbusiness, and then only a handful, they're as strictly divided as any other tribes of New Amsterdam. OK, occasionally some industrialist will take up with some model, and she'll take him to a few nightclubs, and he'll take her to a couple of decent dinners, but his friends' wives won't talk to her, and her friends' boyfriends won't talk to him, and before you can say gold-digger she's back in the arms of some black fag photographer and he's back on the arm of Nancy Reagan's sixth-best friend.' He sipped his coffee. 'Want some? Nicaraguan.'

'*You* drink Nicaraguan coffee?'

'But of course. It amuses me to think of all those European liberal volunteers who go out there to pick it getting blasted by the noble Contras. Yes, the rich are rarely fashionable and the fashionable are rarely rich. Right now, they hate each other as vilely as any other tribe of this barrio. As much as the blacks hate the Koreans or the Irish hate the Jews.' He sniggered. 'Or the women hate the men. Don't you believe that bull about a melting pot – this is the most viciously segregated little fiefdom this side of Jo'burg.' He chuckled happily. 'Which is as it should be.'

She knew that if she didn't take positive action, she was going to be treated to a preprandial discourse on Tobias Pope's Patent Theory Of Racial Superiority, an original body of thought rating the people of the world and their ability to govern on the performance of their female members in bed. She congratulated herself on adapting so quickly to his little ways and learning how to field them, and sidetracked him smartly into what sounded the least offensive and more interesting option, that of Rich v.

Fashionable. Which also, come to think of it, had distinct possibilities as a piece for the *Best*'s style page. She could see it now – CASH OR DASH? By Candida Crewe.

She turned around and leaned against the glass. 'Tell me about the war between the rich and fashionable.'

He looked at her, amused. 'I bet *you* thought they were the same, didn't you?'

'I haven't really thought about it. I suppose I thought there was quite a degree of miscegenation.'

'Only in bed – never on the dotted line. Never where it *matters*.' He clicked his fingers. 'I'll demonstrate what I mean by using a personal example. You've been here before – tell me what you'd do in an average day. For a start, where would you stay?'

'OK. Well, last time I stayed at the Algonquin on West 44th Street.'

He blew a raspberry. 'It must have body-positive walls, all those fags dabbing their fingers in Dottie's dust. What next?'

'I'd have brunch.'

'Brunch!'

'At One Fifth. Mimosas and Eggs Millionaire.'

'No millionaire would eat that garbage. They ought to call them Eggs Social-Climber. Or Eggs Counterjumper. Or Eggs Yuppie. *Brunch* – my point exactly. Go on.'

She wouldn't have countenanced such rudeness from anyone else for a full minute, but Pope was so much larger than life that he made a cartoon out of everything. His words could no more hurt her than Mickey Mouse could mug her. She grinned. 'Then I'd go to Washington Square and watch the fire-eaters and the snake-charmers and that funny man who skips on a unicycle with a fourteen-inch sword down his throat.'

He snorted. 'Very improving. Go on.'

'Some jazz in Central Park, then have lunch at the Russian Tea Rooms on West 57th.'

He snapped his fingers and leaned forward exultantly in his chair.

'Vodka and blinis, right?'

'And caviar,' she said triumphantly.

He laughed, shaking his head. 'Susan, eating croissants when not in France and caviar when not in Russia or Iran is a tell-tale sign of a true nouveau. When in Rome, eat spaghetti. And then you'd go shopping, yes?'

'I suppose so,' she said sulkily.

'Where?'

'The department stores. The East Side is too expensive and the rest is too tacky.'

'And what would you buy from these department stores?'

'I don't know – Adrienne Vittadini sweaters, Kay Unger silk dresses, Liz Claiborne fake Chanel suits.'

He groaned. 'Liz Claiborne! My *secretaries* wear those suits!'

'See the lights go on from the Brooklyn Bridge,' she ploughed on (Pope would probably tell her you weren't anyone until you had a private box in River House for this purpose), 'dinner at Indochine, dancing at Undochine, karoke at Lotus Blossom and then a night at Nell's talking about how you never go to Area any more. Then maybe a drink at Save The Robots.' She looked at him defiantly.

He buried his face in his hands. 'Oh dear, oh dear, oh dear. *Exactly.* That mooching, brunching, self-consciously insider number that all tourists with library tickets do here. I bet you even walk self-regardingly along the picturesque cobbled streets of the Village holding hands with that jerk you live with, am I right?'

'Yes,' she admitted.

'Right. *That's* fashionable New York, Susan. And it sucks. No truly rich New Yorker would do those things. Being fashionable is for people who can't be rich – the consolation prize in the big hoopla of life.' He got up from his chair, turned her around and pressed her so hard against the glass wall that her nose and breasts concertinaed simultaneously. 'Look. Nine million suckers live here, and only the inhabitants of these thirty blocks matter.'

'I'm sure that's not true.'

'It is. We can literally do what we like and get away with it. We can kill anyone.' His eyes glinted.

'That seems a very healthy measure of a man's status,' she said sarcastically.

He laughed, releasing her. 'It's as good as any. But the point is that all those places you read about in your glossy magazines – TriBeCa, SoHo, NoHo, LoBro, the fag bars on the Upper West Side closing at a rate of knots – the people there don't matter now, matter even less than they ever did. Some moron once said that there were nine million New York Citys, one for every sucker that lived there, but there are only four – rich, fashionable, bourgeois and poor – and that's it. And soon, there's only going to be one – rich.'

'How do you work that out?'

He was pacing the room, looking excited – the way he looked, in fact, when he was watching her fuck the local colour. Real estate is the new orgasm, Zero had said in her latest column. At the time, Susan had considered the statement rather facile and flippant. Now she reconsidered.

'AIDS and development. Killing or pushing out the poor, the bourgeois and the fashionable. The carrot and the stick – or rather, the garret and the prick.' He laughed unduly at his joke. 'In ten years' time what's left of them will be in New Jersey or the Hudson. And the ones I personally will be gladdest to see go are the fashionables, those insufferably smug little prigs with more taste than money. Right now they're being pushed out of their lofts in the Bowery by young brokers with more money than sense prepared to pay a quarter of a million for the privilege of gazing through their triple-glazing at the crack-crazed coloureds filing out of the flop-houses. There are million-dollar flats coming up in Alphabet – a couple of years ago this was the worst drug dive on the island. But these yuppies don't care – they're desperate to hang on in there by their fingernails at the heart of the city and of course they can't afford to live here or even over on Central Park West, with the Jews, shrinks and film actors. So they move into the Bowery and the East Village, which is extremely useful. As a type, I hate your yuppie – the men are boors, and the women wear running shoes and make appalling sex partners. But you can't deny they make good shock troops. They move into shitholes and they clean them up a treat. Yes, when you've got yuppies, AIDS and developers, who needs goon squads? Like I say, in ten years' time this town will be like it was in the Fifties. Heaven.'

'Doubling as hell for the poor.'

'You said that in Rio. And probably in Sun City. It's getting a bit repetitive, my dear.' He sighed. 'Anyway, they'll be in New Jersey. I *told* you. They'll be happier there, where everything's horrible. If New York can't belong to you, it's not worth living in.'

'*Some* of New York belongs to everyone.' She gestured at the spectacle beyond the glass wall. 'The skyline does.'

His eyes bugged, and then he gasped in delight. 'Susan! The skyline, for your information, madam, belongs to a small band of men who reside on Park, Wall, Madison and Fifth, plus a couple in Texas. That's it, period. The great unwashed can look, but if they loiter too long by any of these beauties they are very likely to be persecuted with extreme prejudice – beaten up to you – by one or other of the well-equipped armies employed by these men solely for that purpose.' He shook his head, laughing. 'The skyline belongs to everyone! You slay me. And I bet you think the best things in life are free too, yes?' He looked at his watch. 'No, of course not – you're with me. My dear, I have the man from Forbes coming in half an hour. It might be a little difficult to explain your presence unless you get dressed.'

'I could do Museum Mile.'

He sighed. 'Susan, there are more than four hundred art galleries and museums in this town, but not in one will you find anything to compare with the sight of yourself in a beautiful new black dress. Catch.' He fished a battered black wallet from inside his jacket and threw it to her, not at her, she registered in a split-second. 'Here you go. You've done very well at the fucking – here's the shopping. No, don't argue—' (She hadn't been going to: she was sure this had been said sarcastically.) 'Think of it as an investment by Pope Communications Inc. Much as I love your Alaïa, I'm getting awfully bored of seeing it. And dressing for the bedroom in the boardroom really is the height of bad manners.'

She opened the wallet and surveyed the library of plastic within. 'That'll do nicely,' she said.

'Get a good suit, some cashmere, some decent handbags. Don't bother with the West Side – stenos shop there. Walk when you can. If you get lost, or hit a bad barrio, just keep moving; the neighbourhoods change every ten blocks.' He sniggered. 'Or six months, thanks to the yuppies. The Bronx is up and its batteries are down. Don't come back till you've spent a year's wages. Now kiss me. Chastely. Come back before dinner and I'll take you out.'

'The Rainbow Room?'

'What? Art deco and cigarette girls and the assembled media of the Western world watching us? Act your age, girl, not your dress size. No, somewhere dark. We'll see a bit of local colour. You love local colour, don't you?' He laughed and patted her hair. 'Run along now.'

She went into her bedroom, pulled on some Barely Black Lycra tights, some plain black Emma Hope heels and a charcoal wool Joseph button-through. She looked at herself in the mirror as she dabbed a little Amazone cologne – *the* Designer Dyke scent, a predictable present from Zero ('Duty free. The story of my life') – at the base of her throat. The pulse there was jumping.

Local colour. Tobias Pope wasn't interested in local colour – at least not when it was vertical. Tobias Pope said that all local colour was Nicespeak for foreign poor people, and foreign poor people, pigmentation apart, were all the same from the Bronx to Bombay, Bologna to Birmingham; they conned you out of money and sold you salmonella. He was interested in one aspect of local colour. And that was the horizontal hold.

Never mind. It was expecting too much to think he'd brought her here for the sole purpose of shopping. Never mind; come on down, little Susan Street from Nowhere-on-Sea, into the city that never sleeps or says sorry, armed with a collection of cards that say more about you than money ever could – that you're whoring for the boss, for a start. She laughed at her own lyricism and stepped out on to the street, ready to shop till she dropped.

On Madison Avenue, at the soft-tech, Italo-Japanese, black-beige Armani shop, she bought black label, and at Krizia she bought sportswear that would have had a nervous breakdown if one did anything more rigorous than hail a cab in it. She avoided Walter Steiger but did succumb to a pair of pewter, lace and plastic Vittorio Riccis for Zero. She snapped up a brace of six-hundred-dollar sweaters at Sonia Rykiel and half a dozen pairs of cashmere tights at $178 a throw at Fogal, thinking of their less extortionate cousins that David Weiss had wiped his velvet cosh on that night over the dustbins behind the Kremlin Club. She wondered what he was doing, then stopped. It hurt too much. She found Ylang Ylang to be Butler and Wilson by another name and didn't see why she should transport across continents what she could pick up in her lunchtime, but at Helen Woodhull she bought an armload of jewellery that could have been handed down from the Mrs Pope who came over on the Mayflower. She bought forty-dollar earrings that looked as though they cost four thousand at Gale Grant's and four-thousand-dollar earrings that looked as though they'd cost forty at Back In Black.

On Fifth Avenue she ignored Gucci as a matter of principle, bought lots of Micheal Kors black at Bergdorf's and Donna Karan cashmere and a Rifat Ozbek tuxedo dress for under four hundred dollars at Sak's. On East 57th Street she bought a Chanel suit, against her better judgement, for just over two thousand dollars, a three-thousand-dollar handbag at Prada and, after browsing in La Marca for two minutes, understood completely why it was Cher's favourite shop, made her excuses and left.

On Park Avenue she went to Martha, where all first ladies hope to go when they die, and flicked through the Bill Blass, Galanos, David Cameron and Carolina Herrera before deciding she didn't want to look like any First Lady, living or dead, and ignoring Pope's advice she took a cab to West 56th Street where she bought a Norma Kamali dress as blue-black as a bruise and tighter than Nancy Reagan's smile. She self-consciously ordered a Manhattan at the Four Seasons and caught a cab down to Wall Street past the new, beautiful, terrifying skyscrapers: the AT & T, CitiCorp, the Woolworth Gothic and the CBS Black Rock. Then she made her way to the penthouse on the East River, to a man more violent than all the drug dealers in Alphabet City and more vicious than all the art hags in TriBeCa, wondering what was on the menu this evening.

The venue for the menu was a small, unmarked club on the despised Upper West Side, and the proprietress was a woman with the profile of Nefertiti and the figure of Jane Russell – back in the days when men had physiques and women had figures instead of everyone being a body. Tobias Pope left Susan in her hands with a laugh and a leer. 'Maria, Susie. Susie, Maria.'

'What's happening?' she whispered.

'Well, my dear, you've had the shopping – now for the fucking. Don't worry – it's the safest sort of sex there is.' He looked into her eyes, laughed again and disappeared into a long, bare room furnished only with a chair and a long window which covered all of one wall.

The window corresponded with a mirrored wall, Susan calculated as she followed Maria into the bar proper. As a bar it was nothing to write home about – unless your sisters were raving dykes. Because every patron of the bar was a woman.

And hanging from the ceiling was a naked girl, suspended by the wrists and ankles as if in a swallow dive, her long blonde hair hiding her face. She had a strange dark mark on her left thigh, a miniature pineapple, and her small breasts, pointed with sharp pink nipples, were the lowest part of her.

As Susan stared, a middle-aged woman in leather reached up casually with a riding crop and flicked them, never missing a beat of her conversation with a cool, business-suited redhead. 'Oh yeah, Julian's definitely lost it now. He should never have left Mary . . .'

Maria turned to Susan and smiled a smile that could have kept the *Titanic* out of trouble. 'Like what you see?'

'Very nice.' She kept cool. 'Could I have a drink, do you think?'

'Sure.' A consensual path cleared as Maria walked to the bar, not quite a swagger, with her arm around Susan's waist. 'What'll you have?'

'A vodka martini, straight.' *Straight*, that's a laugh. About the only thing in this bar that is.

'Set 'em up, Joanna,' said Maria to the bartender. 'My usual.' She was given a glass of milk with an olive on a stick, which she ate, gesturing vaguely. 'See anything you especially like?'

Susan kept her eyes rigidly from the human mobile. 'I love your banquettes.'

'Well, let's go and utilize one, shall we?' They took their drinks and sat down. 'So, you work for Tobias?'

'Yes. In London.'

'Right.' Maria nodded thoughtfully. As an after-thought she added, 'Do you like to eat pussy?'

'Who, me?' Feeling naive, Susan recovered herself with an effort, though goodness knew what she had been expecting. 'Sometimes. Sometimes in the past.'

'Didn't we all, in our wild youth? Before we discovered the masochistic appeal of men, and made life complicated for ourselves?' Maria laughed easily, her expensive teeth flashing ultra-violet in the stage-managed dark. 'And are you still living in your wild youth, Susie?'

'Sometimes. Sometimes on weekends.'

'I thought so. Strip.'

'What?'

'Strip. Just leave your clothes with me and I'll guard them as if they were my own.' She twinkled. 'Which, as a fellow protégée, they are in a way. Take off every stitch – jewellery, the lot.'

'Are you crazy?' But even as she said it, she feared that Maria was an all too sane mistress of the situation.

Maria smiled without irritation and gestured at the long mirror. 'OK. Tobias says strip.'

She sat and thought for a moment, hearing her heart beat. She thought about what she'd been through, and then she thought about where she was going. Then she reached up, her eyes closed, and unwound her dress from her neck, her breasts, her hips. It came off like a black bandage on a dry wound. Which was just what she was. She sat there in her shoes, tights and Back In Black earrings, thinking.

'All off,' said Maria, looking at her watch.

'Don't rush me,' said Susan slowly. People were looking. Madonna Ciccone was singing 'Dress You Up', which was obviously someone's idea of a joke.

Maria sighed. 'Susie, I'm not trying to get into your pants. I'm trying to do a job, which is to get you out of them. Now *strip*.'

She thought about Pope behind the mirror, laughing at her reserve, relishing her past, weighing up her future. She was fucked if she'd buck at this fence. She wriggled out of her tights, kicked off her heels.

'Earrings off.'

She took them off one by one, laid them gently on the table. Then she looked into Maria's eyes. The nearness and beauty of the strange woman made her realize with a jolt that she was aroused and ready to fuck.

The sensual side of Susan Street was as strong as ever and at that moment she wanted nothing more – well, maybe the editorship – than for this woman, Maria, to push her down on the dog-ended floor and take her by hand or mouth or dildo. But that part of Maria had died a long time ago, assassinated by necessity, and she merely looked at Susan approvingly as if at a child that has eaten its greens.

'Good girl.' She tipped the vodka martini into the milk and drained it in one. 'Same again, please.'

Susan stood up and smoothed down her hair nervously; Maria pulled a tiny comb from her breast pocket and, incredibly, began to fluff up Susan's pubic hair maternally. 'There you go,' she said after a moment. 'Perfect.'

Susan walked out from behind the table and padded down the three steps from the banquette to the bar. The room was very quiet. Madonna had stopped singing. The whole club, more than thirty women, was looking at her.

Thirty women and one man . . .

The crowd parted a little, but not for long. As she reached the bar, the black glass cold against her stomach, they closed around her. One hand explored the contours of her behind. Another hand came around and tightened possessively on her right breast. A knee was thrust between her thighs from behind. And then a hand slid in straight to the meat of the matter.

'A vodka martini, please. And a glass of milk.'

Joanna was a pretty girl, a lot like Beatrice Dalle everywhere but her upper lip, where she bore a distinct resemblance to Charlie Chaplin. She pouted reflexively. 'Vodkatini, milk. Right.' She filled the glasses expertly and before Susan could move or protest, picked them up and flung them, milk first, at her bare breasts.

At this signal the crowd moved as one. She was pushed down on to her back; someone sat on her face, though whether for kicks or to obscure her view of the participants she couldn't decide. She couldn't see or speak or hear; her senses were all in her body as mouths sucked at her breasts, different mouths taking turns and being wrenched urgently away to be replaced by other, rougher mouths. Talk about fast food. When it seemed the whole bar had had their *hors d'oeuvres*, they went for the main attraction, taking her with their hands and mouths till she lost count. Then she was ridden by half a dozen women wearing the longest, hardest dildoes imaginable; two seemed filed to a point, and one spurted something warm and thick into her.

She also lost count of the times she came. When one of the women on the other end of the dildoes tried to withdraw,

Susan cried out and gripped her by the hips, pulling her back in. The whole bar cheered as one, triumphantly yet good-naturedly, their applause ringing in her ears as she blacked out.

When she came to she was being hoisted up into the air by her wrists and ankles. Her dark hair fell over her face as she hung in a suspended swallow dive, her nipples the lowest point of her.

She opened her eyes and looked at the new girl on the floor, the girl who had been hanging from the ceiling when she came in. The insatiable dominatrixes were swarming over her like flies on a Danish pastry. Susan looked at the straight blonde hair, the ski tan, the slight cast in one eye and the sweet, insecure, ecstatic smile in the split-second before the beautiful, cruel-looking Chinese girl who had been sitting on her face took her position once more, bringing new meaning to the phrase 'I'll sit this one out'.

And she knew, in that split-second, that she was looking at the double life of Michèle Levin.

THIRTEEN

Not only had Rupert Grey been ready for the world, but a good part of its population aged between twelve and twenty had been ready and waiting for him. With the decline of the first wave of gender benders, a whole generation of troubled young things in love with their best friends had been left up the creek without an icon. Rupert Grey was the answer to both their prayers and the glaring space on their bedroom walls. His voice, though small, was sweet and true – and his video did him no harm at all. Rupert lying in bed, naked to the waist and covered with a black silk sheet, smoking Sobranies sultrily. Rupert in his shower, swallowing and spitting out shower spray in achingly slow motion. Rupert eating a banana for breakfast and mooching around an expensively spartan waterfront loft ('Can't keep away from the docks, can he?' sniggered Zero when she saw it) miming 'Too Young'.

He went to number one in Britain, Greece and Germany and top ten in France, Italy and Israel. He flew around Europe miming on TV shows, bought a lot of new clothes in South Molton Street, drank pink champagne until he was sick of it and refused all interviews, on Gary Pride's advice.

'The Garbo approach,' said Gary Pride confidingly to Susan as they sat in the Groucho, having met by accident, she waiting for Zero and he for one of the long line of record producers he was engaged in auditioning for Rupert's next record. Since Rupert's success Gary's attitude to her had changed considerably, and he greeted her like an old friend every time they ran into each other. Just *how* old he didn't seem to have remembered, for which she was fervently grateful.

'More like Rin Tin Tin,' she laughed.

He laughed too, slyly, looking around mischievously. 'Steady, gel. Don't bite the bender that feeds me. I like your frock. Don't let Rupee see it, he'll want one.'

'Thanks.' She was wearing a tight, short-skirted pillarbox-red suit by Myrene de Prémonville. 'I liked your *Face* interview.'

He nodded, pleased. 'Yeah, it's best if I handle the verbals. Rupe's a cute kid, bless him, but the man upstairs was taking a tea-break when they put the reckoning gear in.' The vow of silence he had thrust upon Rupert fitted in nicely with Gary Pride's plans to be *the* Mediavelli of the Nineties, a big-time manipulator who aimed to be both more famous and more enduring than his stars.

'What's the next record, then? Another cover? "My Boy Lollipop", "Bend It", "Where The Boys Are"?'

Gary's face darkened. 'He wants to do his own stuff.'

'Oh, no.' Susan was genuinely disappointed. This moment was the one every manager, record company and genuine pop fan alike dreaded; the first stirrings of creativity in their young charges like some malign tumour coming to fruition.

'Happens to all of them,' Gary said sagely. 'Though this one's going to have a fucking fight on his hands with me, I can tell you. He'll be back on the game before you can say AIDS if he plays up. Look, there's your mate.' He looked critically at Zero, who was peering short-sightedly into the club, absent-mindedly twisting her tail around her finger. He liked bleached blondes in tight dresses. 'She's a smart tart. What a waste of talent. What's that bit of old rope she's got stuck on her bum?'

'It's her tail,' said Susan defensively.

He looked at her and laughed, holding his hands up in front of him.

'OK, OK, I'm sorry. I only asked. When's the wedding?'

'Zere! Over here!'

Zero saw them, and pretended she had been peering around merely in the interests of networking. She stopped at three sofas on the way to whisper in the ears of various sharp-suited women and complete the illusion. Finally she got to their table. 'Hello, bach. Hello, Mr Prince. How's it hanging?'

'Going up with a bullet every time I look at you, Zero.'

'Yeah, but what goes up must come down, isn't that so? And in your case I've heard it's fast forward.'

He laughed. 'You got great legs, gel. Legs are a girl's best friend, aren't they? But even best friends have to part some time.'

Zero looked at Susan. 'Did you bring this in on the heel of your shoe?'

'Don't worry, I'm going. I see my dinner. KEITH!' Gary Pride stood up and waved at an anonymous face whose way with a control panel had made him a household sound. 'Be right over! Bye, girls. Don't do anything I wouldn't do.'

'What, think?'

He laughed and left.

Zero stood looking after him. 'I don't know how you can stand to be seen with that. He's got tackiest rep in this town.'

'You shouldn't be late, then. What's wrong?'

'Oh, nothing. He dropped Donna when Rupert Grey took off, and she pissed off back to Paris. I was having a bit of a thing with her. I think I could have liked her, you know?'

'I'm sorry.'

'Forget it.' She looked at Susan and smirked. 'I'll tell you one thing. Don't open your mouth too wide.'

'Why not?'

'Someone might stick a letter in it!' Zero cracked up.

'Very funny.'

'Don't fight it, bach – there is no life after black. It's a rag hag's con trick to keep you buying junk of many colours that you don't need. She who is tired of the little black dress is tired of life.' She looked around impatiently. 'Speaking of which, I feel like getting drunk. Shall we make a night of it?'

'I'm seeing David at ten. Sorry.'

'S'OK. Androna! Thirteen martinis, please. Ta.' She looked at Susan boldly, daring her to say something. She didn't. 'So what was New York like?'

'Very tall.'

'And what did he make you do?'

'Something you'd approve of.'

Zero sat up straight. 'Dykes?'

'A whole lot of them. Anonymously. In a bar.' She leaned closer. 'I hung from the ceiling.'

'Good God, girl.' Zero stared at her.

'Don't tell anyone.'

'My lips are sealed. You'll have to feed me my martinis by drip.'

'And that's not all. *She* was there.'

'Who?'

'*Her*. His girlfriend. Michèle.'

'You sure?'

'Either that or she's got a dyke double.'

'Inside every faithful girlfriend there's a raging dyke dying to get out. The quiet ones are the worst, too. That's what I always say.'

'Frequently.'

'Well – game, set and match, isn't it, bach? And you from Nowhere-on-Sea and all.'

'It would seem so. I'm going to tell him tonight. Postcoitally. And I've got proof. She's got a birthmark. How would I know about that if I was bluffing?'

'Well, congratulations. That's fantastic.' Zero drained one of her glasses. 'And the rest of your problems?'

'I'm waiting for Irving and Lejeune to make their next move and while I'm not exactly looking forward to it like a child to Christmas morning I feel better about it now they've shown me their hand. I'm seeing Moorsom tomorrow and presenting him with my *fait accompli*. And there are only two tasks to go. Things are looking better.'

'Well.' Zero raised her third glass. 'Here's to you, bach. And may all your troubles be curable by penicillin.'

'You did *what?*' hissed David Weiss, springing naked from the bed.

'I saw Michèle. This weekend.'

'In New York?'

'No, in Sainsbury's. Of *course* in New York.'

'What were *you* doing in New York?'

'I was taking a break. Getting away from it all.'

'You were *snooping*, you mean.'

'I certainly wasn't,' she said primly. 'It was complete accident, coincidence, or whatever you want to call it, that I ran into her.'

'Where?'

'In a bar.'

He laughed. 'You're lying. Michèle hates bars. She doesn't drink.'

'I never said she was drinking. I never said it was a drinking bar.'

'What do you mean?' He narrowed his eyes at her. 'What other sort of bar is there? What sort of bar was this?'

'It was a dyke bar,' she said, looking straight into his eyes.

He picked up the TV and threw it at her. She jumped off the bed and it missed. He caught her by the throat and slapped her face twice. 'You EVIL cunt!' he shouted.

She was too exhilarated by her power to be frightened. 'I saw her! I'm telling you, it's *true! I saw her birthmark!*'

He let go of her and pushed her away, moving backwards. He was looking at her as if *she* had attacked *him*, as if she was armed and dangerous. He knew that there had been a switch, and that she had the power now. He looked like a victim. 'What birthmark? You're lying.'

'Shall I describe it to you, David?' Naked and beaten, she felt as though she was wearing six-inch heels and had just had a long all-body massage. She felt great. It was called being in control, and it wasn't at all overrated.

'On the left thigh, very dark, in the shape of a pineapple. About – this big.' She held up a thumb and forefinger a little way apart.

He fell back on to the sofa and, with a loud groan, put his head in his hand. 'Get me a drink. Scotch. QUICK!'

She poured a triple J&B at the bar, feeling like a nurse; it struck her that she was so used to doing nothing for men that even fixing a drink for one made her feel self-sacrificing. She took it to him and laid a hand solicitously on his glossy black hair. Now she had him, she was going to be extra nice to him. She was going to be nicer to him than any woman had been to any man in the history of the world. And it would mean more because she was doing it completely of her own free will. 'Here's your drink,' she said softly.

He groped for the glass. 'What's the name of this place? Who runs it? I'll kill the bastard.'

Patricide, how handy. But much too news worthy. 'I don't know its name, it was very discreet. The club equivalent of the LBD. Somewhere on the Upper West Side, but I couldn't begin to remember where. I don't know New York well.'

'Who took you there?'

'A friend.'

'A dyke?'

'Yes.'

'Then she must know the place.' He grabbed the phone and thrust it at her. 'Call her now.'

'I can't ask her to reveal this just so you can go round and burn the place down, David. That's not ethical. I thought you had ethics.'

He laughed nastily. 'I feel like I'm the only sucker in the world with ethics. I'm pretty fucking sick of carrying them when every other bastard in the world is traveling light.'

That he considered himself to be weighed down with principles while so copiously and enthusiastically betraying his fiancée with her struck Susan as rather self-deluding, self-dramatizing, self-regarding and totally American – an innocence that bordered on psychopathy – but she let it pass. 'David,' she said gently. 'Your argument is not with some poor dyke running a bar and trying to turn an honest buck' – a novel description of Tobias Pope if ever there was one – 'but with your fiancée. Who was not dragged in off the street by the Dyke Patrol, but who went there of her own free will and in a similar manner undressed and hung from the ceiling naked as the day she was born, for all the world like an Allen Jones chandelier.'

He threw his Scotch at her, glass and all. She dodged 'I'm losing my mind here, and you're making funnies! Get me another one.' He grabbed the phone again. 'I'm gonna call her.' He fumbled at the dial and waited.

'Michèle?'

Pause.

'Yeah, it's me. Listen. I know this sounds weird. But it's best if I come right out and say it, Someone' – he looked daggers at Susan – 'told me they saw you in New York this weekend. In a dyke bar. Naked. Hanging from the ceiling.'

Pause.

'Yeah, I know how crazy I sound. But this person described your birthmark.'

There was a very long pause. Susan walked over to the bar, poured herself a shot of J&B, drank it, lit one of David's Camels, put it out and used the toilet. When she came out, the pause was still pregnant.

Finally it reached gestation, and David gave a blood-curdling scream. 'You WHAT? You were LONELY? Christ, you BITCH! You CUNT! You! DYKE! I TRUSTED YOU, YOU, YOU BITCH! HOW COULD YOU DO THIS TO ME?' He slammed down the phone and stared at Susan, breathing heavily. Finally he said, 'It's true.'

She nodded happily. 'I told you.' She went towards him. He held out his hands, palms towards her. He didn't look angry or violent any more, but he did look repelled. 'Keep away from me.'

'What?'

'Keep away from me and get dressed and get out of here. You have completely eviscerated the admittedly shaky foundations that my life has been built on for as long as I can remember. It may not have been perfect, but it was all I had to call my own, the only thing that didn't belong to my father. Now it's all gone, thanks to you. Get out! And tomorrow, in the office, and forever, don't speak to me. I never want to speak to you again.'

He collapsed on the sofa and began to cry.

'I thought I told you I never wanted to speak to you again,' said Moorsom in the House of Commons tearoom the next day when Susan flung down between them on the table like a gauntlet a copy of *The Face*, bearing a cover photograph of Rupert Grey peeping flirtatiously over the top of red framed, heart-shaped Lolita sunglasses and sucking milkshake foam from the end of a pink candy-striped straw.

'I know the girl who did the shoot,' Susan said casually. 'You wouldn't believe what he got up to with that straw later. Well . . . maybe *you* would.'

Joe Moorsom looked at the magazine the way a man on a kill-or-cure diet looks at a cream cake. Then he picked it up and thrust it into her bag 'So?'

'Do you know how Rupert made it big, Joe?'

'I imagine he opened his mouth for someone influential,' Moorsom sneered. 'That's what they all do, isn't it?'

'You're all in showbusiness, Joe. You open *your* mouth to advance yourself and so do these poor starlets. But with Rupert here, it was only a *promise* to open his mouth. A promise to me, if I could get him where he wanted to be. So I introduced him to a friend of mine, who Svengalied him. Geddit?'

'Very clever. I imagine he's very grateful to you.'

'I'll say.'

Moorsom looked at her resentfully. 'It looks like I've landed on Mayfair and you've got the set.'

'That's about the sum of it.' She could feel internally what the cliché meant about your heart soaring. 'Rupert has agreed formally to speak exclusively to the *Sunday Best* about your statutory rape of him.' Moorsom winced. 'If you don't give me a guarantee that you'll stop asking questions.'

'I see.' He looked at his hands. He thought how disgusting they looked; soft, clean, pink. His mother's hands had looked more masculine, more calloused than his. He wished he had become a miner and never left his village. He wished he was dead. 'How do I know that the little whore won't go off and tell another paper anyway?'

'He won't. He's not the brightest boy on earth, and he's still quite concerned about the fact that he tried to blackmail you. Remember that scare I threw into him for you? It stuck. This is just part of a bargain between us.'

'I see.' He was playing with his teaspoon and for time. 'What if I stand my ground?'

'That's up to you, Joe. If you want your union, your wife, your children, your constituents and your party to know that you, Joe Moorsom, champion of children's rights, are the ex-sugar daddy of Rupee, the sensational seventeen-year-old singing sexpot sissy, you're in luck.' She sipped her tea. 'If you don't – well, like you say, Joe, you've landed on Mayfair and I've got the set. *And* hotels.' She couldn't help smirking. 'Stand your ground this time, Joe, and you're very likely to be wiped off the board.'

Question Time came and went that week, and Joe Moorsom's usual denunciation of the Pope empire was conspicuous by its absence. In her office, Bryan O'Brien looked at her calculatingly. 'You did well Sue. You did do this, didn't you?'

'I cannot lie, Bryan.'

'I doubt that.'

FOURTEEN

Susan swirled the Czech & Speake bath oil in her Delafon bath and settled back with a bar of their state-of-the-art grey soap. She looked around at her Zehnder radiator, Schneider cabinets, Cerabati tiles and White House towels and sighed. Her bathroom was the one room of the house in which she felt at home; probably because Matthew never used it, having his own downstairs. If an Englishman's home is his castle, she thought, a career girl's bathroom is her refuge.

Through the double-locked door she could hear Matthew moaning on about the state of the fridge, his favourite conversation piece these days. It was now used so little she had taken to keeping her cosmetic lotions in it, making them refreshingly cool on the face, head and body. Matthew had just come across the Camilla Hepper watercress deodorant, lettuce moisturizer and avocado face cream, and the Body

Shop banana conditioner, strawberry body shampoo and pineapple facewash. He had tried to eat the facewash for breakfast, thinking it was yoghurt that Susan had put there in a rare fit of culinary nurturing, and was none too pleased. 'It's bloody typical,' he was shouting.

She put her fingers in her ears and slid under the water. The house vibrated with the slamming of the front door and she came up for air. She thought again how lazy it was of her to stay with Matthew when she had so little time for either his triumphs or his problems. But she didn't want to live alone; there was something horribly Seventies about it, unless you were a gorgeous dyke with a fan club of lovers. It wasn't swinging for a heterosexual to be single any more; once you got past twenty-five and were still unattached, you didn't look glamorous – but as though you'd been sexually tried and rejected by a generation, as Guy Bellamy said. She needed a man around to change fuses and plugs (she still wasn't sure what the difference was, or even if there was one) and to take out the rubbish. What on earth was the point in feminism if you still had to take out the garbage at the end of the day?

A subtle buzzing disturbed her thoughts. It was coming from the Schneider cabinet, which she had left ajar, and it sounded like her battery-operated toothbrush. But how could it turn itself on . . . ?

As if to give her a clue, the toothbrush bounced down from the shelf and hung twinkle-toed in the air.

'Lejeune!' she screamed.

Like a dog hearings its master whistle, the brush bore down on her and dive-bombed into the bath. She screamed. It rose up, dripping, and dived again, landing between her knees. She felt it wriggling upwards, and grabbed it with both hands, It was surprisingly strong. Holding on to it firmly she jumped from the bath, shoved it into the toilet and closed the lid. She sat on it until the buzzing stopped. Then she ran for the door, unlocked it, slammed it and double-locked it from the outside. Then she collapsed on the bed, laughing hysterically. Assault by a sex-crazed toothbrush! At least Lejeune had a sense of humour.

Which was more than you could say for David Weiss. Ever since she had told him the one about the flying dyke and the birthmark, he hadn't said a word to her. Which is why she was so shocked when he came into her room that day, closed her door and leaned against it.

'David!' She jumped up from her desk. Half in surprise and half, she had to admit, to give him the full benefit of what she was wearing: a beautifully cut, witheringly conservative Nicole Farhi houndstooth skirt topped with a shocking off-the-shoulder black leather jacket by Karen Boyd. The combination of rebel and executive was completely original and, she thought, irresistible.

He looked at her, and she was pleased to see his throat move with agitation. But he didn't come closer and his voice was cool. 'I'm sorry to have to bother you, but I've heard some news which I think might affect your future with this paper. And as managing director, it would be petty of me to keep it from you just because of our personal differences. You've done a lot to make this newspaper into the success it is today, more than anyone now that Charles Anstey's dead.'

She didn't like this; it was too respectful. It was already sounding like an obituary. She sat down. 'What is it?'

'There's going to be a rather embarrassing story about you in the *Commentator* some time over the next couple of months.'

'Really?' So here it was.

'They're in the last stages of putting together a series called "While The Cat's Away: Public Virtue And Private Vice". It's going to be about how half a dozen public figures with an interest in morality, or who are used as an example to others, comport themselves after hours. They've been following a politician, a bishop, a senior civil servant, a minor member of royalty, a marriage guidance counsellor and a muck-raking journalist. I'm afraid that journalist is you.'

'What have they been doing, employing detectives?'

'Something like that. Some regular guy to do the legwork. A few photographs taken with a hidden camera. And they've got Constantine Lejeune.'

She brazened it out. 'That's a little end-of-the-pier for the high and mighty *Commentator*, isn't it?

'I guess they're trying to be a newszine, like all of us.

Anyway, it's going to be in their new supplement. You've got to admit, it's a very daring and clever idea. And the inclusion of the MP and the civil servant do give it a certain subversive clout.'

'Oh yes, it's a fucking brilliant idea,' she said sarcastically. 'Why don't we trail it for them on our front page? We don't want anyone to miss it.' She examined her nails. They lay on her desk still in their little plastic container. 'I hope their lawyers are ready, willing and able. Because they're certainly going to get sued puce.'

David shrugged. 'Whatever you think of that guy Lejeune's shtick, there's no denying he found those bodies. People trust him. He's obviously got a gift of some sort.'

'Yes, for self-publicity.' But she didn't believe it. She knew there was more to Lejeune than clever PR.

'I hear they're pretty confident. Challenging this sort of thing can often be very unwise unless you're one hundred per cent in the clear. And who is, these days?'

She sighed. 'David, spare me another lecture on the decline of the West. PLEASE.'

His jaw tightened. 'I wouldn't waste my breath. But I think you should know that challenging something like this is a tricky business and only one outcome is sure: that you'll attract ten times as much publicity to what they say than if you ignore it.'

She tried to be patient. 'David, if I don't deny this, I'm saying it's true. And if it's true, how can your father give me the editor's job and hope to get that fucking cable franchise he wants so much?'

'What are you scared they've got on you, if you don't mind me asking? I mean, I'm sure everyone knows that you're a complete and total slut by now. Word travels fast, Susan.'

'Thanks.' What am I so scared they've got on me? That I killed my last boss. That's I'm whoring for my present boss, who has had me tattooed with the word SOLD, and that I've sucked and fucked with men and women, black, white and *café au lait*, on two continents. And that's just the story so far. 'I'm not scared they've got anything on me,' she said defiantly.

He snorted. 'I doubt that.'

'Why me?' she burst out. 'I'm not even a journalist. I'm an editor.'

He shrugged. 'I guess you qualify because of that story you did on Lejeune.'

'That wasn't a story! That was an "As Told To"!' It was a wail.

'Well, don't bother telling me. I guess you just tangled with the wrong guy.' He smiled nastily. 'I'm sure you can defend yourself. That's a great bunch of claws you've got there. Though if they've got anything too hot on you, I think you're right about the editorship. But then, if *he's* implicated in your little extra-curricular romps too, I doubt if he'll stay in this country at all with such a blot on his copybook. He'll sell up and go into cable and satellite somewhere else. None of us will have jobs here then – it won't just be you.'

She couldn't resist it. 'And what will you do next, David? Go and get a cushy gig with Levin Brothers?'

He gave her a look that made her shiver with lust. 'That's all over, as if you didn't know.'

'So you need a fuck?' She got up and in a flash was out of her houndstooth skirt and her Keturah Brown black lace underpants. She leaned against the wall in her silk stockings, silk suspender belt, black heels and black leather, sticking out her pubis.

'You disgust me,' he said quietly, going out and leaving the door wide open.

She got back into her lower clothes hastily, but not fast enough to prevent Max Sadkin from seeing a sight which quickly replaced Serena Soixante-Neuf as the main feature of his sweetest dreams. She sat down at her desk and put her head in her hands, dizzy with desire and worry. Lejeune on the warpath, and she was still thinking about sex. She didn't know what had got into her.

If only it had been David Weiss.

Susan lay on her stomach on the living-room floor wearing a cotton nightshirt, waiting for Rupert Grey's return appearance on the *Jack Black Show* and eating a Pot Noodle with her eyes closed in delight. After the years of designer cuisine which had been her exclusive diet, supplemented with Marks & Spencer's sublime sandwiches, the Pot Noodle tasted impossibly exotic and wholesome.

Matthew said he was having an affair, but she knew he was really just working late, as usual. Fancy trying to make her jealous! As if you could be sexually jealous of your teddy bear . . .

Jack was going through his usual lame routine with the sound down: raising an eyebrow, parading jokes so old they should have a preservation notice slapped on them and cracking up his audience with monotonous regularity. They loved him passionately and Susan thought that it might be his very banality which endeared him to people. She'd noticed this in many entertainers and immediately began to think in headlines – CALL OF THE MILD. By Sean Macauley.

'Ladies and gentleman, without further ado, please welcome back our very own – well, he must belong to somebody! – singing sensation of the year, and you saw him here first – RUPEE!'

To the strains of 'Too Young' Rupert walked on. But something was different. *Everything* was different. For a start, he *was* walking: not wiggling, prancing or sashaying, as was his wont. He was wearing no feathers, no lamé and no lipstick, but a sober slacks and sweater ensemble which could have come from British Home Stores. And, even more incredibly, *Rupert wasn't pouting*. Was he sick? A terrible thought struck her – had he sprained his lips? In which case, his career was surely over.

The audience, a good half of whom were the teenage fans who called themselves Rupettes, gasped. One girl, obviously the leader of her pubescent peer-group pack, began to sob loudly.

Jack Black whistled softly. 'Well, Rupee . . .'

'Please, Jack, call me Rupert. I was christened Rupert Grey. Rupert . . . is my *Christian* name.' The accent on the denomination was unmistakable and Susan sat up quickly, spilling her Pot Noodle on the Persian rug which had come from Raymond Bernadout and was Matthew's pride and joy.

'Rupert, you told me earlier that you came here tonight specially to talk about your recent experiences . . .'

Rupert held up a hand firmly. There was nothing limp about *that* wrist any more. 'No, Jack. About my recent rebirth.'

Jack raised both eyebrows and looked at the audience. They cracked up.

'You were recently born again, Rupert?'

'Yes, Jack.' Rupert waited serenely for Black's fans to desist. In the old days he would have stamped his platform-booted foot and flounced off camera. 'Introducing me, Jack, you joked that I must belong to somebody. Well, until recently, I didn't. Like a lost lamb I wandered the backstreets of the city being used and abused by all sorts or men—' The crowd gasped. 'From the highest to the lowest.'

Susan wondered whether he was going to baptize his dirty linen on prime-time TV.

'Like a lamb to the slaughter I went to their sumptuous homes when their wives were away.' Even in his hour of confession, Rupert couldn't admit to having had a bunk-up in the Elephant and Castle. Some things never change. 'I knew grief. But now I know Jesus. And I've come home. I've given myself to him.'

He's about the only one you hadn't got around to, Susan thought grimly. What did this change of heart mean to Rupert's pact with her? He probably looked on it as a pact with the Devil in his current frame of mind.

'And when did this wondrous occurrence take place?' asked Jack Black respectfully.

'Two weeks ago. Two weeks and one day. I was in Spain promoting my latest single, "Sweets From A Stranger" – it's my own composition,' he said pointedly. One in the eye for Gary Pride. 'It was ten minutes to airtime. The biggest live pop show in southern Europe. And then – it happened.'

'You found Jesus?' said Jack Black reverently.

'No – my hairdryer fused. My *lucky* hairdryer – the one I *always* use before I perform. I was distraught. I yelled that I couldn't go on, that life was a sick joke. And then I heard a voice.'

The crowd murmured.

'The voice, which was very deep and masculine, said "Rupert. Don't worry. You will get your hair dry. Trust me." And when I tried my hairdryer again, it worked.'

The audience applauded.

'Yes,' affirmed Rupert. 'It worked. And in those moments, I gave myself to Jesus.'

'Why do you suppose Jesus spoke to you about your *hairdryer*, of all things, if you don't mind me asking, Rupert?'

'Well, I couldn't swear to it.' Rupert looked as thoughtful as it was possible for him to look. 'But from the pictures I've seen of him, he seems to have had a little trouble with his hair, too.'

In the audience, the adults cracked up and the teens swooned and screamed. Obviously Rupert's conversion was going to cause them no philosophical problems. Susan remembered the fiercely Mormon Osmond brothers from her youth; girls had gone crazy for them. Forbidden fruit and all that jazz – literally, in Rupert's case.

'So from this moment in time,' continued Rupert triumphantly, 'I am a new man, born again. I have ordered my record company to withdraw "Sweets From A Stranger" from the shops, and instead I plan to record a concept album dealing with the anguish and temptations of the young Christian in the modern business, which makes Sodom and Gomorrah look like Marks & Spencer. It will be called *Forbidden Fruit*. Furthermore, I have decided to handle my career myself and plan to dismiss my alleged manager – a real money-changer in the temple of my career, if ever there was one—'

Susan groaned, and began to count. At the beat of eleven, the phone rang and Gary Pride's voice shrilled on to her answerphone: 'Susan, gel, can you believe what this little bender's pulling? I'm being murdered on live TV in front of more people than anyone since Lee Harvey Oswald! Call back soonest, Gaz.'

'But that's not important,' Rupert went on, frowning slightly. 'The real reason I'm here tonight, Jack, is to make my peace with a man I have wronged. Do you mind?'

'Be my guest.' Black's eyebrows went into orbit.

'Hello out there.' Rupert leaned forward. The camera still loved him. 'I can't call you by name, but you know who you are. And so does Jesus. You wronged me, but I have wronged you, or at least threatened to. And two wrongs don't make a right – they make' – He paused dramatically – 'a bigger wrong. I want to say that I forgive you and so does Jesus. I hope you forgive me. Let bygones be bygones. And let those who seek to profit from our trespasses against each other do their worst – God is on our side. I will never act against you. Goodnight, and goodbye.' Rupert sat back composedly in his seat and looked at Jack Black. 'Thank you, Jack. May I sing now?'

'Certainly, Rupert. And what are you going to do for us?'

'Well, Jack, unfortunately the songs for *Forbidden Fruit* have not been written yet, although I have designed the cover. So I'll have to sing a song pre-dating my salvation.' He stood up. 'This is the B-side of "Sweets From A Stranger" – "Baby, Bite My Bum".'

'So you see, darling, it's *pointless* to pretend that you can do anything macho like bluff us out or negotiate,' said Ingrid Irving, biting into a cream cheese sandwich at Brown's Hotel in Dover Street. 'Because, to be common and nasty about it, we've got all the aces.'

Susan stared at a stained-glass window and offered up a prayer for something sharp to say. A stiff quip was the stiff upper lip of the urban modern, signifying insouciance and no surrender. 'Really, darling. All the aces, eh? Well, you've certainly got a few good diamonds, and if you count your swarthy sidekick you've even got a spade. But you certainly don't have a heart – and I can't think offhand of any club that would have you.' She smiled to herself and sipped her Earl Grey.

Ingrid laughed sweetly, but she was stung. 'Keep it up, sweetie – you're going to wisecrack your way on to the front page very soon. Or rather, on to the supplement centrespread.' She paused for effect, chewing on a crustless cucumber sandwich. 'And I do mean *spread*.'

'OK.' Susan put down her teacup and drew off her Cornelia James gloves. 'Let's stop sharpening our claws and messing about. What exactly have you got on me?'

Ingrid laid her Chanel gloves on the table. 'The works. The tattoo, for a start. If you deny it, and sue, you'll have to show your forehead. Either the court will see SOLD in black and white, or they'll see a dirty great scar, which is just as incriminating. The tattoo, for a start, is going to be pretty hard to explain.'

'OK, it's an embarrassment. But who's to know it's not a private joke between some man and myself?'

'Exhibit B. Her name is Thalia.'

'That bitch!'

'She sends you her love, too. She claims you had various forms of sexual congress with six Brazilian prostitutes for the eyes of Tobias Pope in Rio earlier this year.'

'I see.'

'Exactly. Then we have a testimony from one Washington Brown that you were travelling in South Africa with Mr Pope a month later.'

That dirty, washed-up has-been. 'Sorry to point it out, Ingrid, but I *work* for Mr Pope. I'm allowed to travel with my employer on business, aren't I?'

'Of course, darling. I go for wet weekends with Mark in Manchester all the time, and everything's perfectly above board. But having proof of what you got up to in Rio, it doesn't take a Mensa man to guess what you were up to in Sun City, for heaven's sake. The place is a brothel with roulette wheels.'

'I see.'

'I also believe you have a recent New York stamp on your passport. Constantine says he smells a fish – lesbian sex, with about three dozen women, and he can see a two-way mirror.'

'He must have very good eyesight.' Susan sighed and replaced a glazed strawberry tart on the cake-stand. She'd lost her appetite. 'OK. What do you want?'

'I want to be first,' said Ingrid with admirable simplicity. 'I want to be the youngest-ever female newspaper editor in this country, which means the world. Mark's leaving for Hong Kong next year, and there'll be a big reshuffle on the *Comm*. I know I'm in with a chance, and I know he's going to recommend me to the board. I want to be first, and you're the only obstacle. So I want you to resign.'

'I see. And if I don't?'

Ingrid laughed. 'Susan, I don't think you fully understand. You can resign, and leave on your feet, and get a good job in magazines – any of them would welcome you with open arms. Or you can refuse and let me go ahead with my story. Then, you'll have to leave on a stretcher. You'll be a joke, a dirty joke. You'll be a cinch for a job at Madame Claude's, but no newspaper worthy of the name would touch you. And Pope, what with his heart set on a cable franchise – isn't it funny how that word sounds like some sort of cream cake? – won't touch you with a six-foot dildo; he'll sell up before you can say SOLD.' Ingrid was making short work of a potted meat sandwich, which was highly appropriate under the circumstances, and she smiled as though the black ball had just dropped into the net. 'Susan, *you* understand; you're as ambitious as I am and in opposite circumstances you'd do the same. I ask you as a meritocrat, what's the point in neither of us getting our heart's desire? I could run the story out of spite regardless, and you'd lose your job anyway. What I'm doing now is giving you the chance to walk away instead of crawl. To resign honourably and save face.' She smiled again. 'Because we're women. And I think women should stick together – don't you?'

FIFTEEN

'There's a man here,' hissed Matthew, intercepting her at the front door. 'A strange man. He won't go. I had to let him in because he was leaning on the bell and yelling at the top of his voice. The Adamses came out to see what was going on, and the Wises. I've never been so—'

She pushed past him, her heart missing a beat. Lejeune? DAVID? The description pretty much fitted him. No such luck; it was Gary Pride, gazing at her with all the betrayed loyalty of a whipped puppy.

'Hello, gel. Why didn't you call back?'

'Did you call me, Gary? I didn't get the message. Damn that girl of mine.' She busied herself taking off her raincoat. 'Would you like a drink?'

He made a retching noise. It was reassuring to see that even in his hour of loss and confusion he was as urbane as ever. 'Leave it out. I've had a fucking skinful.' He stood up, swaying. 'What I want – right now – is a guarantee that you'll get that little bender back for me.'

'There's nothing I'd like more, Gary.' Susan poured herself a large J&B. 'But I'm afraid I can't do that. Rupert is his own person.'

'Bollocks!' He belched. 'He's been brainwashed by the God Squad! Can't your paper do some investigative story on it – nap him back and de . . . deprogramme him?' He laughed. '*I'll* deprogramme him. With a fucking pickaxe handle!'

'That's the Moonies, Gary. You can't do that to a Christian.'

'Oh, no?' He smiled at her. 'Susan, gel, we're friends, aren't we?'

'I hope so, Gary.'

'Right. Now, you were very keen on me handling this little bender, as I remember. So keen that you offered to get me back Candy and her crew if I helped you – an offer I graciously didn't take up seeing as young Rupee was such a smash hit and that all *they* ever gave me was the pip. But Candy's a Pope property, which meant that Pope had to be getting something out of me making Rupee. I can't quite put my finger on what. But I'll tell you this for nothing, gel – I might be green, but I ain't grass-coloured. I saw that penitence routine young Rupee did – and all that stuff about people who seek to make trouble. Now I can't prove it, but I know you, Sue – and *you're* trouble. I'd say whatever young Rupee had been asked to do, he was asked by you.' Suddenly he looked sober, or was it just shrewd? 'Am I right?'

'Come now, Gary. We're both adults. What do you expect me to admit to?'

'I'm not sure. I haven't been thinking that clear. But pretty soon, I'm going to start thinking. I'm going to start thinking very hard if my time isn't occupied, know what I mean? The Devil finds work and all that.'

'I see.' Was she ever sick of saying that. Zero maintained that seeing the other man's point of view was the start of moral decline, and Susan was beginning to see what she meant.

'Yeah, the Devil finds work. It's true, that. Me, I'm a workaholic, you could say.' He was warming, like a hot toddy, to his subject. 'When I've got work to do, I don't give a damn what other people get up to, so long as they don't do it in the street and frighten the couriers. Live and let lech, I say.' He frowned. 'But when I'm forced to be idle . . . I don't know. Something happens. I come over all moral. I guess it's to do with me roots.' He threw back his shoulders. 'The English working class are a highly moral people.' This was a line left over from his prole pop-star days, Susan recognized dimly. 'And like . . . it's a morality thing with me. If I hear something that my supposed elders and betters are getting up to, I feel I've got a moral duty to pass it on to whom it may concern.' His eyes lost their spiritual cast and fastened on her greedily. 'Get my drift, gel?'

'I'm beginning to, Gary.' She most certainly was.

'I've been around, Sue, y'see? I especially been around that gaff in Lowndes Square with Candy some nights when the sister of 'ers has been nodding out. She's got a loose mouth on her, that Caroline, as well as everything else. And I've kept my head, when all around me were getting stoned out of theirs – that's Kipling, you know. Yeah, I've picked up a few things, sitting there drinking ponce-water when they've been getting smacked up to the gills.' He smiled. 'Are you receiving me, Sue?'

'I think so, Gary.'

'Right, then. That's settled. You know which side your croissant's buttered, gel. I'll lay it on the line: you got me Rupee, you can get him back. Or if not him – because to be frank, now the God Squad have got him, he'll never write another decent pop song again – then another one like him. Pop stars, they're all the same. Come and go. But you got an *eye* for talent.' He leered alarmingly. 'That's 'cos you're talent yourself. Fancy a bunk-up?'

'No, thank you,' she said primly. 'I have a boyfriend in the next room.'

'Suit yourself.' He stood up. 'But remember – I want some product and I want it *now*. I'm not planning on going back to being the world's forgotten boy in a hurry. Thanks, I'll let myself out.' He twinkled. 'I know my place.'

'Sure. Have them,' said Tobias Pope when she called him in Munich the next morning. 'Good thinking, girl – very

282

ecological, though I don't usually approve of the waste not want not line. Waste not, taste not is more like it. Still, if it's saving me money and trouble . . .' He thought for a minute. 'And why not take the darkie off my hands? He's a fucking pest and well past his best. Isn't there some sort of vogue in your quaint country for Negro crooners from the nineteen-sixties?'

She couldn't help laughing. 'Why, Mr Pope, you've been reading your *NME*!'

'It's my business to know things, madam. You'd be surprised at what I know.'

'Such as?'

'Well, I know that you're taking it down the throat from my son and heir as often as you can. I also know that said heir's bimbo fiancée has eaten more pussy than she has hot dinners.'

'Oh.' She was shocked. 'Well, doesn't good news travel fast?'

'It's no skin off my nose. You're all little insects to me. Just don't do anything stupid, that's all.'

'Like what?'

'Like fall in love and get married. I was married to a broad who did that. It ruins a woman.'

'I'll bear that in mind.'

'Heard anything more from the Commie germ?'

'No. I don't really think the *Jack Black Show* is on Joe Moorsom's agenda, Mr Pope. He's a very busy man.'

'He'll be busy dodging car-bombs if he uses this as an excuse to get back on my case.' He paused. 'I liked seeing you in New York.'

She was silent.

'I mean it,' he insisted. 'I know I laughed at your starry-eyed view of the skyline but the old neighbourhood has been known to affect the most intelligent of young moderns in that way. Anyway, I enjoyed it – it was the cerebral equivalent of having the soles of one's feet tickled by geisha. Good for the digestion.'

'Thanks a fucking *bunch*.'

He laughed. 'Anything you want from here? What a dump, like your delightful Birmingham with serious money. And their eating habits! They put pig in everything, even the finger-bowls, and as far as wine's concerned they bottle their own piss. The women probably have less idea of how to undress than anywhere else in the world, including Canada. Still, my secretaries tell me the shops are quite nice. Can I bring you anything?'

She couldn't resist it. 'Only yourself,' she husked, straight-faced. He was still laughing when she put the phone down, and she found she was smiling.

She automatically felt well-disposed towards anyone who could make her smile these days, anyone who could make her forget for a moment the name of her new constant companion: Fear.

Fear was with her all the time, since tea at Brown's Hotel.

After her initial burst of adrenalined insouciance, it had turned up early the next morning and stayed close to her ever since – shadowing her with all the silky skill of the new signing to Napoli. She woke up with a start at dawn, and the dawn chorus she heard was Fear, lying between herself and Matthew, happily humming the Lilliburlero – Fear was a stickler for tradition. Looking into the rear-view mirror of her morning cab, she saw Fear driving behind her – Fear drove a Jaguar, of course, and his bumper sticker read 'MY OTHER CAR IS A HEARSE'. And inside the *Best* building, absorbed in her morning paper, she sensed Fear from the corner of her eye as he got into the lift with a cheeky PING! Yet when she got out at her floor, the elevator was empty. Fear moved fast.

In her office, the serious Fear began. What had once been an altar to action, decision and dynamism had become a high-tech waiting-room: every phone call could be a diarist asking her if she would deny or confirm The Rumours, every messenger might be bearing proofs of the piece sent by Ingrid to taunt her, every strange man with a camera might be there to shoot her as opposed to taking orders from her. So when Kathy tapped on the door and came in carrying a large brown paper parcel, she was not her usual contender for the Perfect New Woman Boss title.

'Sue, this—'

'Kathy, what's that around your neck?'

Kathy's hand darted to the incriminating garland of small blue bruises.

'Is it some sort of state-of-the-art necklace from Lesley Craze? Or did someone jog your arm in the tube while you were trying to put on your eyeshadow?'

Kathy flushed. 'Sue, you know my boyfriend's in the Israeli army. He drives a tank. It's awful, we never get to see each other from one month to the next. And he's on leave—'

'And on heat, judging from the state of your neck. Really, Kathy – you're how old?'

'I'm twenty-five.'

'Well, take a tip from one who's been there – love bites don't look good on anyone over fifteen. They especially don't look good on a senior secretary and personal assistant who's angling to get an NUJ card sometime next year. Do you get my drift, Kathy?'

'Yes.'

'Right. Now for God's sake wear a high neck until your condition heals, or you can get a skin graft, or something. Or at least ask him to take his teeth out before he attacks you. You look as though you're auditioning for a white-collar remake of *Dracula*.'

'Right, Miss Street.' Kathy's soft West Country voice was cold and dull. 'Sorry, Miss Street.' She put the parcel on Susan's desk. '*This* just came by messenger.'

The door slammed, and Susan's sigh was almost as loud. She was behaving like a man, in the worst possible way – taking it out on her secretary, indeed! How low could you go? She'd be being rude to waiters next; real suburban middle-management slob stuff. And what a *nerve* she had, complaining about a few kosher love bites given in all good faith by a member of the Israeli Armed Forces – no wonder Kathy wore them like medals. And here *she* was, sitting with a *brand* on her head. And all because the lady *loves* ambition . . .

Wearily she reached for the parcel, automatically checking the SCANNED stamp in the corner. It wouldn't do to let herself get blown up just before the *Commentator* spread came out, would it? And spoil it for everyone . . .

A game of Monopoly lay on her desk, with a note on House of Commons paper. She picked it up.

SUSAN, LOOKS LIKE I'M BACK IN THE GAME AFTER ALL. I DON'T KNOW WHICH PIECE YOU WANT, BUT I'LL BET ON THE (UNDER) DOG EVERY TIME. REGARDS, JOE.

There was a noise from the corner of the room – a whispering. She didn't look up, but she knew straight away what had happened. Fear had found a friend.

'Beigebeat?' Gary Pride looked suspiciously at Candida Malaise across the table for four at the Dorchester. 'Whass that when it's at 'ome?'

Candida played with her treacle pudding, pouting. A summer in South Africa had not darkened or diminished her Poohsticks appeal. 'Washy, why don't *you* explain?' She giggled. 'I'm *so* stupid.'

'Don't call me Washy, girl.' Washington Brown sat back in his chair and looked around the grill room with stupefied satisfaction, as well he might considering that he had just finished a bottle of 1959 Margaux which Gary Pride had been forced to spring three hundred pounds for. He could smell success coming back down that lonesome trail, and he was well pleased by the aroma of it – even more so than with that of the steak and kidney pudding he had just demolished, complete with a side-dish of Branston pickle. 'Right . . . Beigebeat is the sound you get when black and white unite.' He closed his eyes. 'It's the cacophony of confidence underscored with a backbeat of suffering. It's agony and ecstasy. Chalk and cheese. Day and night. Put them together – and what you got yourself is Beigebeat.' He opened his eyes and smiled triumphantly at Candida.

On cue, she bounced in her chair. 'Washy, that's practically *poetry*!'

'*I'd* be fucking poetic on a bottle of *that* plonk,' muttered Gary to Susan.

'Isn't he great, Susie?' Candida squeezed Washington's gnarled hand. 'You're so lucky to have heard all his great stuff the first time around. Me, because I'm so silly and young, I had to search it all out! But it was worth it!' She gleamed at him. He glinted back. 'Isn't he *ace*?'

'Ace.' Susan looked at Washington suspiciously.

His eyes met hers with only a hint of mockery. 'Hey.'

He spread his hands, pantomiming his innocence. 'If your boyfriend wants to take me off ice, I got no quarrel with him. I'm just sick of sitting on my black ass by some bad swimming pool, is all, doing nothing but getting bedsores and chilblains from all that ice and idleness. And Candy feels the same. He wants to cut us loose, we can't be bothered to badmouth him? Whatchoo say, sweet Sue?'

'Can we really go, Susie?'

'You most certainly can.'

'And will you handle us, Gary? Like you did with Rupee?'

'It would be a pleasure,' said Gary graciously, but his eyes were hard. Hearing Gary try to talk when his mind was in this mode was like watching a pocket calculator trying to chew gum. His brain had been flicking through the index of pop trends over recent years, and had put one and one together and come up with the answer – megabucks. The biggest white acts were all trying to sound black and the biggest black acts were all trying to sound white. Duets were back. And of course, all the pop world loves a lover. Sensing a new twist, he looked at them slyly. 'You two having it away, then?'

Candida giggled. 'Gary! You'll always be an oik!'

'Hey, man.' Washington held up a shaky though still impressive finger. 'Speak like that again and I may just have to take that space-phone of yours and stick it where that sun don't shine. That's a lady you're talking about; one very *special* lady.'

'Sorry, mate. No hard feelings. Let me get you some fine port.' Gary clicked his fingers urbanely at a waiter and lowered his voice to Susan as Washington and Candida smooched over their dessert menus. 'Hear that? *Special lady*, my foot. When a spade calls a white chick a special lady, he's poking her. Law of nature. What d'you think? The new Sonny and Cher?'

'Which one's which?'

'Very funny. I got a name already – Coffee and Cream. What do you think?'

'How about Bubble and Squeak? Her temperament and his voice, by the time he's been through the wine list.'

'God, you're right. Got to start looking after my investment.' To the waiter who had materialized, he gave his order for Washington's drink. 'The gentleman would like warm water with a little honey.'

'Hey – I thought you said port.'

Gary patted his own throat reverentially. 'Your larynx, Mr Brown. Think of it as a temple. You wouldn't throw shit on the walls, would you?'

'What . . . well, I guess not.'

The light of mutiny died in Washington Brown's eyes, and he turned to smile at Candida. He was under new management and over the moon, no longer an angry man. One less bullet in the gun that Irving and Lejeune were holding to her head. Susan finished her white port with a slightly lighter mind.

'You're late,' said David Weiss from her Kioto chair with his feet on her Turbeville-Smith desk.

She closed the door and leaned against it. 'I know.'

'You're late and you're drunk.'

'Perk of the job. Like getting free drugs if you're a doctor.' She took off her raincoat. 'Can I sit down? I have work to do.'

'Suit yourself.' He got up. 'I just thought I'd warn you. I've seen the proofs of the *Commentator* story.'

'What? Where?'

'Your friend Miss Irving was kind enough to show them to me last night after a party at the Polish Club.'

'She had the proofs with her?'

'No. They were at her flat.'

'You went back to her flat with her?'

'Yes.'

She lunged at him, her nails out, aiming for his face.

He caught her wrist. 'Now you calm down at once or I'll slap you.'

'You stupid, evil, ugly prick, how COULD you?' she screamed.

'Would I be right in assuming that you believe I had carnal knowledge of Miss Irving?'

'You certainly fucking would, boy.' She glared at him. 'Why else would you go back to her place?'

'I told you. To see the proofs.' He let go of her. She rubbed her wrists resentfully. He sat back down, in the visiting chair this time. 'Susan, I would not consider sleeping with Miss Irving, or indeed any Englishwoman again, now knowing the depths of malice and duplicity they can habitually sink to. It's not *your* fault; you're a nation of spies, it's in the blood. I went home with Miss Irving – who, I think, was similarly under the impression that I was going to sleep with her – purely to see what she had on you in black and white.'

'Oh. I see.' Lying bastard. 'Well – what has she got?'

'The goods. There's a blow by blowjob account of an orgy from this Brazilian hooker. There was a guy in Sun City who saw you with my father, but he's withdrawn his statement. But they do have a killer photograph of the tattoo—' He leaned across the desk and brushed her fringe aside, staring at her forehead in disbelief and shaking his head. 'Christ, what a thing to do to yourself, Susan. Yeah, the photograph; you're getting out of a cab, and your bangs are blown to one side, and it's there in black and white, like a *Best* banner headline: SOLD. Long lens, hidden camera – whatever they used, they can take *that* to the bank.'

She groaned.

'Then there's a testimony from some dyke bartender in New York.' He looked away. 'That dive you filled me in on, I guess. All in all, one number it doesn't add up to is an editorship within a corporation who're currently engaged in proving what upright, uptight citizens they are. And of course, they've got Lejeune.'

'Him!'

'Come on – *we* thought he was newsworthy enough to put on the front page. He *was* playing the market cleverly with that weird mind of his. He's their ace in the hole; people believe *him*. I'll tell you, Susan, it's a salutary reminder just how far hacks have sunk in the public's esteem that they now have more respect for and faith in witch-doctors than journalists. A hooker and a dyke's testimonies, one or both of whom are highly likely junkies into the bargain – they're not worth the tape they're recorded on. But with *him* – he found those *bodies*, Susan. The police go to *him*, now. They call him Mr Lejeune.'

'I see.' She looked at him, wanted to run her tongue over his hair, his hands, his shiny black Church's shoes. 'When will they run it, do you know?'

'In three weeks' time.'

She looked him in the eyes. 'If you were me, what would you do?'

He stood up. 'I'd leave London. Pronto, Tonto. And I wouldn't bother to come back. You're finished in this town.' And with that, he closed the door on her dreams.

She went out into the street, and she walked until she was clear of the ghost town. Then she walked into an ordinary pub and sat with ordinary people and drank ordinary vodka. She had forgotten that it was possible to get drunk so cheaply – a double for the price of a glass of water in the bars and restaurants she had become used to. She thought of her parents. Their cheap drink, their cheap food, their cheap labour. Everything was cheap about the people she had come from, except their souls.

She drank until she was dizzy, got up and walked out. A man followed her; white, middle-aged, badly dressed. He put out his hand. She drew back and offered him her three-thousand-dollar Prada handbag. She felt beat.

He looked at her, shocked and appalled, and put up his hand. 'Taxi!' Slouched inside it, she saw him gazing at the vehicle in drunken, chivalrous dismay. She had forgotten what kindness looked like, and upon seeing it had recoiled, as though from an alien.

She got home, fell into bed. At four in the morning she was massively sick into the Practical Styling wastepaper basket beside the bed. Afterwards she lay there, tears running into her ears. She cried and asked theatrically, 'Why was I born, God?' Only she was so drunk she said 'Dog'. 'Oh Dog, how could you do this to me?'

Matthew woke up fractiously. 'We're not getting one, I told you. They moult. And Muggins here would have to clean up after it. Go back to sleep. You stink of drink.'

With Matthew on her case and tears on her pillow, she fell asleep. Her last thoughts before blackness were: all that ambition, all that work – all for nothing.

Then it was dawn and the phone was ringing. 'Dog?' she said stupidly into it.

'What? Stop babbling, girl. It's me. It's Zero.'

'Zero? Oh, it's so *late*.'

'Late it's not, girl. It's *early*. It's the dawn of the first day of your ninth life, bach. Constantine Lejeune's been shot, by a demented disciple, at a rally in Leeds last night. Susan, he's dead.'

SIXTEEN

'Mark Kemp's a clever bloke, and the *Commentator*'s skint – that combination always makes for wise editing, in my experience.' Bryan O'Brien lifted Susan off her feet and sat her on his desk. She blinked at him, surprised, and he smiled. 'Clever girl, having him offed!'

'Bryan! How can you say that?'

He winked. 'Your secret's safe with us, darling. Isn't it, Dave?'

David Weiss nodded reluctantly.

'Yes, from what I hear they're pulling the whole series now. Without their corpse-finder gimmick all they've got to take to the bank, and the libel lawyers, are the tall stories and grudge matches of assorted lowlife – a bit flimsy and downmarket, especially for the *Comm*. Face it, these girls will say anything for the price of an ounce.'

'Girls like Miss Soixante-Neuf, you mean?' put in David Weiss sarcastically.

Bryan flashed him a condescending smile. 'Oh no, Dave – that was legit. Public interest as well as human interest; ethics as well as morals. You remember the first rule of popular journalism from when you learned it at the school of hard knocks, don't you? – ethics is money and morals is sex. Our Lejeune scoop was an *ethics* story – the sex was a side-dish, as it were.'

'Well, you certainly didn't leave any on the side of your plate for Mr Manners, did you?'

Bryan sighed with infinite, weary patience. 'Dave. What sort of paper d'you think we're running here?'

'Well, Bryan.' David Weiss looked serious. 'I wish I could answer that without sounding rude. All I know is how I'd like the paper to *be*. You know that old Hays Office maxim from the Thirties about couples on beds keeping one foot on the ground at all times? That's what I'd like the *Best* to do. I know that people want escapism, and that they want a little sleaze too. But we shouldn't either have to be in the clouds with the royal family or in the gutter with Serena Soixante-Neuf all the time. I think we should try to keep one foot on the ground.'

'Suggestions?' If Bryan O'Brien had moved one more muscle, his set smile would have become a sneer.

David Weiss looked at Susan. 'Miss Street. When Anstey was editor, isn't it right that the *Best* was something of a campaigning paper?'

'In a modest way, yes. But Charles certainly didn't rule out anything that smelt of fun. He didn't think that if it tasted bad and bored you it was necessarily good for you – the take-your-medicine school of journalism.'

'I'm not *looking* to be one hundred per cent serious – you've got me wrong.' That note of exasperation which Susan had noticed came so quickly into American voices when they couldn't get their own way had crept into his. 'Keep the royal family. Keep the sleaze. But can't we have a little more *investigative* journalism? A little more *campaigning* journalism? Are those the only words too dirty for newspapers these days?'

' 'Course not, Dave. You're absolutely right, mate.' He turned to Susan. 'Sue, I want a big investigative piece on how many Page Three girls aren't getting it regularly. And then we'll run a big crusading campaign to match them up with eligible young royal blokes – Edward, Linley and the gang.' He smiled at David. 'That the sort of thing you wanted, Dave?'

Their only answer was the slam of the door.

'Look at me, I'm Sandra Dee,' said Bryan and they laughed. '*He's* a bundle of fucking laughs these days. Needs a good seeing to.'

She shrugged. 'Not my job.'

'Can you believe its front? Waltzes in here from a *book publishers* and tells *me* how to run a newspaper. ME! Fucking colonials.'

Susan laughed. '*You* say *that?*'

'Ah, it's true. The Aussie hates the Pom until the Yank butts in. Then you see what we've got in common.'

'Such as?'

'Seeing things on the slant. Whereas they come barging in like a bull in a china shop. Thinking that so long as the bull wears a white hat it doesn't matter if everything gets smashed to buggery. Look, you know and I know, despite the difference in our ages and backgrounds, that a lot of popular journalism is a joke. But the readers *know* it's a joke, and they know that Brit papers tell that joke better than any other popular press in the world. They laugh *with* us when we tell the joke and they laugh *at* us when we get our asses sued. Either way they get the last laugh. But a Yank can't see that. He thinks we're putting one over on the poor buggers. Why does he think they buy the bloody thing, because we're at the newsstands with cattle prods? They love being lied to. It makes them feel important.'

'They place a lot of importance on telling the truth over there, Bryan,' Susan said, getting to her feet. 'Wee Georgie Washington and the cherry tree. Nixon murdering all those poor people by proxy in Indochina and then getting the sack for telling a fib. They've got a passion for honesty.'

'Mmm. That's a bastard, isn't it? Talking of which, your pal Moorsom plans to come back with a bang this afternoon. Andrew called from the lobby. He's tabled another question.'

'Oh dear.' She sat down.

'Never mind.' He gave her a smile she couldn't quite decode. 'This honesty . . . you can't catch it from toilet seats, can you?'

Very soon she saw the announcement in the *Independent*:

Mr W. Z. Brown
and Miss C. M. Malaise
The engagement is announced between Washington Zebedee, son of the late Mr C. Brown and the late Mrs H. Brown of Louisville, Kentucky and Candida Maud, younger daughter of Colonel A. and Lady Sasha Malaise of Somerset.

Not long after that she turned on the television to see the upper-class white girl of twenty and the battered black man of forty-five sing a smoochy, saccharine shadow of a soft soul song called 'Born Again Beige', a hymn to the healing power of love which the pampered girl and the calloused man sang with such conviction that a sentimental Western world wept long and hard enough to turn the record from plastic to platinum.

And not long after that, Susan received the wedding invitation from Truslove & Hanson at Sherratt and Hughes, announcing a quiet civil ceremony at Chelsea Town Hall, brought forward to accommodate Coffee and Cream's forthcoming European tour.

Candida, radiant in black, and Washington, ridiculous in white, greeted her warmly that Saturday morning.

'Hey, Suze.' Washington looked like the black panther who had got not just the cream but the milkmaid, every well-fed white inch of her.

'Hello, Washington. Congratulations on your record.'

He shrugged happily. 'Just beginner's luck.'

'Washy, don't *say* things like that!' Candida flung herself at Susan. 'Hi, Susie!'

'You look lovely, Candida.'

'D'you think so?' She peered down at herself, squeezed into a boned black dress. 'Hyper Hyper. I've come to the conclusion that it's silly to spend a lot on clothes. I can't *believe* I was such a little breadhead when you first met me – remember? Lindka Cierach frocks, the Café de Paris, Fuck U – it all seems like such a long time ago!' She giggled. 'Now all I care about is making music and fucking Washy!'

'Language,' said Washington automatically. 'That's no way for a special lady to talk on her wedding day.'

'Are your parents here?'

'Oh no. Listen Susie, this is really funny. I told them I was marrying a black man and they were really sweet. And then I told them I was planning to wear a black wedding dress! They freaked! Refused to come. See, they don't care

302

what you do as long as you remember protocol. And a black wedding dress is not protocol. But we're going down to stay at their new place in Somerset for our honeymoon, before we go on the road. We had to sell our seat, you know. To *Americans*.'

'Yes, Caroline told me.'

'Sue!' Gary Pride, who was doing business as usual, broke off from a bullying phone call and made a thumbs-up sign. 'Dig you later!'

'Is Caroline here?'

'She's over there.' Candida pointed, frowning.

' 'Scuse us, Susie. We must mingle.'

Susan turned to look for Caroline and saw a shadow instead. The radiant blonde of the early Eighties soft-focus skinflicks, the hothouse hybrid of Diana and Deneuve was gone, replaced by an ageing waif in a rumpled houndstooth Chanel suit. Her hair was chopped short and ragged, and she was living proof that you can be too thin. She was leaning against a wall, warily and wearily observing the wedding preparations.

Susan walked over to her. 'Hello, Caroline.'

'Oh, hi.' Caroline pulled nervously at her fringe. 'Haven't seen you in yonks. How are you?'

'Fine. Working hard. How are you?'

'Not fine. Not working hard.' Caroline laughed. 'But I'm sure you'd deduced that already. Been seeing much of Tobes?'

'I've only seen him once since we had lunch.'

'But I bet he calls you up a lot, wherever he is.'

'I spoke to him in Munich recently.'

'I spoke to him recently, too. Last week.'

'Oh?'

'Yes.' Caroline lit a cigarette with shaky hands. Susan didn't remember her smoking. 'I'm going to tell you this story, just so you'll know what kind of man you're dealing with. I picked up the phone one morning, and his first words were: Caroline, it's me. Listen. I could have got a lackey or a lawyer to do this, but as we've known each other for so many years I thought you deserved better. A more human approach. So I'm telling you myself; pack your things and be out of the flat by Friday. Post the keys through the letterbox. So I said, Why, Toby? And he said, I wish you hadn't asked that, but because we've known each other so long I'll do you the courtesy of telling you. The reason I want you out is that I need a thirty-year-old junkie with no visible means of support like I need cancer of the rectum. Goodbye.' Caroline looked at Susan both triumphantly and defeatedly. 'What do you think of *that*? – that's his idea of the human touch.'

What Susan thought was that if Caroline had welched on her side of the bargain – which had been presumably that she would be the perfect London mistress of a millionaire and that he would support her accordingly – then she deserved nothing better, and to look at her, welched on it royally she definitely had done. But she knew this sort of thinking was highly unsound and masculinist, and she tried to think of a sympathetic comment – 'That bastard!' or 'Men!' But all that came out, true to form, was, 'Have you got any money?'

'A bit, I s'pose. A couple of thou left in trust. But nothing serious – it's all in here.' She rubbed her left arm resignedly. 'I'm staying with a friend in Clapham – she was an actress too but she married a racing driver. Now they're divorced and she's trying to bring up a kid alone. *He's* legged it to Lanzarote. I have to sleep on the sofa and babysit in lieu of rent while Camilla goes out on cattle calls.' She shook her head quickly. 'It's *so* depressing, I can't tell you.'

Susan thought. 'Can't you go back to your parents for a bit?'

Caroline sniggered. 'Oh, *yah*. It's really easy to score in Somerset. I mean, you can just walk into a field and pick it – like scrumping for apples when you're little. It grows on trees, dontcha know?' She sighed exaggeratedly. 'Of *course* I can't go to the country.'

'Caroline, I don't want to sound like a girl-guide leader. But surely the first thing you want to do to get your life back on track is lose your habit?'

'What?' Caroline looked confused, then thoughtful. 'Well, no, actually. I don't think I do.'

'What do you mean?' Though her expression remained concerned and sympathetic, Susan was coming to believe more with each minute that Tobias Pope had his head screwed on, not least of all where Caroline Malaise was concerned.

'Well – I haven't put it into words before, but I'll try. It's like – if I kicked the habit, I don't think I'd exist any more. I shoot up therefore I am. If I wasn't a junkie, what would I say at parties when people ask me what I do? I'm not an actress. I'm not a mistress. I'm not even a housewife. I'm just a thirty-year-old woman with a past and no future.' She shook her head determinedly. 'No, I'm not giving up junk. If I do I'll disappear.'

'Well, I don't know what to say.' She did, but it was very rude.

'You could offer me a job.' Caroline almost smiled.

'I'm sorry. It's not that easy.'

'OK.' She made a show of gathering her gloves, lighter and bag together. Her hands were still shaking. 'I understand. But you don't know how lucky you are, coming from where you did. You had everything: poverty, provincialism, no friends in high places. Everything to kick against. Me, I had nothing except what was given to me on a plate. That's why you're on the bus and I'm under the wheels.'

Susan thought that this analysis was a little blurred around the edges, but she let it pass. 'Didn't you ever have an ambition, Caroline?'

'Me?' She paused, pulling on a short, dirty white glove. 'No, I had money instead. The great thing about ambition is that it doesn't depreciate or end up in your arm: it's much more bankable in the long term. Well, shall we join the wedding party?'

Susan looked at Candida, sashaying into the register office on the arms of Washington Brown and Gary Pride. The three of them were chattering loudly in their comically differing accents – upper-class English, black American Southern and Cockney. They sounded like an idea for a sitcom. But somehow, the three voices were made eerily alike by the same note of satisfaction and anticipation in each.

'Look at them,' said Caroline softly. 'A few months ago they were ready and willing to blow Pope's brains out. If he walked in now, they'd pat him on the back and ask him to be best man. How fast the happy forget.'

As the plane touched down, Tobias Pope looked up from his papers and wondered for a moment where he was. Rio, Munich, London? Sonya, Sigrid, Susan? He hoped it was London.

It was, the weather assured him as he stepped out of the plane, descending the steps slowly with a tall black twin either side of him. When one of his best bodyguards had died after falling out of a window into an empty swimming pool during a crack party in a Sun City hotel, the chance of getting two perfect physical specimens for the price of one had been irresistible.

And the twins were as quick on the draw as they were on the erection, as good at fighting as they were at fucking. He laughed, thinking of Susan's face when she recognized them. He had his line ready: 'But my dear – I thought you said that matt black went with everything!'

Thinking up little teases for a girl – he must be going soft in his old age. But she was worth making an effort for. He liked her. And her impenetrability was the one thing which titillated him these days. He had other girls whom he placed in situations, a pawn in every port, and liked to watch, but afterwards they went all quiet and morose. They got what he thought of as 'the guilts', a virus like flu. Catholic girls were the worst for that. They usually ended up taking various sorts of sordid drugs because they 'couldn't live with' themselves. Fair enough. *He* couldn't live with them either. But drug-taking women were so messy and unappealing. For one thing, they stopped enjoying the sex, the banquet of flesh he placed before them. Then they had outlived their usefulness.

Some talked about respect and how he didn't have any for them. He didn't. But not because of what they chose to do with their genitalia. He hadn't respected his wife, and she'd been a virgin. He hadn't respected Caroline and she, despite her habit of shedding her clothes before cameras, had been a faithful girlfriend whom he had never involved in any of his tableaux. He didn't respect Sigrid and Sonya, who were by now more or less whores. But the chastity or promiscuity of these women hadn't come into why he didn't respect them; he didn't respect them because they were *soft*.

Susan was hard. Beneath the satin abundance of skin and hair, it was like biting on silver foil; you couldn't get through. He put her into situations which would have curdled the blood of any normal white woman and she didn't just endure them to please him, as the others did; she *took* the situation away from him and turned it towards her own pleasure. He had never known that before. It was a challenge. But one day . . . one day she'd break. And that would be the greatest thrill of all. Then, and only then, he'd fuck her. And then he would be free of her.

Pope turned to Warren. 'OK, boy?'

Warren smiled back frankly. 'I've never been to London, sir. Lots of pretty girls, right?'

'The prettiest,' said Pope with a surge of misplaced patriotism. 'The finest women in the world. As yours are the finest men.'

'Thank you, boss,' said Warren, bowing.

Pope laughed. The boy was being sarcastic; he had spirit, and a sense of humour. Even that hellhole he'd grown up in hadn't bashed it out of him. Unlike that po-faced bastard *he'd fathered*. Pope thought of his son and frowned. His mother's son, all right.

A thought hit him. Wouldn't it be a great joke – a *black* joke! – to leave Pope Communications to this illiterate darkie from shanty town when he died? He could just see the look of horror on David's face, and Maxine's when they got through the layers of tranquillizers. They'd soon stop their liberal crap then; they'd soon start talking about *schvartzes* like the bigoted bourgeois German Jews they were at heart. He laughed again, and turned to Warren to share the joke as they reached the bottom of the steps.

But before he could open his mouth, a shot rang out. And Tobias Pope hit the ground.

SEVENTEEN

'Yes, I have this man to thank for my life,' said Tobias Pope, standing up and reaching across the aisle to slap Warren on the back yet again.

'Well, I'm glad I know who to blame,' said Susan moodily. He hadn't told her where they were going, and she was mildly annoyed.

'He'd pushed me down and blown Montes's head off before you could say Wetback,' went on Pope admiringly.

'Congratulations.'

'Always aim to please, miss.' Warren twinkled at her.

'What did this man Montes have against you anyway, Mr Pope?' She wondered if he'd tell her the truth.

He shrugged. 'The outraged papa bit: very big in Lat Am. Some silly girl I asked to a couple of parties – she got a liking for cocaine and fell in with a bad crowd. Bought the building in some gang war crossfire. They bring it on themselves, these girls, they really do. Drugs. Messiness. Silliness.'

'I saw Caroline last week.'

'Oh yes? And is her career as a screen siren progressing apace?'

'That's hardly likely, now she's thirty.'

'No, Susan. That's hardly likely now she's a *drug addict*. Which I certainly did not encourage her to become. On the contrary.'

Susan looked out of the window. 'I don't think it was very conducive to staying off drugs, just waiting around a flat for your boyfriend to visit you once a month.'

Pope sighed. 'Susan. I never *asked* Miss Malaise to do that. When I met her she was a film actress. A bad one, but a film actress. When I started paying the rent on her flat, I presumed she would continue to be a film actress. I didn't know she was going to throw in the make-up towel and give me a poor imitation of a mad housewife giving away the best years of her life, now did I?' He looked thoughtful. 'I've been meaning to ask you something. Do you think I'm a New Man?'

She turned and looked at him, incredulous. 'What?'

'A New Man. I've been seeing things about them in some of my publications. See women as equals, want women to enjoy sex, want women to work and be tough. All that jazz. Don't respect women who are chaste and don't despise women who are whores.' He preened. 'I think that's a perfect description of my personal self. Yes, I'm definitely a New Man.'

She fell against his shoulder, laughing helplessly, her bad mood gone. He put his arm around her and pointed at the window. 'Look.'

The sky was red, like a delight or a warning or both. 'Where are we?'

He pushed her away, straightened up and smiled. 'We're in Bangkok, Susan. Where else?'

In the master bedroom of the suite at the Hotel Oriental, the girl looked at Susan. She was tall for a Thai, a few inches under six foot, but with the distinctive skin; skin only marginally less golden than Shirley Eaton's in *Goldfinger*. She had long slender limbs and long, dark, heavy hair cut in a fringe; her eyes were delicately slanted and unusually pale. She was probably Amerasian, though she wore the traditional Thai woman's national dress: a shiny black monokini and high black heels.

Susan turned away from the mirror and looked at Tobias Pope. 'Will I do?' she asked sarcastically. 'Do I need contact lenses? Liposuction? A lobotomy?'

'Who'd know the difference?' He looked over his copy of *Fortune* at her. 'You look great. Too beautiful, in fact. Thai women are too short, and most of them are titless wonders. They aren't actually the raving beauties that the maladjusted men who frequent them make out. Sure, they look pretty good if no white woman has given you a tumble in ten years, and of course the Elephant Man himself could find a girlfriend out here if he had the spending cash. But basically they're for men who want boys or children or both.' He yawned. 'And, of course, they're basically very *decent* girls, which is always unattractive in a woman to any red-blooded man. The majority of them won't suck cock, for instance. They say it's a crime against Buddha.'

'I thought they did everything. Can I put my raincoat on now?'

'No, you won't be dry for another ten minutes. Also your nipples are the wrong colour. Sungita, see to it. No, everything but. That's why they have these fancy routines, pulling strings of razor blades and Pershing ground-to-air missiles out of their twats. To distract from the lack of blowjobs. Personally, I know what I prefer.' He put down his magazine. 'What do you say, Sungita? Take your hands off that white woman and answer me.'

The chic Thai girl in the black smock was pouting fiercely with concentration as she put the finishing touches of brown body make-up to Susan's nipples with a small brush. She had already applied the golden all-over tan with a small damp sponge, and artfully attached the liquid plastic at the temples to Chinese the eyes. Now she smiled at Tobias Pope, politely rather than flirtatiously. 'Thai girls always pleased to see friends from West.'

'You like us *farangs*, Sungita? Why's that? Our pasty skins?

314

Our paunches? Our hairy legs? Drives you women crazy, does it?' He smiled slyly. 'Or is it our dollars, our *deutschmarks* and our *yens*?'

Sungita laughed. 'I personally am married Thai man.' She began to pack away her brushes. 'I finish. I go?'

'Yes. Beautiful job. My man outside will settle. I've told him to give you one hundred American dollars. Make sure he does.'

Overcome, Sungita left the room backwards and bowing. Susan watched her go.

'Hey big spender,' she said sarcastically.

'You may mock. But I could fuck her for five dollars. As a gentleman and a hygienist, I prefer not to. Have you heard of Vietnam Rose?'

'What's that? Disinformation with discharge?'

'Nearer than you think. It's a vile Oriental venereal disease whereby one's organ turns outward, like a rose, and one urinates as from a watering-can.'

'And they said romance was dead. Can I put my raincoat on now?'

'Relax, I've seen it all before. Come and sit down.' He patted the sofa beside him and looked petulant. 'We never talk any more.'

'You sound like a wife.' She sat beside him on the paisley *eau de nil* satin sofa, an Oriental idea of English restraint.

'Is it any wonder I sound like a wife when all you're interested in is that career of yours?'

The satin was slippery against her high gloss monokinied behind.

'It's your career as well, Mr Pope.'

'Tobias.'

'I can't call you Tobias.'

'Why not?'

'It's a . . . it's a silly name.'

'You see? Always an insult. That's why men come here – it's the last capital of conceit for Western man, the last bastion of an illusion that women have trampled all over in their stilettos. Here, men can kid themselves that the girls don't do it just for the money – I've actually had smart men say this to me – but because they love Western cock. Like hell they do. They leave school at twelve, or they're refugees, or they're sold by their families. But one reason they certainly don't do it is because they love their work.' He rolled *Fortune* into a tight tube and rapped her smartly on the nipples with it. 'Unlike you, madam.'

'Don't, you'll smudge me.'

'You wish. Yes, prostitution is prostitution – it's shit work, like cleaning out sewers. No one who had an option would do it. Your thick Westerner says it's in the blood of Thai women, to fuck like rabbits – garbage. It's an economic thing, as straightforward and unerotic as *that*. You look at your middle-class and upper-class Thai women – do they fuck like rabbits? Do they hell – they don't even fuck their husbands unless they say please. The poor fuck for money because they're poor, not because they like it, in every country. And these girls are less suited to it than most – they're a very religious people, like all stupid peasants.'

'Aren't they supposed to smile rather a lot? Maybe that's what gives Westerners a false impression.'

He sighed at her stupidity. 'Of *course* they smile. *You'd* smile if you were one step away from the gutter and you saw your next meal coming. Not to mention the next bowl of rice for your family back in the country. That smile hides a thousand frustrations. It's a mask. But we like it, because we know our own prostitutes too well. We've seen the repulsive fly-on-the-wall documentaries: we know they hate fucking us, we know they're all dykes and junkies because they hate it so much. We know their heartaches better than we know those of our own wives. And that's not the biggest aphrodisiac in the world, especially for the inadequate geeks who come out here. Here they can still pretend that the hookers are happy. They're not, of course – just foreign. Which often seems the same thing to stupid fucking Westerners.'

The windows were open, and across the balcony came the smell of incense and sweat mingled with the sound of wind-chimes, tuk-tuks and disco music. She pulled on her raincoat and walked out through the French windows, shivering.

'Hot to trot, my dear?' Pope called from the sofa. 'You should pardon the vulgarism. We Americans, you know.'

'Just restless. And nervous.'

317

He came up behind her. She felt his sinewy hands on her neck, an attempted murder disguised as a massage, and he briefly removed one to gesture at the sparkling city.

'Look at it. Thailand was practically the only South East Asian country never to be colonized. Too clever, they thought. And now it's the world's brothel. Too clever by half, I'd fucking say. There's a lesson there, young lady.'

'Which is?' She leaned back against him. In a way, he was home in a strange land. She knew his methods, and his madness. She couldn't be mad at him.

'You have to lose control to gain control.'

'Which fortune cookie did you get that out of, Mr Pope?'

'Very funny.' He gestured again. 'But look. Ten million people on a mud flat. Every time someone flushes a toilet it sinks down a centimetre. And talking of toilets, there's half a million whores in Bangkok and not one orgasm per night between them. There's a madam in this town, a charming woman – earned twenty million dollars from bars and massage parlours. One night over cocktails at the Embassy, I asked her the secret of her success. She threw back her charming head – and she had a chignon that my wife *never* got quite right – laughed and said, "I run the greatest acting school in the world." There you go – straight out of the whore's mouth.'

'I see.' Looking too long at the city lights had made her dreamy and docile. Neon – that was what modern female hormones reacted to, *not* testosterone

He put his hands on her shoulders, turned her round,

opened her raincoat and looked at her. 'You look wonderful. And you're going to have a great time.' He laughed, closing her coat and buttoning it paternally. 'Just think, when you're up there on that stage tonight, you're going to be the only girl in town not faking an orgasm.'

The Faster Pussycat Go-Go Bar's exterior was pink, Susan noted, as she alighted from the tuk-tuk, reeling from the mingled scents of orchids and open sewers. But inside the air was blue, as men in the uniforms of the US Marines ordered their drinks and girls for the evening. Girls were everywhere: beautiful and plain, tall and small, aged from fifteen to around thirty. Many of them wore what looked like National Health spectacles, giving their bikinis and high heels a look of perverse respectability.

'Come, my dear.' Tobias Pope made for a door marked PRIVATE. Susan followed him. A tall, dark Marine, the only handsome man in the room, caught her by the wrist.

'Hey, sexy girl. You want drink? Sit down and take your coat off.'

She shook her head and broke away.

'Can't you wait till we get inside the door?' Pope laughed. He rapped smartly three times, then opened the door. Susan followed him inside.

A woman of middle age, her hair short and blue-black, her dress a high-necked, black and skintight satin cheongsam, was standing behind a large desk. She came out from behind it now, holding her hand out to Pope. She displayed an expensive pair of French court shoes and ridiculously good legs; her figure was unimpeachable. She reminded Susan, in both luscious looks and dry manner, of Maria in the New York dyke bar – Pope obviously had a series of such managerial madams stashed all around the world.

'Monsieur Pope!'

'*Enchanté*, madam.' He kissed her hand respectfully. 'You look excessively well. And business?'

'Business is always good.' Her English was clipped, high and excellent. She looked at Susan. 'Is this your friend?'

'Yes. Open your coat, Susan, and let madam set what you're hiding in there.'

Susan felt her face burn. She closed her eyes and held her coat open, feeling like a flasher. She could feel the woman's eyes stabbing into her like the cold steel implements of a surgeon.

'Hmm.' The woman nodded. 'Very good. Very, *very* good.' She walked back to the desk and picked up a telephone. 'Hello? Yes. Will you send Oon in, please? Thank you so very much.' She replaced the receiver.

'Oon's still here?' Tobias Pope raised his eyebrows. 'Wasn't she going to marry that Australian dentist and live a life of suburban bliss in Sydney?'

'Ah, she got bored. She came back within eight weeks. She's the one girl I have who really loves her work. For Oon it's a vocation, not a job. Like being a nun.' The woman sat on the desk and smiled at Susan. 'So you have a fantasy to be a bar dancer for a night.'

Was that what the lying prick had told her? 'Yes.'

'OK. I take it you can't do any tricks?'

'Tricks?'

'Have you ever pulled a string of razor blades out of your vagina? Can you smoke cigarettes with your anus?'

'Sorry. There wasn't much call for that sort of thing where I came from.'

Pope and the woman laughed. 'Have you ever been fucked by a donkey?'

Her stomach plummeted. 'No. Never.'

'Well, you're out of luck tonight. Our donkey died last week and we haven't bought a new one yet.' The woman lit a black Sobranie. 'The girls are climbing up the walls. OK. I'll buy it. You don't need tricks, I have Oon for that. You have a good body and I take it you can dance?'

'Yes.'

'Right. You'll do.'

There was a knock on the door. It opened and a girl stepped soundlessly into the room.

She was genuinely and undeniably beautiful, the Thai dream girl that Westerners seek and so very rarely find. She looked like a model for some Oriental airline, with waist-length, poker-straight black hair, delicately slanted eyes and classic, almost Western features. She was pale gold all over, wearing white slingback high heels and a white bikini bottom.

'We meet again, Oon,' said Tobias Pope. He sounded almost lustful.

'Sure,' said Oon, She had an unusually low voice for a Thai. She looked questioningly at the woman in black.

'Oon, a favour if you please. This young lady wishes to join you for the night's entertainments. Will you take her under your wing?'

'Sure.' She turned to Susan. 'Wanna come and make up?' She had a slight American accent.

'Go along, my dear.' Pope held the door open and ushered them through. 'I'll leave you in Oon's very capable hands and see you in about fifteen minutes.'

'Will you be in the club?'

He pointed upwards. 'Walls have ears, my dear, but ceilings have eyes. There's a two-way mirror above the stage. Madam and I will be up there. I'll be watching over you the whole time. Like God.'

The woman in black laughed, went over to a cabinet and took out a bottle of whisky. Tobias Pope closed the door behind them.

'This way,' said Oon. They passed through a hot, narrow corridor to a small room lined with mirrors and hung with clothes. 'You English?'

'Yes.'

'I've always wanted to go to London. I really like your pop groups. Curiosity Killed The Dog.'

'Cat.'

'Cat. I like the Police too.' She lowered her lids and looked at Susan with a parody of lust. 'That Sting. I'd like to eat out his asshole.'

'I'm sure he'd be very flattered. Why don't you come to England?'

'Ah, it's too far. I've just come back from Oz. I married this guy. I thought it might be quite like England. But it sucked.'

'You speak great English.'

'I only go with Aussie and American guys. We all have our own speciality. Lots of girls go with the Germans and Japanese. Often they've got more money. But the Germans are fat and the Japanese are short. Most bar girls don't really like fucking. But I do. I'd rather be with a good-looking guy who can fuck than some rich ugly German.' She sat on a dressing table and fumbled in her purse, pulling out a cigarette. 'Thai stick – want some?'

'I'd love some. I feel quite nervous.'

'It's OK.' She lit up and inhaled deeply. 'You like to fuck?'

'Yes.'

'Then it's no problem. Lots of Thai girls, they don't like to fuck. For them it's a problem.'

Susan sat down next to her and accepted the reefer, holding down the smoke until she spluttered. But the calming, euphoric effect was almost immediate.

Oon handed her a glass of water. 'Let's have a look at you.'

Susan let the raincoat fall from her shoulders.

'Mmm!' Oon inhaled and bounced enthusiastically. 'Fantastic! Is that a tan or make-up?'

'Make-up. Will the men realize I'm not Thai?'

'Oh, don't worry. They won't be looking at your face. They'll be *sitting* on it.' Oon laughed, bitterly but with a kind of lustful relish. She pushed a tray of cosmetics at Susan. 'You're welcome to share these if you've left yours behind. Red lipstick, lots of eyeliner.'

'Thanks.' Susan took another lungful of Thai stick and selected a red lipstick.

Oon got up, smoked the last of the reefer and put it out. Picking up a hairbrush, she stood behind Susan and began to groom her. 'OK, here's the schedule. We go onstage and dance to a couple of records. Then we take off our pants. You keep dancing, I do my act. Then we make love together. Then guys come up and fuck us. OK with you?'

'OK.' She felt dreamy and distant. 'Do we have any choice in the men?'

Oon shrugged. 'First come, first served.'

'We can't pick them?'

'Why? See someone you like?'

'There's a Marine out there . . . tall, dark. Looks a bit like Michael Douglas.'

'Oh, *him*. That's Italian Johnny. He's great. He's a fantastic fucker. OK, I get him for you. Though that means I get his short friend Vinnie. They go everywhere together.' Oon sighed good-naturedly. 'OK. As it's your first night.'

'Only night.'

'You might like it, you never know. You might decide to stay. Wait a minute. Open mouth.' The Thai girl put down the hairbrush and blasted Susan with Mint Spot from a small aerosol. 'Don't want you to stink when I kiss you.' She smiled mischievously and pinched Susan's nipple, hard. 'Come on. It's show time.'

The small stage was a catwalk, running down the middle of the room. As Susan and Oon stepped out on to it, disco music began to play – Anita Ward singing 'Ring My Bell'.

Oon whispered, 'You stay this end, I go other. Just keep dancing till I come to you. Good luck.'

She felt both calm and mildly excited as she began to dance dreamily, straight-backed and on the spot. Oon was more energetic, waving her arms above her head and kicking her legs; obviously she had learned to dance from Americans, Susan thought smugly. Men were drifting at a rate of knots from the bar to the stage, looking up with frank, interested lust at what appeared to be the two beautiful near-naked dancing Thai girls. The bar girls on their arms looked bored, allowing their façades to slip for a moment while the attention of their meal-tickets was temporarily distracted.

Susan saw the tall, dark American shouldering his way to the stage, casually shaking off the two bespectacled bar girls who clung to him as if they were flies. Italian or not, he looked enough like David Weiss to make her throat contract and her mouth water. The other men were disgusting – she wouldn't touch them with Ingrid Irving's. But with him . . .

She and Oon were by far the most beautiful girls in the bar, she decided; this fact, and the Thai stick, and Oon's friendship, and the presence of the tall American combined to make her feel good. She began to move a little less dreamily; she began to grind her hips, shaking her long, dark hair back from her breasts. A Marine whooped appreciatively and flicked beer at her. Oon flashed her a grin of approval. She threw back her head, looked up at the ceiling and smiled wryly for the eyes of Tobias Pope. He'd done it again. Or had she?

The music changed – 'Shaft' by Isaac Hayes. Oon was pulling off her bikini bottom and lying down on the stage. The crowd strained forward, or rather the thirty or so men in the crowd did. The girls remained immobile; Susan saw one of them yawn openly and raise her eyebrows at a friend. Obviously they had seen whatever Oon was going to do a thousand times before.

Oon parted her legs, and pulled out a string of razor blades. The men cheered. The razor blades were followed by five ping-pong balls, spat into the crowd as if from a machine. More cheering. Susan danced on, amazed.

Someone placed an unopened Coke bottle on the stage. Oon stood up, put it between her legs and then triumphantly brandished it in the air, fizzing and foaming. Incredibly she had removed the top without using her hands.

What does she do for an encore? thought Susan, dazedly – pull out the Empire State Building? But no. Oon was scrabbling in her discarded bikini briefs for cigarette and matches. She got on her hands and knees, lit a cigarette, stuck it into her anus – sticking boldly in the audience's faces – and smoked it down to the butt, in both senses. The crowd went wild and she jumped to her feet, grinning and bowing quickly two ways.

The music changed – 'Love Hangover' by Diana Ross. Oon beckoned to Susan, who walked as if in a dream down the catwalk to her. They faced each other and embraced. Oon fell to her knees and removed the shiny black monokini. The Marines had gone dead quiet. Susan stood there in her stilettos as Oon parted her vaginal lips and began to suck her clitoris.

I'm getting a blowjob, Susan thought surreally. I thought Thai girls didn't do that. She stroked Oon's head, winding the long heavy hair around her hands. If they were alone, she knew she could get into it. As it was, the presence of the paying public was something of an inhibitant. Thoughts of the orgy in Rio, the twins in Sun City and the dykes in Manhattan flitted through her mind; it wasn't group sex she objected to, it was lack of audience participation.

Oon was whispering, 'Am I pleasing you?'

'Yes,' she whispered back. But it was only half true. Oon was beautiful and good, but far too gentle for her. Guiltily she fell to her knees and took Oon in her arms, kissing her as she pushed her backwards on to the floor. She slid down between her legs and found her clean, silky and sweet to the tongue. Oon's narrow hips thrust up and she began to wail loudly. *Someone's* having a good time, thought Susan, sarcastically but without rancour.

Oon shrieked and then was still. As Susan lay between her legs, panting for breath, the crowd cheered and threw their hats in the air. When the noise subsided, Oon sat up and stared down challengingly from the stage.

'Who wants to fuck my friend and me?'

You'd have thought, as Susan said later to Zero, that she'd been offering the last place in her nuclear shelter just as the three-minute warning was going off. There was a roar as the men pressed forward, waving their hands and hats in the air. Susan thought they looked like a bunch of little boys waiting for the teacher to give them permission to go to the lavatory. Which, in a sense, they were.

Only the tall, dark American didn't move. He stood there, leaning silently on the stage, and as she looked at him he smiled slowly. Fear that Oon might forget her request made her brave, and she sat up quickly, pointed at him and squeaked in what she hoped was a Thai voice, 'You.'

He vaulted up on to the stage, knelt down, grabbed her and kissed her. His haste reminded her of a TV film she'd seen of American housewives with just two minutes to get around a hypermarket and pile as much loot as they could into their trolleys. Maybe he had to get back to his ship; but anyway, he wasn't one to mess about. He was hustling her on to all fours, unbuttoning himself, pulling on a condom and mounting her.

He wasn't exactly built to Davie Weiss dimensions and there was no pretending he was, but he was strong, clean and thick and he felt good. She smiled and threw back her head, moving with him.

'Feels good, huh, sexy girl?' he whispered.

She nodded quickly, not trusting her accent. Out of the corner of her eye she saw Oon, kneeling before a short, light-haired man who was obviously the less-favoured Vinnie, every boy's mandatory Ugly Best Friend.

Behind her, the Marine was making noises which sounded ominously like the ones men make when they're about to come. She closed her eyes, trying to concentrate on the matter in hand – or somewhere – and ride in on his coat-tails. But it was too late; he groaned and they collapsed on to the floor. The crowd cheered.

After a minute she felt a small soft hand pulling at her. 'Get up,' Oon was whispering. 'Show not over yet. Stand up, stand up. You too, Johnny.'

They got to their feet; he was still hard.

'Go back in,' hissed Oon. 'From behind, standing.' Johnny slid back into her vagina; Oon resumed her position in front of Susan, and Vinnie, kneeling behind Oon, entered her. As he fucked her, and she sucked Susan, and Susan thrust against

Johnny, the music changed. Call it coincidence, or call it a DJ with a sick sense of humour, but as Susan Street reached her first orgasm in front of a paying public, the record they were playing was 'She Works Hard For The Money'.

In the part of her mind that wasn't obliterated by sensation, she recognized once again the mischievous hand of Tobias Pope.

EIGHTEEN

'You SLUT!' shrieked Zero Blondell, jumping up from the armchair and on to Susan's sofa and beginning to beat at her with bony little fists. 'You SLAG! How come every time you're in the mood for muff I'm on the other side of the world?'

'Ah, Zero – maybe that's why!'

'You PIG!' The blonde lunged at her, but half-heartedly this time; Susan caught her wrists and they lounged there in companionable enmity, exhausted from an evening of true confessions and martini cocktails.

'So how many to go?' asked Zero after a while. 'Lessee – Rio, Sun City, New York, Bangkok – two?'

'One. You forgot the tattoo.'

'So I did. What'll you do with the tattoo when you've got your stilettos under the editor's desk, bach?'

'By then I won't care and it won't matter.' Susan threw her head back and closed her eyes, smiling dreamily and drunkenly. 'I'm going to be such a great editor that they wouldn't sack me if I had 'BUBONIC PLAGUE – INFECTIOUS' printed on my forehead. I *think*, I *dream* in headlines; I was *born* to edit this paper. All I need is a chance to prove myself and I can do the rest.'

'That's what they call bootstrap feminism.'

'Yeah, well, you know what the alternative is – sackcloth and ashes feminism. Sit in a squat licking your wounds and raising your consciousness at a womb workshop while men go out and get all the fun, love and money the world has to give. Wouldn't they just love that, having no competition? No, cringing in the ghetto is never a good idea.'

'OK, bach, you don't have to convince me. I'm hardly the belle of the Radical-Feminist-Lesbian-Separatist ball, with my satin and tat and my wicked ways.' Zero stretched. 'Know what I think of you as? A smash-and-grab feminist. You've got to have it *now*. You know what Madonna said when some man asked her what she thought of feminism, expecting her to put it down? She said, "Oh, I believe in everything they do. But I was too impatient to wait." That's what you're like.'

'That's right, Zere – I can't hang about waiting for men to change, or trying to change them myself, like they say we're meant to. It seems that if we agree to that, we're letting them off the hook of being responsible for their own behaviour all over again. I'm not a nurse or a nanny; they can change themselves, they're big enough and ugly enough. I've got too much to do, I just want to get on with my life.'

'I'm with you, bach, believe me.' Zero sniggered. 'Though I dread to think what the sisters would say if they knew about your bargain with the ugly American.'

'Christ, I didn't come this far so I could worry about what a bunch of bellowing, bullying dykes think of me.' Susan slopped vermouth into her glass and then looked at Zero. 'But what about you? Aren't I colluding with the enemy?'

Zero shrugged. 'That's pretty much par for the course in wartime.'

'Wartime! Zero!' Susan threw back her head and laughed.

Zero nodded seriously. She didn't seem drunk now. 'No, it is a war. But it's a guerrilla war, and that's why life seems to be going on more or less as usual. But it's all there: the rapes and the raiding parties and the goon squads and the losses. You'd have to be a pit-pony who believed in the power of positive thinking not to see it. It's a dirty little war, and they've got the arms.' She shook her short hair and smiled falsely at Susan, crossing her legs so that her short black micro slid all the way up to heaven. 'We, however, have the legs. Not to mention the other parts. And like all armies of the night we must use them for all they're worth. Of course I'm not going to condemn you for what you're doing. It would be as futile as arguing with God.'

'So you don't think I'm – immoral?' The word didn't feel right on her tongue; she was back at school, speaking bad French.

Zero shrugged impatiently. 'War and murder and child molesting are immoral. That being so, I don't see how the word can be used about consensual sex. Some words are sacred.'

'I don't know what it means when they use it about sex, either. It's one of those words that's lost its meaning – like sinister for left.'

'Or left for progressive. No, when men use "immoral" about women, it means "Cleverer or richer or more successful than me". Like "plastic" means "Better-looking than me". These words, they're the pop-guns of the powerless, and these days that's starting to mean men.' Zero drank dry vermouth from the bottle. 'But I'll tell you honestly what I think about your bargain, without recourse to portable pulpits.'

'Go on.'

'First you've got to level with me. You *have* slept with him—'

'Cross my *heart* I haven't. Wherever it is.'

'Yeah, the smart money says it's hanging around the lobby at Claridge's. But you know what that means, of course? He's impotent.'

'I don't know.'

''Course he is! You know my line about impotence?' Zero began to bounce excitedly, as she always did when thinking back to her best lines.

'"It's Nature's way of saying you're a bad fuck,"' Susan recited dutifully. 'I'll say I know it, Zero. I cut it from your copy about twice a month.'

'Ah, it's a great line.' Zero pouted. 'You're a bunch of old women up there.'

'Go on. Tell me what you think.' It struck her that Zero was the only person in the world whose opinion mattered to her, and she thought drunkenly how strange and beautiful modern life was, the way it took you from your family and tossed you up high in a blanket, so that you ended up with the weirdest and most wonderful creatures of the species as your spiritual next of kin.

'Well, all right.' Zero was making the most of it now she had her audience. 'One, I think that if a women is as chaste as a Poor Clare and makes it to the top of her profession, then wherever men gather to spread their slime, be it private club or public bar, she will be talked about as though she sucked and fucked her way to the top; such sad specimens are their pathetic little egos that their worlds would collapse if they had to believe she got there on merit. So they'll talk anyway – you may as well be hung for an editorship as for being a personal secretary plucked from the typing pool.'

'Go on.'

'And two, which gets top billing: since I was sixteen, I've seen the way men crawl round the big boss man. I've seen it in Wales in insurance offices and I've seen it in London in newspaper offices, and only the accents are different. In every workplace in this country, the majority of men spend their time crawling, rimming and kissing ass to the boss; and the ones that don't, they're eventually singled out and sacked for supposedly making trouble. Well, I've seen these men crawl, and you can't tell me that if they weren't so ugly, and the boss wasn't so straight, they wouldn't bend, blow and bugger, too. They'd do *anything* to get ahead. And as white, well-fed, male people, they are hardly the wretched of the earth. They have *no* excuse, and yet they do it. It's called capitalism.' Zero touched Susan's forehead, tracing the SOLD with her fingertip. 'My child, you are absolved. Just say three Hail Marys, suck me off and we'll say no more about it.'

Susan laughed weakly, though she felt like crying. 'Oh Zere, *you* understand. All I need is one shot. Then I can do it properly.'

Zero looked at her nails with more attention than they merited; they were short and cracked, from typing and from other acidic activities best not gone into. 'Actually, you might get your chance sooner than you think. Before your chores are over, so to speak.'

The words were like ice-cold water in the face and Susan sat up straight, instantly sober. 'What do you mean?'

'Me? Oh, I say nothing.'

'ZERO!' She grabbed the girl by the shoulders.

'Mmm.' Zero wriggled. 'Why don't you slap my face?'

'*Please*.'

'Slap it silly, till I beg for mercy—'

'Be *serious. Tell.*'

'Well.' Zero looked at her flirtatiously from under her lashes; then, seeing the desperate ambition so alien to her, almost backed away with fright. Instead she stopped stalling and lowered her eyes, speaking softly.

'A couple of days ago, Yasmin told me that Bryan wanted to see me. I thought it was for a scolding, look you, because I'd sent little Rachel up the ladder in the reference library for something – and then on impulse I'd gone up after her. I didn't mean to, but she was wearing Chantilly by Houbigant, and it brought back some very pungent memories of cheap girls who wear even cheaper scent. Just a bit of fun, mind you, nothing dirty. But who should walk in but Bryan! And Rachel only married last month. He gave me such a look. So I thought Yas meant straight away, and I knocked and walked in. But I was wrong.'

'Why?'

'Well, there was your beloved and Bryan facing off over the desk – one step from coming to blows, I'd say. They looked round when I walked in and backed off. It was very novel for me, coming the Grace Kelly bit from *High Noon*, I can tell you. So I stood there trying to look sort of Quakerish – not easy in a sideless dress – and then your beloved left the room, snarling at Bryan that the way the paper was going, he wouldn't wipe his behind – only he said "butt" – on it soon. And Bryan ran to the door and yelled after him that he hadn't known that Pope Junior – that's what he called him – *did* wipe his behind: he'd thought he wore nappies, and that his father changed them for him.'

Susan winced, thinking of David Weiss's sensitivity concerning his father. 'What then?'

'Well. Bryan told me to piss off and keep my cruising out of the office. So I burst into tears.'

'You did *what?*'

'Oh, I cried. Being Welsh I cry very easily. And I'm very good at it. I can cry from either eye alone, and I can make the tears stop halfway down. Tears are a deadly weapon with a certain sort of man, and that big ox O'Brien's one of them, bless him.'

'But why did you cry?'

'I wanted to find out what was going on, didn't I. So I detonated myself, as it were. A bleached blonde dyke is Threatsville – but a weeping woman isn't. Sure enough Bryan came over, threw his arms around me and began to sort of heave. The Aussies are very like the Welsh – I'd call it *maudlin macho*. He said he was sorry and he wasn't himself these days. He went on about Wagga Wagga and how he knew how hard it was to feel Different. He said he was having a difficult relationship with a sheila – no, I'm being mean, he said woman. And he said he wasn't happy on the *Best* any more. "As Weiss has got more confident, he's got more opinionated," he said, "and like all Americans he's serious, and he wants a serious paper. I can't do serious,

338

Zero, because I'm aware of what a fucking tragedy the world is. Like all sensitive people – though I'll cut your clit off, you little bleached twat-tickler, if you breathe a word of this to anyone – I can't get serious, or I'll break. I'm off as soon as I can find another foxhole. And you will be too, Zero, if you don't want that po-faced Yank cutting your gags." And I quote.' Zero sat back, looking pleased and expectant of praise.

'I see.' Her mind flicked back through her memory, all thumbs in its impatience, and came up with a scene just before Candida Brown's wedding; the contained but nasty skirmish over editorial direction in Bryan's office when David had previously flounced off in a huff. 'They don't work well together, do they?'

'Do men ever? All that stuff about women bosses is just a decoy. But it's not just personal chemistry, bach; Bryan's a great editor. He's *so* good that Pope keeps him on tap, like Red Adair, always ready to fly off and sort out some new mess. But he's sick of being an understudy; he wants a real job. And he knows now that he's just keeping that seat warm for you: English, and young, and a girl. It *hurts* him.'

'I can see that,' said Susan slowly. 'But he's never mean to *me* . . .'

'Of course he's not – he's an Aussie, and a pro, and a gentleman. Besides, he doesn't blame *you* – he understands ambition. He blames *Pope*, for fucking him about all these years. But don't sweat it – it's a storm in a can of Fosters.'

Zero leered. 'So forget that. Let's talk about the important stuff. What do slant girls taste like?'

'Sushi?'

'Hello?'

'Susan, I've got Joe Moorsom on the line.'

'OK, Kathy.'

'Hello?'

'Hello?'

'Susan. It's Joe.'

'Joe who? Joe Blow?' She felt used (T. Pope), bored (D. Weiss) and insecure (B. O'Brien).

'Joe Moorsom.'

'Oh. Joe *Blowjob*.'

There was a sullen silence. Fags couldn't even take a joke any more. Wasn't that a perversion of nature? – fish gotta swim, birds gotta fly, and fags gotta take a joke?

'Very funny. Still, you won't be able to make funnies at my expense much longer.'

'Why? Are you having your face done?'

'No. But maybe you should.'

'Oh yeah?' His working-class, masculine smugness really brought out the worst, the *brat*, in her.

'Oh yeah. Because I've got the goods, Susan. I've really got them now. And your little sex bomb's been detonated good and proper. Now nothing can stop us.' The line went dead.

She stared at the receiver. 'Us?' she said stupidly. This she didn't like *at all*; in fact, she was damned if she was going to try to handle it herself any more. Jumping up, she bolted from her office and flung open Bryan's door. Then she gasped.

Sitting in the editor's chair, his Hush Puppies on the desk, was Oliver Fane – looking like the cat who not only got the canary but the entire contents of the aviary.

'What are YOU doing here?'

'Keeping your seat warm.' He winked at her. 'You can do the same for me sometime.'

She slammed the door, marched to David Weiss's office and flung open his door without knocking. 'What's going on?'

'How so?' He didn't look up from his papers.

'Don't get piss-elegant with me, you,' she snarled. 'Why is that meathead Fane sitting in my chair?'

'The *editor*'s chair, Susan. He's sitting there because my father instructed me to put him there upon hearing of the situation.'

'Situation?'

'Haven't you heard?' He laid down his New York Yankees fiber-tip pen – a pathetic affectation in a middle-class, bookish Jew, she thought – and looked at her. 'O'Brien's gone. No notice, no nothing. I could sue his ass within rights, but I'm glad to see the back of him. The man wanted to edit a funny paper, not a newspaper.'

'He was a damn good editor.' She glared at him. 'And your *father* told you to put *Fane* there? I don't believe you. What about *me*?'

'Ah. I mentioned this. Despite your low opinion of me, and mine of you, you *are* the deputy editor of this paper. I mentioned this to my father when I spoke to him. But he didn't seem to believe you were ready yet. "She's got to prove herself one more time, and then she gets the gig," he said.' David shrugged. 'I guess that means you have to persuade yet another hooker to spill the beans for the benefit of the front page – either that or off another carny act. My father acts in mysterious ways, his blunders to perform.'

Her head began to spin. She felt dazed, drunk; she staggered forward and caught hold of a chair back. Tobias Pope . . . the mystery was not why he was behaving in this way, but why she had expected anything else of him. Officially, her side of the bargain wasn't complete. But she had thought they were friends now . . .

Friends! Did a rattlesnake have friends? Her gullibility and disappointment overwhelmed her, and she burst into tears.

She stood there, weeping and hating this weak side of herself. Any minute she expected to hear David Weiss laugh and tell her to go and pull herself together. To talk to her as if she was a *woman*.

But he didn't. He came out from behind his desk, put his

arms around her and said in a voice of sheer amazement, 'Susan. You're human. You're *human*.'

'I love you,' he said grimly as he smoked his king-size cliché afterwards.

'What?' She sprang up in bed and knelt, staring at him, her hands on his shoulders.

'I love you. I'm in love with you.'

She got up, wandered around the room, took her hairbrush from her bag and smoothed her hair. 'I don't understand.'

'It's very simple. I realized that night after you left – that night you told me about . . . Michèle, and I called her. With the mirage of her purity out of the way, I could see very clearly that I loved you. But I was scared. I'd gone overnight from loving this girl who I thought was an angel – however misguidedly – to loving this girl I *knew* was a monster. I was terrified. So when I saw you crying – I don't know. I still think you're sort of half-monster. But I guess you're half-human too. All in all, you're either more or less than human – I can't figure out which.'

She stood and looked at herself in the full-length mirror, then at him. 'Both?'

'Whatever. Who needs the love of a good woman when you can have the love of a bad one? It's in the good woman's nature to give love. A bad one – well.' He patted the bed beside him and smiled. 'That's the challenge. That's the only game in town.'

* * *

She was walking on air, on cloud nine, in seventh heaven and thinking in a ceaseless stream of clichés – white wedding, happy ending – instead of the usual headlines when she walked into the *Best* next morning. She even put her head around the editor's door and wished Oliver a good morning and a crucial day. He gaped at her in horror and disappointment. Damn the bitch. She wasn't meant to bounce back like this.

When she found the message to call Caroline Malaise, she was mildly surprised. She had trouble visualizing Caroline rising before noon, let alone calling before ten. Obviously, being downwardly mobile concentrated the mind wonderfully. She called Caroline and was persuaded by her surprisingly brisk urgency to cancel lunch with a motor-mouthed ex-model who had distinct possibilities as a gossip columnist.

She was nevertheless surprised to find Caroline waiting when she walked into Le Caprice at ten past one. She was even more surprised to see Caroline sitting at a table for five. Two of whose seats were occupied by Ingrid Irving and Bryan O'Brien.

She fought panic, greeted a waiter, walked over and looked at them one by one – Caroline, Ingrid, Bryan. Caroline looked at her hands, Ingrid looked back, grinning, and Bryan looked embarrassed.

'What's going on?'

'Sit down, Sue,' said Bryan.

'You'll need to,' said Ingrid, downing her Pussy-foot in one go and slamming the glass on the table triumphantly. 'Poor baby. You got so used to picking the sweet soft centres in the big chocolate box of life, didn't you?' She giggled. 'Well, this time it looks like you've been well and truly left with a choice between the Montelimar and the Praline.'

'Who's the extra chair for?' Susan asked Bryan earnestly. 'Miss Irving's liposuctionist?'

'No. It's for me.'

She turned around and saw Joe Moorsom.

NINETEEN

What followed could best be described as a *fait accompli* in four courses. Her usual numerical vertigo came on quickly, but she could still understand enough to see that Tobias Pope, tycoon, entrepreneur and publisher, would soon be able to add convicted felon to his long roster of titles.

It was Caroline who had first heard him conspiring with his money men in the flat in Lowndes Square; it was Bryan who, after a long round of liquid lunches with Pope Communications corporation men who felt they had been unfairly passed over for promotion, confirmed the story. It was Ingrid who had the front page ready, willing and able to roll and Joe Moorsom who was ready to ask questions in the House about Pope's suitability to hold a cable franchise.

The meat of the matter was a number so large that when Susan first heard it she mistook it for some phone number on a far continent, vital to the plot. When the words 'tax evasion' were added as a dialling code, the number suddenly looked even bigger. Big enough to spell out the end of Pope Communications' irresistible rise; big enough even to put a big man behind bars.

Bryan finished his narration, and they all looked at her. Their faces were proud and eager, as though waiting for praise.

'Well,' said Susan Street, looking down into her third empty martini glass, 'let me first congratulate the four of you on your act. You work incredibly well together – a seamless dream. You're quite a bit like the Beatles, all things considered.'

'Why's that, Susie?' asked Caroline curiously. Ingrid shot a daggers glance at the gentle blonde.

'Well, there's the pretty one –' She looked at Caroline. 'And the clever one –' She looked at Bryan O'Brien. 'And the boring one –' She held Joe Moorsom's stare. 'And the plug fucking ugly one. Who shall be nameless.'

'I'll push your face in, you bitch!'

'Isn't that a coincidence? I'd push yours in, only no one would notice the difference. Yes – between the four of you, you just about make up one whole person. Congratulations, as I say.' She raised her empty glass to them, mockingly.

'Do you know what Gore Vidal calls irony?' spat Ingrid Irving. 'The weapon of the powerless.'

'That wasn't irony, you stupid bitch, it was sarcasm. Which you'd know if you ever read anything more taxing than *Horse And Hound*.'

Ingrid lunged across the table at her.

'Ingrid, Susan!' said Bryan urgently. 'Stop this! We're grown up people – we shouldn't be behaving like this. Strewth, even I know that!'

'Then how should we be behaving?' Susan turned to him. 'Excuse me, Bryan, but what exactly was the point of this? Why are you and Caroline doing this to me? I can understand the motives of those two twisted bits of work – of course *they* hate me. It's called envy and misogyny. But what did I ever do to either of you? Answer me that.'

It was Caroline who answered. 'Oh Susie, I'm sorry. It's nothing personal. It's nothing personal. It's him we want. You're just in the way.'

'Think of yourself as the John Connally of journalism,' said Joe Moorsom with an excruciatingly smug smile. 'You'll feel better that way.'

It was a smart line, Susan reflected as she left Le Caprice at a trot. Still, he didn't look quite so smart with a raspberry pavlova running down his face.

'So he did it.' David Weiss smiled coldly and whistled slowly. 'Ooo-eee. The crazy bastard really went and did it.'

'You're talking as if you knew he would.'

'I knew he *wanted* to. Tax – it was his big thing. *Being*

made to do something – only the IRS had the power. As he got richer, so fewer people could tell him what to do. But the richer he got, the *more* they could take from him. It drove him crazy. I remember when I was a kid, these big dinners at our place in Connecticut; he'd take a drink too many and, instead of going on about the Russian or the blacks, he'd go on about tax. It was his demon. Compulsory communism, he called it; the malignant tumour in the tender flesh of freedom. The noose that squeezed the juice from the nation's finest. Oh, he was a real poet when it came to tax. I remember Maxine weeping into her vichyssoise at dinners for twenty-four people, most of them New York Jews and New England Democrats. Well, they were all loaded but they weren't used to that kind of crazy talk; they had a sense of *noblesse oblige*. My father didn't.'

'Because he basically believes that all men are born equal and therefore no one owes anyone anything,' she said, surprising herself with the indignation in her voice.

He looked at her nastily. 'You're entitled to your opinion. All I know is what I saw and heard with my own eyes and ears. Tax was his Rosebud in reverse – what made him tick. But I thought he'd be content just mouthing off and offending polite liberal company. The crazy bastard . . . with all his money, dodging doesn't make a speck of difference.'

'It was a matter of principle,' she said stubbornly.

'Principles? My father thinks a principle is the head of a college.'

'You think that because you think the only principles are liberal ones.' She reached for the phone. 'You don't understand him, or this world we're living in. I've got to call him.'

'No.' His hand covered hers stiffly. 'If you pick up that phone, you may as well get out my Swiss army knife and cut my balls off.'

'But—'

'*No*. I've got to work this out myself, Susan. *You* got rid of Moorsom the first time; *you* had the clairvoyant killed.'

'I didn't!'

'No.' He held up a hand. 'Don't deny it. I know you. Just spare me the details, that's all I ask. But *I've* got to do this: I've got to earn my pay for once in my life. I can't be Maxine's little boy, or Michèle's little boyfriend, or Susan's little sidekick, or my father's little son and heir forever. And I'll *always* be his son till I can be his saviour.'

She giggled.

'Does that sound melodramatic?'

'A bit. A bit like one of those biblical Bruce Springsteen songs.'

'Hey, I *love* Bruce Springsteen. Don't you? Say you do. I always think a marriage can go horribly wrong if the parties concerned can't agree over Bruce Springsteen.'

There. He'd said it. She knew he would. Once you knew how to bring out the worst in a boy, a proposal of marriage was only a scruple away. 'I love him. But I'm wary of his position in modern life. Isn't Bruce Springsteen what men believe in when they stop believing in God, politics and football?'

He roared. 'Baseball, you bitch! Susan, you slay me.' He kissed her, holding her face between his hands. 'Listen, I'm going to work this out. Don't tell Dad, OK?'

'Don't tell me what?' asked Tobias Pope.

They turned to gape at him.

He raised one hand, wiggling his fingers in slow motion. 'Hi, children. What's this you're not going to tell me? Never mind, it'll keep – I'll have it as a nightcap. I love surprises. Come along, Susan. I'll be in the car. And quick. You know how I hate to wait.' He closed the door. Automatically she began to gather her things together.

David Weiss stared at her. 'Where do you think you're going?'

'I have to.'

'Why?'

'He's my boss. I have to go with him.'

'To fuck?'

'NO!'

'But you told me you were fucking him. Remember? You told me how much *better* than me he was.'

'I was lying.'

'So I'm better than him?'

'I don't know. I've never slept with him. I was lying about that.'

'You liar.'

'I'm *not!*'

'Then why should I believe you now?'

'I have *never* fucked your father. Or your mother. Or your girlfriend Michèle, even though she *was* hanging there like a human buffet ready to take on all comers.'

He slapped her.

She backed off, rubbing her cheek. 'I'll say it one more time. I have never fucked Tobias Pope. I was lying when I said I had. I'm not lying now.'

'Then why are you going to him?'

'Because . . . we have a deal.'

'About fucking?'

'I can't say.'

'So you *are* fucking him!'

'NO!' She screamed it.

'Go on.' He opened the door and pushed her out. 'Go to him, you lying bitch. Go and do all the pair of you are good for – go and roll in the stinking mud and rot. I could forgive you for fucking him before, when I wasn't playing straight with you – but not now. Forget it. Don't worry, though – I'll save this lousy paper for both of you. He'll have his investment back, and you'll have your precious little editor's chair to come back to. But I won't be here. I'm not working for that man any more. The man who stole my life. The man who stole my *wife*. I'd rather lick out toilet bowls for a living.' He came after her and pushed her skidding down the corridor. 'Go on. Go and make an old man happy. You can't make anyone else happy, that's for sure. Because you're *evil*. You're *evil*.'

'*You are*' screamed Maxine Weiss Pope in 1958 as she slammed the door of the master bedroom of the penthouse on Central Park West. 'EVIL!'

'*But why?*' asked the young Tobias Pope quietly, as though reasoning with a crazy person. 'Why, darling?'

'*Asking me to sleep with a* whore! A negro whore!'

'*But Maxine, you're a fully paid-up member of the NAACP. What's the problem, angel?*'

'You do not ask that thing of a women you love, Goddamnit!'

'*Then who do you ask it of? Someone you've got no feelings for? Isn't that a pretty cold and exploitative thing to do, Maxine?*'

'Just go take a walk, you crazy sick bastard!' *Maxine was at the end of her tether now, he could tell; the fruity, yeasty rasp of Brooklyn had at last burst through the taut refinement of her uptown voice with all the subtlety and relish of a cheerleader bursting through a paper drum.*

'*Maxine, Maxine.*' He fell against the door, his blond face snubbed by it. 'Oh, Maxime,' he said drunkenly, though he hadn't touched a drop; his wife always had that effect on him. He pictured her leaning against the door, her fists clenched, her wrists scarred: golden-skinned, black-haired, with eyes the colour of a hot toddy. She looked like one of those beautiful

354

mid-western brunette WASPs who were always chosen by Hollywood to play Hebrew heroines in its best biblical epics. In her white silk peignoir, her flesh would shine with righteous indignation; he could almost taste its colour and sheen. How he loved her.

'Maxine, I've got to talk to you!' *he shouted urgently. He could see things slipping away before his eyes.*

'Just go and get a lousy whore to do those dirty things, you cheap bastard!' *she shrilled, Brooklyn triumphant.* 'I ain't playing! Get a whore to do it!'

He slumped against the door defeatedly. 'But it's no fun that way,' *he said, almost to himself.*

'Am I evil?' Susan Street asked Tobias Pope blankly as the car slunk from EC4 to SW1.

He looked at her pure, perverse profile and laughed softly. 'Did he say that? He didn't mean it. He's just jealous. It does terrible things to people.'

'Am I, though?'

He sighed. 'I don't know, Susan. Maybe I'm not the best judge. I can tell you this – you remind me of me. Does that answer your question?'

'No. Not really.'

'Why? Don't you think I'm evil?'

'No,' she said, surprised. 'No, I don't.'

In the lift at Lowndes Square she asked him, 'What's going on? I thought I wouldn't be seeing you for another month.' He noticed that she had the dazed, distracted air that survivors walking away from car crashes often have.

'I have to tell you something,' he said. And he thought he could feel his heart almost burst inside him, just like in trashy books. They went into the flat and he locked the door.

'I came to London, and I brought you here, to tell you I love you,' said Tobias Pope. 'Go into the bedroom and get undressed.'

'I've always thought that sex spoils a relationship,' she said weakly.

'That's funny, I've always thought that a relationship spoils sex. Get to it.'

Stunned, she walked into the bedroom. He followed her. Out of her Alaïa, her tights, her heels. She got into bed and pulled the covers up to her chin.

'I have to tell you I love you, and I want to marry you,' he said. He left the room, and when he returned he was wearing silk pyjamas beneath an old, worn dressing-gown, and carrying a white cup.

She stared solemnly at him over the bedclothes as he sat down beside her; Miss Muffet and the spider.

He laughed. 'Don't look so scared, I certainly don't intend to sleep with you before I marry you. Not now. Not now I respect you. Drink this, it will help you sleep. I just want to tell you a story.'

'What.' It wasn't even a question.

He laughed again. His new laughter made his face look very young, something which only served to accentuate how old he looked in repose. How old *he was*. 'An old, old story. Stop me if you've heard it. Two stories in one – romance and redemption. Boy meets girl and finds faith – if you can call a man of fifty-five a boy or a complete monster a girl, which I doubt. But I digress. Semantics are not romantic.' He stood up and began to pace the room.

'When I met you, I had neither romance nor redemption on my mind. What I had in mind was sport. I've found sport in you, but I've found more; I've found love, and faith in the human spirit. To see your strength, and your faith in yourself, and your utter lack of self-loathing no matter how squalid the situation you find yourself in – for me, it's been an education.'

'You make it sound like a sexual *Jeux Sans Frontières*.' She shivered with memory.

'Well, I didn't think they *made* people like you any more – a rebel without a doubt. Not women, not in the West. Not now it's closing time.' He sat down and searched for her hand under the covers. 'I don't just want you for my editor, I want you for my wife. What do you think?'

'I think you're crazy,' she said slowly. But she didn't really know any more. All she could see was the winning tape, turned to liquid gold in the sunlight of her success; all she could feel was it breaking, like a perfect, meritocratic, wave across her body.

Again he laughed. 'No you don't. You think I'm fascinating. Which I am. And worse, much worse, you care for me. As I care for you. Will you marry me?'

'I'm going to marry your son,' she said, looking into his eyes.

He laughed sadly, shaking his head. 'No you're not. Not because I'm going to stop you, but because your will to survive and thrive will. That route's not for you; you know as well as I do that romantic love is always either a living death – those are the ones they call *happy* marriages – or a battle to the death – they're the ones that end in divorce. Boy meets girl, and their hormones act as a sort of magic carpet carrying them up, up and away to all sorts of weird and wonderful places. Oh, sweet mystery of life, at last I've found you!' He blew a loud raspberry and stuck out his tongue. 'And then one day the young ones wake up with a crash landing and they're yelling at each other about whose turn it is to put the garbage out. Susan, young love is a lemming: it's born to die. And you're left with that resentful boredom you last experienced as a teenager living *en famille*; why don't you leave me alone, why don't you understand me, why don't you *die*? Until one day you just walk away, and as you sit on the bus finding your fare, you count your loose change and find that you've spent ten whole years of your life. The only difference is that this time you did it voluntarily – and that as a teenager, you could afford to kill time. But now, when you look in the mirror, you see time's been killing you. You see that you're not so unimpeachably *young* any more; too much bullshit and too many bullshots have left stretch marks on your mind and body.'

'I am beside myself with fear,' she said sarcastically.

'You will be, when you walk out on my son and you're not SUSAN STREET in upper case any more; when you're not upwardly nubile, just another divorced broad living on begged alimony, borrowed time and stolen kisses. Susan, you're too good for that. *You don't want that.*'

'I want your son,' she said.

He shrugged. 'Have him. On the side, as they say. Who's stopping you? God knows, I'm a New Man . . .'

She hooted. And then she threw her arms around his neck. Like an American Fifties B-film, he was so bad he was good. How could she let him get away just for a pretty face and a big cock when he was the only person she had ever met who didn't make her feel like a Martian? Her head on his shoulder felt like home. She squeezed him tight.

'I'll make you rich beyond the dreams of avarice,' he promised.

'Who's she? Your new girlfriend?'

'Will you marry me?' he asked patiently.

'I think that might be a distinct possibility.' She laughed.

'Well, sleep on it.' He patted the pillows. 'Drink your milk. And let me tell you a bedtime story.'

She smiled at him indulgently. He was beaming like a boy.

'Let me tell you about your next task. The next task is the last, isn't that so? And then you get your heart's desire. I want to tell you now what the last task is so that you may prepare yourself for it. And thus relish it all the more.'

Her smile faded. Her muscles tensed. She watched him as he stood up and began to pace the room once more. The long mirrors scattered around the room threw him back at her wherever she looked, this old man with his new love. He was everywhere. He was everything. Right now, nothing existed beyond this room. She felt reality, struggle, even ambition slip away. His words sounded like a mantra.

'For our last task, we're going to Haiti. The beautiful island of Haiti, Susan – it's received a lot of bad publicity over the last few years, most undeserved. Home of AIDS, my foot! – why everyone knows that San Francisco is the home of AIDS. OK, so a rich American fag *can* buy a native there for the price of a piña colada – but so what? It's a free country. And in a free country, everything has its price. Who are we to sit in judgement? Live and let live. They're a charming people, too; so *obliging*. Make the Thais look like iceboxes. I, my personal self, like to watch the goings on at one particular house of joy where the girls and boys drink a punch whose base ingredient is seminal fluid – I'm sure you'll enjoy it, darling. I'm told it's rather like a margarita. Only thicker.' He laughed reassuringly. 'And the hangover's worse.' He looked at her, his eyes gleaming. And he started to laugh again.

She lay under the thick covers in the warm flat, frozen from head to toe. She felt as if she were lying in her own grave. This, for him, was the final twisted kick: to use her as gun and target both, to play Russian roulette with the girl he loved – and she knew now that he really did – which made it much more exciting, a game played for much higher stakes than if she had been some faceless pro.

She couldn't believe it. She couldn't do it. But to have come all this way . . . done all those things . . . to have lost David . . . dear God, why had she ever trusted this man? He *was* evil; at last she understood the meaning of the word.

But too late.

A single, solitary tear ran down her face.

Tobias Pope stopped laughing. He leaned towards her with the rapture of a scientist discovering DNA and said, 'My God.' His voice was the voice of a man in the heat of the act of worship as he said, 'My God. You're *crying*, Susan. You're really *crying.*'

She began to bawl, loudly and unbeautifully. He watched her, mesmerized. Through the fluid fog she saw him fumble with the belt of his dressing-gown and pull at his pyjamas. And then she felt him climb on to the bed.

'I've broken you. *I've broken you!*' he cried in a voice full of reverence, regret and agonizing excitement. 'I'VE BROKEN YOU!'

She felt how hard he was; how hard, big and rich he was. He was all American, all man and all men, and that made her suddenly and maddeningly aware of how soft she was – how soft, European and powerless. It wasn't fair, and it stirred something inside her; some swampy instinct of aggression and survival.

His face was already red with excitement, and as he fumbled at her opening he said, 'Your money. The tax. They're going to take the tax. *They're going to take your money.*'

He stared at her, stopping. Then he clutched her by the shoulders and yelled into her face, as though she were an old trusted family physician who had just told him he had an incurable disease and six months to live, 'IS THIS TRUE, GODDAMNIT?'

'Yes!' she screamed.

With that the will left him. And he gasped, stiffened and was still.

She pushed him off, got out of bed and looked at herself in the mirror. And she said, 'My name is Susan Street, and I am the youngest-ever female newspaper editor in the world.'

The man on the bed jerked one more time, as if in agreement.

And then, for good measure, he jerked again. Because the late Tobias X. Pope had always done everything to excess.

The police came.

TWENTY

In the morning, when she woke up, she realized that she actually probably wasn't the youngest-ever female newspaper editor in the world at all.

Her mixed blessing of a benefactor was dead, his son and heir hated her and Pope Communications was due to go up in moral and fiscal flames the minute the IRS lighted the touch paper.

And her career with it. And as everyone knew, there were no second acts in modern careers.

From that moment she became immobilized by grief, lying in bed neither sleeping nor really awake. Occasionally she would go to the bathroom and pass or drink some water. When Matthew spoke to her, she just looked at him.

He started to sleep on the sofa.

The only game in town was over, and she'd lost. *She'd lost.*
So now there was really no point in going on with anything.

On the sixth day she want into the office at lunchtime to clear
out her desk and give in her notice. But as she passed David
Weiss's office on the way to hers, automatically looking in,
she saw that his door was open and he was at his desk. She
stood there, looking at his head bent over some papers.

He looked up and stood up. 'Oh. It's you. I was wondering
when you'd have the nerve to show your face. You'd better
come in.'

'OK,' she said dully. She looked lousy, in an old raincoat
and with nothing on her face but twenty-seven years of
thwarted ambition. She didn't care. She went in and shut
the door behind her.

He stood looking out of the window, his back to her.
'Susan.'

'Yes, David.' She sat down.

'Susan, you may be aware that my father is dead.'

'Yes, David. I know, David.'

'Of a heart attack. Killed in the throes of what is
fancifully known as love-making with a young English slut
and alleged employee.'

'It wasn't the throes,' she muttered.

'What?'

'I said IT WASN'T THE THROES. He never even got
it in. And I mean *never*.'

'So you keep saying. Anyway, while you and my father were so industriously engaged working yourselves to death, I've been busy doing humdrum things like saving Pope Communications from the tender mercies of the Supreme Court. Just in case you were interested.'

'WHAT?'

'I did what I said I'd do. It's business as usual. Well, almost as usual.'

'But HOW?'

'Not without a good deal of crawling, capital and courage, I can tell you. It hasn't been cheap, in any sense. But we won't be hearing from the fab four again.'

'How did you do it?'

He came around and sat on the desk. 'For a start, some time late next year will see the launch of Pope Communications' mass-market Sunday paper, to be called – don't retch – the *Sunday Sauce*. Don't make that face. And to be edited by Bryan O'Brien, who can run sex scandals and serial-murder centre-spreads to his heart's content. The *Sauce* will effectively look after the downmarket end of sales, leaving the *Best* free to pursue its original ideals. The wedding will also take place next year of Bryan O'Brien and Lady Caroline Malaise; the happy couple will honeymoon at the Sunny von Bulow Clinic, where Lady C and her monkey will attempt a surgical separation.'

'And Joe Moorsom?'

'Ah. When not evangelizing on the healing power of

nudity, the *Sunday Sauce* will be editorializing on the healing power of unity that only a Labour government can bring to this great nation of yours. Mr Moorsom will also have his own weekly column, from which not one word may be expurgated.'

'A left-wing *Sun*? But that's blackmail!'

He shrugged. 'A good majority of the British press has been in the pocket of the Conservatives ever since its inception. Just think of this as redressing the balance a little.'

'And Ingrid?'

'Here's the bit you're not going to like. It's now almost certain that we'll get our cable franchise. Miss Ingrid Irving will join Pope Communications as Controller of PTV. A post she specifically asked for. Because, and I quote, "Everyone knows newspapers are finished now – it's cable that counts." ' He shuddered. 'I only hope her judgement as Controller will prove a little more sound than her judgement *per se*.'

'She's getting the cable?' Susan was horrified.

'She's not the only one. As a sweetener to the Honourable Mr Moorsom, PTV will be a little different from the wall-to-wall, round-the-clock, patriotic nude female mud-wrestling my father had in mind. It will have a heavy news and current affairs bias.' He walked to a video machine in the corner of the room and switched it on. 'With one exception. Miss Irving's first signing.'

The screen flickered for an instant before a silky fringe and sulky pout materialized. Then she was staring at the face of Rupert Grey; which was standing up very well, considering the number of times it had been sat on.

'His screen test,' said David with a smile.

'Good evening. Rupert Grey reporting. I am pleased to preview my forthcoming new show for PTV, *Repent with Rupee*.'

Susan turned to David with a look of disbelief; he nodded, grimly.

'*Repent With Rupee* will combine the best of the talk show with the religious broadcasting currently so popular in the USA. Each week I will be talking to a celebrity who had the good fortune to find God and renounce their wicked ways; sins as diverse as drug abuse, embezzlement and—' Here a barely audible sigh escaped Rupert's raspberry lips. '—oral sex. Nevertheless, *Repent With Rupee* will sidestep tacky voyeurism by virtue of its immaculate presentation, and will stand as a tasteful, poignant yet positive document of our time. God bless you. Byeee!' The screen went blank.

'This is a joke, right?' she pleaded.

David shook his head. 'Joe Moorsom moves in mysterious ways, his pound of flesh to get.'

'Is there any more?'

'One more thing. Pope Communications will take immediate steps to withdraw from South Africa. All in all, we are about to embark on a major revamp and

367

revitalization programme which will make certain that we take a leading role in the new caring capitalism crusade of the Nineties.'

'What's black and white and Green all over,' she muttered.

'What?'

'Nothing,' she said sullenly. 'Well. Aren't you clever? You won't be needing me now.'

'That's right.' He went back to the window. 'I suppose I don't need to tell you how shamefully unprofessional your conduct has been ever since Charles Anstey died. And before, if office gossip and the coroner's office are to be believed.'

'Yes, David.' The crunch had come and she was feeling faint. She put her head between her knees in order to revive herself.

He turned around. 'What on earth do you think you're doing, Susan?'

'Trying to revive myself.'

'Oh, I'm sorry. I thought you were attempting auto-lingus. You realize that you are now widely and indelibly regarded as a complete nymphomaniac, I hope?'

'Indelibly.'

'So I'm giving you ten minutes to clear out your desk.'

She gaped at him stupidly. Tears came to her eyes – this was becoming a habit. 'Yes, David.' She got wearily to her feet.

'And another ten minutes to transfer the contents – G-Spot vibrator, Chinese love balls and piña colada-flavoured condoms and all – into the editor's desk.'

'DAVID!'

'I'll call for you at home – sorry, at your *house*; it hasn't been a home for a long time – at nine sharp tonight. I'd prefer it if you were packed and ready.'

'But Matthew . . .'

'You left Matthew years ago. Quite frankly – and I don't mean this in a negative way – he'll be glad to see the back of you at last.'

'He will not!'

'He will so. I know it for fact. The night you were making an old man's last minutes happy, I called Matthew on impulse and we had dinner. I wanted to get to the bottom of you – I thought it would help me get you out of my system. Well, we got juiced and talked about pretty well everything. And Matthew took it pretty easy. He's got a girl, you know, a nurse; very pretty girl, blonde, a little overweight but she wears it well. He's very proud of her – showed me a photograph. Told me he carries it everywhere. If you cared about him, you'd have found it. He said that. He's a smart guy.'

'Why, that two-faced—'

'Susan!'

She laughed, feeling light-headed – feeling all-conquering, and therefore all-forgiving. Then she looked at him thoughtfully. 'But your father . . . aren't you angry with me?'

He crossed the room and stood in front of her 'Look at me, Susan. Look at me for once without thinking about who my father was. What do I look like?'

She looked at his waving black hair, his dark eyes, his brown skin. 'I don't understand.'

'What race do you think I belong to?' he asked, impatiently, imploringly.

'You're Jewish. Well, half. Your mother . . .'

He laughed. 'Susan, to a WASP everyone the wrong side of beige looks the same. Yes, I am Jewish, half. But the half that isn't isn't white. Because my father was black. Well, half. Susan, Tobias X. Pope wasn't my father. And it was the worry while she was pregnant that drove my mother crazy.'

'But your father – Pope—'

'Pope was such a crazed egotist that he never even noticed; like you, he thought Jews were coloured – marry one and your son and heir's bound to come out with a touch of the tar brush. Or maybe he did know – maybe that's why he treated her the way he did. But anyway, my *real* father is a light-skinned mulatto who was a servant at our place in Connecticut. I've known for the past ten years, and I've been doing all I can to support him. He's a wonderful man – everything Pope wasn't, including poor. Now I can really do something for him. And my mother – who knows?

370

Now at last maybe she'll have the nerve to come out of that place.' He looked down at her. 'Stand up.'

She did so, and he put his hands on her shoulders.

'Susan, I have no illusions about you. You are the most amoral and unprincipled human being I have ever had the misfortune to tangle with, and that includes the late Tobias X. But you are also the most sexually desirable and the most singular, and maybe these two sides of you are not unconnected. Anyway, you've made me see the light: that lust is just love with the gloves off, and that I don't want some pure ideal any more. By way of a fringe benefit you've also killed a man I've hated all my life, thereby making my poor demented mother as happy as she'll ever be. You've given me an empire. The least I can do is give you a job.' He put his arms around her.

She looked searchingly into his face; his beautiful, familiar, strange face. Something in her stare made him pull back and narrow his eyes. 'But I warn you, I have a heart of US Steel!'

She hugged him tight, laughing.

How she loved him!

And he had an empire . . .

And she'd be an editor!

And they'd be married . . .

Loving him with all her heart, she couldn't help but wonder what proportion of healthy young men died on their honeymoons from coronary collapse.

And when they kissed, his eyes were closed. But hers were open, staring out through the window and up at the sky – the bright blue Big Top under which so many opportunities just lay, waiting to be taken.

Staring onwards and upwards; staring up, up and away.

THE END